Igniting His Flame

REDWOOD BAY FIRE
BOOK ONE

HJ WELCH

Igniting His Flame
Redwood Bay Fire Book One

✿ Created with Vellum

Contemporary Fairy Tale, Folk Tale and Classic Literature Adaptations

The Fairy Tale Collection Box Set (Beauty and the Beast, Cinderella, Rapunzel)

Daddy's Fairy Tales Box Set (Daddies and kink – Goldilocks, Little Red Riding Hood, The Three Little Pigs, Puss in Boots)

In Good Spirits (Daddies and kink, Christmas, MMMM – A Christmas Carol)

Sweet Tooth (Christmas – Hansel and Gretel)

Jacked Up (D/s – Jack and the Beanstalk)

Rise and Shine (Novella – Sleeping Beauty)

We're All Mad Here (Novella – Alice in Wonderland)

Content Warning

A main theme throughout this book is Dario recovering after escaping an extremely manipulative relationship that turned physically abusive. No violence occurs on page.

As with all of my HJ Welch and Helen Juliet books, no harm will ever, *ever* come to any fur (or scale) babies.

CHAPTER 1

Lochlan

MOST PEOPLE RUN AWAY FROM BURNING BUILDINGS, NOT INTO them. But I'm not most people.

Also, I'm kind of a dumbass.

"I don't like the look of that roof!" Cap yells.

The One-Thirteen dismounts the truck and the engine that just came screaming to a halt. The old warehouse in front us is currently succumbing to roaring flames. I whistle and shield my eyes from the sun, assessing the situation.

It's not engulfed yet, but it's getting there. Luckily, we're kind of in the middle of nowhere, but that doesn't mean the situation isn't still urgent. There's a reason the saying goes 'spread like wildfire.' This is California. We don't fuck around when it comes to this shit.

"Anyone inside?" I ask.

Cap shakes his head. "Dispatch spoke to the owner who called it in. There shouldn't be, but we don't know how this started. Could be kids messing around."

"Worth a look, then," Lieutenant Rico Flores chips in.

Captain Valentine nods. "Bell," he shouts at me. "Go with

Flores and do a sweep inside. You've got three minutes before we open the hoses. Be fast, be safe."

"Yes, Captain!" Rico and I reply, already hustling towards the gaping open doors.

I think this place might have been used to store ship-building parts back in the day from what our driver, Gene, was telling us in the rig, but I wasn't really paying attention, if I'm honest. Dispatch would've told us if there's anything in here likely to go 'BOOM,' and that's all that really matters to me.

Tugging my mask over my face, I listen over the comms as the rest of the team coordinate tackling the blaze. However, my mind is already preoccupied with scanning the area as Rico and I start our assessment.

"Fire department!" I bellow at the top of my lungs. *"Call out!"*

Rico's doing the same as we move through the area. There's a ton of old crap. This place obviously hasn't been operational for a while. As I move through the aisles of boxes and conveyor belts, I'm aware of the flames licking at the walls, especially to my right and overhead. It looks like a section up ahead has collapsed, but whether that was before the fire started or after I really couldn't tell right now.

There's creaking and groaning all around as the flames ravage the structure. "I'm not feeling good about this roof, Bell," Rico tells me over the radio. "You see anything?"

"Nah, man," I say, despite the fact I'm still moving farther inside the building. That pile of rubble is bothering me for some reason. It's probably nothing, but until the captain tells us to move out, I'm going to keep doing my job.

Look, I know I'm not book smart. I struggled with all the written crap back in my academy days and was damn lucky to graduate. But once I made probie and was out in the world...damn. It's like I speak fluent fire or something.

There're ways I can read what that monster is trying to do, and I always manage to sneak in one step ahead of it.

I know this guy around us right now has a few minutes before he gets real ugly.

The trouble with going on my gut, though, is explaining what the fire's saying to other people. Like my captain.

"Okay, that's it," Valentine calls over the radio. "I'm calling it. Flores, Bell, get your asses out of there."

"Just one more minute, Cap," I reply. "We've barely searched half this place."

"Bell," he says in a warning tone.

I shake my head even though no one can see me. "There's still time," I assure him. "I want to—"

That's when I hear it.

Don't ask me what 'it' is, okay? Just something out of place. Something that's not roaring or crackling or groaning or snapping. Something…desperate.

"Wait a second, Cap!" I say, already hauling ass closer to that big old pile of debris. It's all bricks and metal beams and torn boxes stretching several feet in various directions. Is this where the something came from?

"Bell?" Rico says questioningly.

"Bell, that roof is coming down any second," Valentine snaps. "I'm not telling you again. Get out, now."

"I know, I know, Cap," I grumble, starting to pull bricks away from the mini landslide. "Just give me a sec, okay? I swear I heard something."

"Yeah, you heard the fucking *building coming down*," my best friend, Lili, scoffs over the comm from outside. "Beast, move your ass!"

Out of the corner of my eye, I can tell that Rico is making his way over. I wave at him, shooing him off. "Go! I'll be right behind you!"

"I'm dragging your sorry hide out of here, Bell," he growls over the comm at me. "Cap says leave, we leave."

That's when I hear the something again, though. Except this time, it's not a something anymore.

It's a whimper.

"There's someone here!" I cry, yanking at more of the debris. "Fire department! Call out! I'm coming!"

"Bell?" Valentine says, but I ignore him.

My heart is pounding. We don't know what started the fire, and Cap was right in what he said before. A kid goofing around could have done something stupid and made a mistake. If there's a chance someone's still alive in here, I'm not leaving.

Neither is Rico, despite how he scowls at me when he appears by my side, already shifting a rusty old girder that was pinning down a bunch of crap.

"You swear there's someone here?" he asks.

"I heard what I heard," I say, panting as I scramble through the chunks of brickwork as safely but also as fast as I can. "Come on, buddy. Tell me where you are."

Behind us there's a terrifying ripping sound as parts of the burning ceiling start to fall. I know we have to go, like, yesterday. But if I run off and save my own skin without knowing for sure there isn't someone just beyond my reach, I'll never forgive myself.

That's not what firefighters do. I've always said I'll give my life trying rather than take the easy way out. I show up to this job day in, day out, because I can be there for someone in the worst moment of their life. I can make a difference.

Today is just another day at the office.

It's my decision to make, though. No one else has to go down with me.

"Get out of here!" I yell at the lieutenant, flinching as fresh flames burst out to our left.

"Not without you, asshole," he grinds through his teeth.

"Bell, Flores, I'm giving you a direct order," Valentine shouts. I hate disobeying orders, but I'm here and he's not. I know I've still got a couple more moments before shit really hits the fan.

"Beast, if you die, I'm going to kill you," Lili warns over the radio.

"Not helping," I tell her, wrapping my hands around a sheet of metal, hauling it back with a grunt.

And there he is.

The puppy isn't much bigger than my damn hand as he trembles against a hunk of wall, his tail tucked all the way under his belly as he cowers from the destruction raining down around him. His ears and paws are so big compared to his tiny body, which I'm sure is supposed to be white when it's not covered in a thick layer of soot and grime. Although, I think his short fur does have some natural black spots as well…

He's a fucking Dalmatian.

"I got you, buddy!" I assure him, wrapping my fingers easily around him. "Let's blow this Popsicle stand."

"Bell, move!" Rico commands, already sprinting back toward the light blue square of daylight I can still just about make out through the smoke.

"Right behind you, Lieutenant!"

Cradling my charge close to my chest, I run and jump my way through this hellish obstacle course, stumbling back outside just as the hoses let rip and a deluge of water starts tearing through not only the flames but what's left of the warehouse itself.

Once I'm clear, I fumble to a halt and lift up the little guy to give him a visual inspection. My EMT training didn't really cover dogs, but I think that aside from being dirty and probably hungry, he looks okay. The sooner I can get some water into and on him, the better, but I think that pile of crap he was hiding under most likely prevented him from inhaling too much smoke.

I use my free hand and yank my helmet and mask off, dropping them on the dry grass. "Hey, there, little man. Are you doing all right?"

His tail gives a feeble little wag, then he stretches forward, his tiny tongue flicking out and licking the very tip of my nose.

My heart melts into a puddle at my feet. I don't care if Cap fires me or Lili murders me.

I've just found myself a new best friend. And you bet your ass I'd run into a hundred burning buildings again for him.

CHAPTER 2
Dario

What the hell am I doing?

I grip the steering wheel of my parked car, breathing slowly in and out. My therapist has assured me that this is a good idea, and my family agreed enthusiastically. But I can barely take care of myself. What makes them think I can possibly be responsible for anyone else?

Rubbing my chest, I try and calm myself by cataloguing what I can see. I look out at the building attached to the lot. Having grown up in San Diego, the Spanish colonial revival architecture all through Redwood Bay is a familiar sight to me. The cream walls and reddish-brown terracotta roof tiles aren't all that different from the suburbs of Phoenix, Arizona, either.

Not that Shane ever really let me leave the city much to take the scenery in. He never really let me leave the apartment at all.

Shaking my head, I try and let go of those memories. That's in the past now. The whole reason for making this move was to get a fresh start. I was lucky enough to get a job reasonably close to San Diego, but it'll still be an hour's drive to see most of my family. During the week, I'll be on my own.

That thought scares me.

So, apparently, this is the answer. I tighten my hands, making the leather on the wheel squeak. The only reason I don't turn the ignition on and drive the hell out of here is because I know I won't be able to face my mom's disappointment if I don't go through with this.

Instead of bailing, I close my eyes and take several long deep breaths. "I am worthy," I say out loud, cringing even though no one else can hear me. I hate saying these affirmations, but begrudgingly, I do admit they can help when I'm spiraling. "I am strong. I am loved."

The words taste like bitter lies in my mouth. But I promised my family I was going to take therapy seriously, and this is part of it. So would getting out of my damn car and making my feet move toward the front entrance of the building I've taken time out of my Saturday afternoon to visit.

"What's the worst that can happen?" I ask myself out loud, trying another technique that my therapist gave me.

Unfortunately, my traitorous brain has plenty of answers to that it helpfully supplies. *I'll fail and hurt someone. I'll get it all wrong and embarrass myself. I'll prove Shane right that I can't do anything without him.*

"Fuck that," I mumble, jabbing at my seat belt clasp and opening the car door. It might be difficult for me to believe a lot of things about myself. But I know without a shadow of a doubt that my life is a hundred times better without my ex in it.

The air is warm, and the sun is shining, as is pretty typical here in California. Closing the car door, I take a moment to close my eyes and breathe. "I can do this."

Gravel crunches under my feet as I cross the lot, pulling

the glass door open so I can step inside to the much cooler air. There. That was the first step, and it wasn't so bad.

Behind the desk is a young blonde woman whose face lights up as I wipe my feet on the welcome mat.

"Hi there! Can I help you?" she asks cheerfully.

"Um, yeah," I say, shuffling closer and trying not to get distracted by my pounding heart. I'm still terrified I'm going to make a terrible mistake, and everything in me is screaming to turn around and run away. But one foot after the other, I approach the desk. "I was thinking about making an adoption. Maybe."

If it's possible, the woman's smile gets even bigger. Her name badge tells me she's called Paisley. I'd guess she's only a bit younger than me, so perhaps mid-twenties? I hope she's not judging me for being so hopeless. I bet she doesn't have to give herself a pep talk every time she walks into a new place. Or maybe she does? How would I know, right?

In any case, she beams at me for a second before grabbing some forms. "That's wonderful! We'll need to take some details first. If you're approved, we'll also need to do a home visit before you can take an animal home. But that's getting ahead." She laughs and passes the forms to me, pinned to a clipboard. "You'll need to come out back and have a look and see if anyone tickles your fancy, first. Did you have anything in mind for your new four-legged friend?"

I try and stop my hands from trembling as I take the forms and a pen. "Um, a dog?" I say, sounding unsure even though that's what I've already decided on, rather than a cat. Not that there's anything wrong with cats. They're awesome. I just think the energy I need right now needs to be a pet that's (hopefully) excited to see me. Not one who treats me like a disappointing butler.

I half expect the nice lady to scoff and tell me I can't

handle a dog so I should get a goldfish instead. But of course, she simply nods.

"Yep, we've got all kinds of dogs here. Do you have a particular breed in mind or age or temperament or anything like that?"

If I say 'no' will she tell me I can't have one? I take a couple of seconds to fill out my name, address and telephone number on the form, then decide honesty is usually the best policy. "I'm not sure what I'm looking for. I've never owned a dog before."

Sure, we had dogs in the family when I was growing up, so I'm not totally clueless. But *I've* never had one all by myself.

"So maybe, um, one that's easygoing?"

Paisley nods happily. "We've got a couple I can already think of for you to meet. Is an older dog okay? A lot of people want puppies."

I shake my head, handing back the completed form. "I want to give a dog a good home, that's all."

She sighs and places her hand over her heart. "Good answer—" She glances at my form. "—Dario. Let's go take a look, shall we?"

It's funny hearing people using that name out loud. Not that it's wrong. I'm just still getting used to it.

But a thought occurs to me, and I don't move even though she's rising to her feet. I point at the form I just gave her, my pulse quickening again. "Um, sorry. Silly question. But do you keep your records confidential?"

She blinks at me before waving her hands at me. "Oh, of course! We have a closed CRM system, so it's all kept private."

I relax and manage to give her half a smile. "That's great, thank you."

I'm grateful she doesn't probe into why I asked that. She

just comes out from behind the desk with a big bunch of keys and ushers me toward a set of double doors to the right.

"Here's where all our pups live. It can get a little noisy, just to warn you."

"That's fine," I assure her as she unlocks the door and leads the way.

Immediately, my heart breaks at seeing all the dogs living at the shelter. They each have little rooms behind wire doors. They're reasonably sized, though, with a bed, water and food bowls, and some toys, so it's not completely bleak. Some of the dogs have roommates, but most are by themselves.

How am I supposed to pick just one? How do I decide who's worthy? I want to save them all. But I tell myself that them being here is far better than them being on the streets, or worse. Practically speaking, I can only take responsibility for one. Hopefully this nice lady will help me find a good match.

"So," Paisley is saying, "we have a lovely little guy who joined us recently. I think he's going to go fast, so I'll show him to you first. If you follow me this way, then—"

"Hang on," I say, freezing in my tracks. "Who's this?"

It's the eyes. They're so sad. I step closer, peering through the wire at the bundle of white and tan wrinkles looking up at me. One lower canine tooth pokes up over a top lip before its owner gives me a low, little 'woof!' The dog looks tired as they get to their feet, their wide shoulders sturdy as they steady themselves on their massive paws. Most of the wrinkles have smoothed out over their solid body now they've stood up, but the face is still rumpled and the mouth downcast. The tooth is poking up again.

"Oh, this is Queenie," the woman says. "She's been with us quite a while."

"Queenie?" The name doesn't seem to suit this unhappy, hulking dog all that much.

But the woman nods. "She's an English bulldog, so we named her after the late Queen Elizabeth. But a lot of people rename their new friends when they get them home."

"You don't know what her name was before she came here?" I ask as I crouch down, lacing my fingers through the wire frame of the door. Queenie shuffles closer to me, and I catch a short corkscrew tail giving a little wag as she sniffs my hand. Her nose is cold when she bumps it against my hand.

"No, unfortunately not," the nice lady informs me. "Queenie was left on our doorstep in a cardboard box. We think she was used for a couple of rounds of breeding before…well, we're just grateful that whoever dumped her did so responsibly."

I can tell from her tone what she thinks of anyone who would abandon a living creature like that, and I feel exactly the same. But she's right. There are far worse alternatives.

"Hi, Queenie," I say softly, managing to give her chin a rub through the wire.

"Oh, she drools quite a lot," Paisley warns me.

I don't care.

In fact, I've changed my mind. I think this majestic dog suits her name perfectly. She's a survivor, and that makes her royalty in my eyes.

"It's okay," I say, standing back up. "Actually, can I, um, hang out with her for a bit? What do people usually do?"

Paisley's eyes go a bit glassy. "You're interested in her?"

"Very," I say firmly.

She nods and clears her throat. "Of course. Let's get her out and on a leash, then you two can spend some time in our yard. There's space if you want to walk around and some toys to play with."

Queenie barks again as the woman opens the cage door. Because, if I'm being honest, that's what it is. A cage. Not a home. How long does she have to stay in there every day for her wellbeing and so the shelter staff can manage all these dogs?

The thought of taking her for long walks in the woods or on the beach makes my throat tight with emotion. I know I shouldn't jump into anything without proper consideration, especially with how apprehensive I was before coming in here. But I don't need much more time to make my mind up. As soon as Paisley hands me the leash and Queenie looks up at me, I know it's a done deal.

Queenie deserves rescuing just as much as the adorable puppies and prettier dogs that are here, all of which I'm sure will get picked way faster than her. I look into her dark eyes, positive that I see them brighten a fraction. Her little curly tail gives another tentative wag.

I might still not know what the hell I'm doing, but that's okay.

Queenie and I are going to work it out together.

CHAPTER 3
Lochlan

IT TAKES US ALL NIGHT TO WRAP UP THE WAREHOUSE FIRE. IT'S all we can do to get the rigs back to the station in time for the next watch, wash up, and get out of their way before we all stumble home.

So it's not until a couple of days later, when I'm barely twenty minutes into my next shift, that Cap's voice comes tearing through the house.

"BELL!"

It's not only me who whips their head up to the balcony where Valentine is leaning, staring daggers at me.

"Uh, yeah?" I croak, knowing full well what's about to happen, but playing dumb anyway.

He arches an eyebrow at me. "My office," he says smoothly. "Now."

As he walks away, all my asshole colleagues—who I would have called friends up until approximately five seconds ago—let out a chorus of *"Oooooh!"* Like I'm some kid being sent to the principal's office.

I mean, that's exactly what's going on, but I don't want them rubbing my face in it.

"All right, all right," I grumble, waving my hands and deliberately flicking water over the guys closest to me. I was washing down the truck's bumper when I was summoned, so I obviously couldn't help it.

"Asshole," our probie, Teddy, hisses as he wipes droplets off his face.

Rico chuckles. "You'll live."

"Dibs on all your shit, Beast," Lili calls after me as I grab a rag and dry off my hands.

"No way I'm ever dying before you, Kwon," I fire back at her.

But the truth is my stomach's in knots as I jog up the stairs. I hate letting people down, and Valentine's like a second dad to me in a lot of ways. I never want to make him or my actual dad disappointed in me.

Okay, so maybe Cap isn't quite old enough to be my dad, unless he'd been a wild teen, which I know he wasn't in a million years. I would never think of my old man as being hot, either, and it's impossible not to notice how dreamy Cap is.

Not that I'm into guys like that. Not that there's ANYTHING wrong with that! Half the damn One-Thirteen is gay or queer or something, and if anyone has a problem with that, they'll have to go through me first. I'm just not wired that way. Into dudes, I mean.

But if I was…yeah. Julian Valentine would get it.

Warm, dark skin. Bee stung lips. Long cheekbones that could cut glass. And on a normal day, I'd say his eyes have this way of sparkling. But as I walk into his office, they look distinctly stormy, and I try my best to shrink in on myself. Difficult, when I'm six-five and 'built like a brick shit outhouse,' as my gramps affectionately says. But my cheeks heat and I certainly feel sheepish as I close the office door. I take a seat opposite the captain, his mahogany desk between us.

"Captain—" I start, my apology ready to go.

"Can it, Bell," he snaps. "You know why you're here?"

"Yes, sir," I reply automatically.

He crooks that eyebrow again, and I do my best not to squirm. "And?" he asks.

I blink, not sure what he's saying. "…and?"

He sighs. "And why do you think you are sitting in my office right now, Firefighter?"

Oh, right. I quit squirming and just slump. "Because I disobeyed a direct order and almost got my ass flame-grilled like a ribeye steak."

Cap rubs his forehead for a second before fixing me with that disappointed stare that makes me want to melt between the floorboards with shame.

"It wasn't just your ass on the line, Lochlan. That's why I'm mad. Rico stayed with you. I was about thirty seconds away from charging in and dragging you both out."

Before he's even finished speaking, I'm sitting up straight in my chair and frowning at him, wagging a finger his way. "Naw, wait a second, Cap. I *told* Rico to get out of there. And I would've never, *ever* expected you to come in after me, even if things went sideways. That was *my* call to make. I heard the sound, so I took the risk. I'd never—"

But he's already waving me down, shutting me up. "That's the thing, though. The thing I need you to get, Bell. We don't leave anyone behind. Not now, not *ever.* If I make a call, it's because I'm a fucking dinosaur and I've seen everything there is to see on this job. I know when shit is about to hit the fan. I am never going to stand by and let you get swallowed up on my watch. Do you hear me?"

I squirm again, but I nod. It gives me all kinds of feels, knowing I've got a team here who really are ride or die.

However, I do have to stand my ground, even if it gets my ass chewed out even more.

"I knew I had time, though, Cap," I protest. His eyes get stormy again. However, I push on. "I read the fire. I knew there was another minute or so before it got too bad, and that's the only reason I didn't scream at Rico to haul ass. But I heard what I heard, and I wasn't leaving until I'd found whoever was making that noise."

Valentine sighs and folds his arms over his chest. "You don't have the authority to dismiss your lieutenant. I do, but he didn't listen, because he wasn't going to abandon you, either. Do you see the dilemma?"

I shrink down again. "Yes, sir." God, if anything happened to anyone on my crew, I'd literally never forgive myself.

Valentine puffs his cheeks out and squints at me. "I hate seeing you look whooped. You're a dick, okay? Just…don't do it again."

I practically vault out of my seat as I sit up straight and nod like a maniac. "I promise, sir. I won't."

"I give you three weeks," he grumbles, a hint of a smile tweaking at the corner of his mouth. "All right, enough of this bullshit. I assume you're keeping the little rascal." He arches that eyebrow again, and I chuckle and squirm for slightly different reasons.

"Um…he might be under the kitchen table right now."

Valentine looks skyward and mutters what I assume to be a brief prayer under his breath. "Of course he is. You pick out a name yet?"

I grin. "Sure did, Cap. His name is Rocky, coz he's a fighter. I washed him up real good, bought him top shelf doggy chow, and took him to the veterinarian for a check up and all that. He's not chipped, and he's only about ten weeks old, so they were sure he's a stray and I can keep him. They gave him some shots and he's got more scheduled next week."

Cap is waving me to shut up again, but I can tell it's good-natured. "All right. I'm down with it. But you can't just dump him in a tub and get him jabbed. You gotta train with him, for real. Take classes. If he's going to be around the house, he needs to be a model citizen."

"Yes, sir," I promise. "He'll be the goodest of good boys in no time. You'll barely even notice he's here."

He rolls his eyes. "Yeah, yeah. I think we can officially declare this ass-whooping done. Introduce me, already."

I jump to my feet. "Yes, sir!" I cry a lot more enthusiastically.

When I yank his office door open, Lili and Teddy are scurrying along the balcony toward the stairs. "Oh, hey, Cap!" Lili calls, spinning around like she wasn't trying to pretend the two of them weren't eavesdropping. She shoves Teddy one-eighty as well. "Uh, Probie here was just wondering, uh…"

"What you'd like me to cook for lunch!" he supplies pretty smoothly. "Enchiladas or chicken pasta." For a baby-faced blond, I'm not sure our youngest team member is as innocent as he seems most of the time, but especially now.

Valentine scoffs, apparently agreeing with me. "Nice try, Probie," he says as he ushers me past the threshold of his door and closes it behind him. "I believe there are some latrines that need cleaning, hmm?"

"Oh, I already did—" Teddy begins. Then he catches Valentine's expression and clears his throat. "I mean…yes, sir. I'll get right on that."

Sheepishly, he turns and starts jogging down the stairs.

Lili joins him…for about two seconds. "Uh, Firefighter Kwon?" Valentine calls out, a touch of amusement in his voice.

She flinches for just a second before spinning back around with a big smile on her face. "Yes, Cap?"

He snorts. "Probationary Firefighter Foster will get the job done a lot quicker with some help."

Lili grimaces, but nods all the same, probably knowing full well that she deserves a little punishment for trying to snoop on me getting my butt kicked. "Yes, sir," she says before disappearing after Teddy.

Valentine laughs and claps me on the back. "See. No one's ever in my doghouse long, Bell."

Having been under him at the One-Thirteen since I was a probie myself, I know that all too well. I just prefer it if I'm not the one in trouble for too long.

I'm grinning as I hurry down the spiral staircase and march into the kitchen. Aside from the bunks and bathrooms, the whole ground level of the house is an open space held up by thick supporting pillars. So the gaggle around the dining table has nowhere to hide as we approach, but that doesn't matter anymore.

"Cap!" Sawyer squeaks, immediately looking guilty. "We were just, um…"

Valentine chuckles. "It's fine. The cat's out of the bag. Or the Dalmatian, I guess. But speaking of cats, where's Smokey?"

A couple of people point to above the refrigerator where the station's gray kitty, Smokey, is glaring at us all with her orb-like yellow eyes. "Ah, sorry girl," I say with genuine chagrin. "I promise I'm gonna teach the new guy some manners."

Our driver engineer, Gene, is already pulling out the cardboard box where Rocky's been hiding. His little face immediately pops up and his tongue lolls out of his mouth as he wags his tail. "Told you Cap couldn't say no to such a cutie," Gene grumbles with half a smile. "You're all worse than my kids. Bell, get over here and take this little guy outside sharpish. He's making 'I need to go potty' noises."

"Oh, yikes," I cry, lurching over and fishing both my puppy and his leash out of the box I'd lined with newspaper. "Good boy, Rocky! Daddy's here. Let's go tinkle out on the grass and not in Captain Valentine's house, all right?"

Sawyer sneaks in a quick scratch on Rocky's head as I pass. "He *is* a good boy! So, Cap said he can stay?"

"Cap did indeed," Valentine says ruefully. "Lord help me. As if this place isn't chaotic enough."

I know the alarm could sound at any moment, so I rush outside with Rocky and gently place him on the lawn, trying to be calm for him. I've never had my own pet before and I've been trying to research as much as possible, but it's only been a couple of days so far. I know that I need to be his alpha, though. His pack leader. That means I need to be in charge and set an example for him.

In other words…I'm gonna have to fake it till I make it.

"Okay, little man. Do you need to go potty? Here's where you do that. Daddy has poop baggies and everything, so you just feel free to do your thing."

Rocky scratches one of his big, floppy ears with an equally large paw, then looks expectantly up at me.

I sigh. Gene has almost as many dogs as he does kids, so if he says Rocky was making those kinds of noises, I believe him.

"Let's just stay out here for a while and see if you change your mind, huh?"

Rocky yelps, wags his tail, then rolls over and starts fighting with the end of his leash.

I sigh again, reminding myself that this is still very early days—for both of us. I'll get the hang of this and so will he.

Hopefully.

"Mr. Bell, is that you?"

I turn and grin to see the station's neighbor approaching. Mrs. Sylvia Bloom's satin pumps click-clack along the sidewalk as she raises her arm high and waves at me. In her other hand she primly holds her own leash, connected to the one and only Miss Margot Fonteyn, her prize-winning floor mop. I mean…shit zoo. No…shih tzu! That's it.

"Mrs. Bloom!" I call back as she gets closer.

Wide, light-purple pants billow like a parachute as she walks, and her crisp white blouse shows off her tanned arms. I can already catch a whiff of her expensive floral perfume before she even reaches me, and her bling is dazzling as usual, catching the Californian sunlight like a disco ball. I'm not sure how old she is, but she's certainly from a generation that wouldn't consider it polite to ask.

She's a widower with too much time and money on her hands who long ago decided that the firehouse was hers to fuss over. It's not unusual for her to drop by two or three times a week with stacks of freshly homemade cupcakes, a giant lasagna, or a vat of Szechuan noodles.

But I believe her primary joy in life is telling everyone what to do because she knows best, and honestly? A lot of the time she really does.

"Oh my goodness," she coos, immediately spotting my currently uncooperative puppy. "And who is this, then?"

"Rocky!" I tell her proudly, puffing up my chest. "He's mine!"

"Is that so?"

She watches with me in amusement as Margot trots up to my gangly baby, her floof shimmering like a cloud. I'm glad I won't have to worry about brushing Rocky every day like Mrs. Bloom does for her. That sounds annoying. Rocky flips himself back on his oversized paws, automatically sniffing Margot back.

Then he barks at her. Loudly.

"Oof, he's going to need to learn some manners," Mrs. Bloom comments with a laugh. She doesn't seem bothered as Margot growls at my rude son, standing her ground.

"Yeah, I know," I say, rubbing the back of my neck. "I've been reading stuff online but he kinda just fell into my lap, so I wasn't prepared."

Mrs. Bloom tuts and arches her signature sculpted eyebrow at me. "Books will only get you so far, you know. What this young man needs is a training class. Not just to learn, you understand, but also to socialize."

I blink before grinning at her again. "Hey, that's a great idea! He can make doggy friends and maybe I can make human friends, too."

She hums and gives me a wink. "You should be aware by now that I only have good ideas, Mr. Bell. And it just so happens that I know a very good class in the area. It's run by the granddaughter of one of my SCUBA-diving friends." She points a manicured nail at me. "The granddaughter is engaged, so don't get any funny ideas in that direction."

I hold my hands up. "Whoa! Yes, ma'am. But I'm not the playboy. That would be Sawyer. Your friend's granddaughter's virtue is safe with me."

She hums again, not sounding convinced. "All you kids are allergic to settling down, I swear. This whole damn house is single."

"Gene and his wife have enough kids for all of us," I promise her, genuinely unable to recall if their last baby was number four or five.

She hums dubiously again, sounding not all that dissimilar to Miss Margot's growls. But speaking of our four-legged buddies, Rocky still seems determined to try and make friends with the show dog. He's yapping and jumping and wrapping his leash around my legs. Margot scuffs her feet and barks back, not having any of his nonsense.

"I better get back inside," I admit, twisting around to try and untangle myself.

Mrs. Bloom laughs. "I'll send you the details for the class. Make sure you sign up right away. I believe the next group is starting next week, and Zoe is always popular. She trains animals for Hollywood, you know. And guide dog puppies."

"She must be great then," I enthuse.

"I wouldn't recommend her if she wasn't," Mrs. Bloom says with a tsk, but her eyes are warm. "If the class is full, you just tell them I sent you and you'll get in. Best of luck, Mr. Bell. Goodbye, young Mr. Rocky."

My Dalmatian barks, then flops over to start licking his balls. I resist the urge to facepalm.

A smile quirks at Mrs. Bloom's glossy lips. "Come, Margot." The shih tzu obediently trots by her mom's feet as both of them waltz away.

Before I can think of anything else, the alarm blares through the house, the dispatcher's voice calling for both the engine and the truck as well as the ambulance. Sounds like a pile up on the interstate, so we'll no doubt be teaming up with a few of the nearby San Clemente units.

"Okay, buddy!" I cry, tugging at Rocky's leash. "We gotta go!"

He races back into the house with me, where I hot foot it to Nancy's office. As our administrator, she'll be here during the day when we get called out and has already promised to watch over Rocky for me.

"Hey, Nance! Can you—?"

The older lady's eyebrows raise as she peers over her glasses to my feet…where Rocky is relieving himself all over the linoleum floor.

"Aw, man," I groan.

"BELL!" Cap hollers from where he and the rest of the team are jumping into the rigs. He's pointing at me with a triumphant grin. "Looks like you better stay here and clean that up."

"You can't leave me behind!" I shout back, but the damn engine is already pulling out. "What the hell should I do after that?"

"Make lunch!" Lili yells at me.

"Latrine duty!" Teddy gloats.

I sigh and watch my whole team haul ass until it's just me and Nancy left with my naughty puppy and a skulking kitty. Rocky has apparently finished tinkling and is wagging his tail at me again. I huff and run to get some paper towels and disinfectant before the mess can spread too far, mopping it up in record time while Nancy plays tug-o-war with my dog.

Once I'm done, I look around the quiet house. Who knows how long they'll be?

I look at our administrator and decide I've probably cleaned up enough icky stuff for now. "Enchiladas and last night's Traitors?" I suggest.

She laughs and jumps to her feet, Rocky dancing by her side. "Now you're talking," she says with a snap of her fingers.

Who cares if I'm missing out on all the action. I've got a hot lunch date and a training class to book. I'm going to be the best doggy daddy Redwood Bay has ever seen.

CHAPTER 4
Dario

I'M STILL FINDING MY WAY AROUND TOWN. I'D REALLY HOPED that the doggy training class that the shelter suggested I sign up for was going to be, you know, at the shelter. Or maybe at the local high school. Anywhere really with an address that I could put into my phone to guide me.

Instead, I was told to find 'the big tree by the water fountain in Memorial Park.' That did not fill me with much confidence.

But it turns out this place really is that small. There's just one memorial park, the biggest tree is pretty obvious even from a distance, and as Queenie and I approach, there's the water fountain. I breathe a sigh of relief that I'm probably where I'm supposed to be. The problem now, though, is that I'm ridiculously early.

"That's okay," I say to Queenie. She looks up at me, panting with her pink tongue lolling out of her mouth. "We can just chill in the shade until other people and their doggies get here, right?"

If they come. What if I got the day wrong or the time or there's some other park with a large tree, after all. What if—

Queenie woofs and wags her tail at me. She's so happy to be out in the sunshine, on the grass, and smelling the ocean breeze, nothing else matters. I need to be more like her, don't I?

"If I got it wrong, then we'll still have had a nice walk, and we can try again next week, okay?" I tell my dog. She's still a miniature tank made of wrinkles, but her whole demeanor is so much happier since I brought her home from the shelter. With a better diet, her eyes are brighter and less watery, her breath less like garbage, and she's even slobbering less.

It breaks my heart to think about all the time she sat all alone in that cage, waiting to be picked. But I'm doing my best not to dwell on the past—for both of us. We're here now, living our best lives, and I need to make sure we're both making the most of it.

First, I get Queenie's collapsable bowl out of my messenger bag and fill it up from my bottle of water, then I settle us in the shade where we can both have a drink. I have carrot sticks for us both, as she surprisingly loves them. I also have a Frisbie to play fetch together. It's already getting pretty chewed up, so I don't know how much longer it's going to fly, but that's okay. She'll only want to chase it for a while before she'd rather wrestle me for it and then eventually just lay down and munch around the edges before having a nap.

I love that it's only been a week, but I know her so well already. I was nervous about adopting a rescue dog because they might be, well, nervous. Who knows what kind of life they've lived beforehand? But Queenie's attitude is kind of like her body: sturdy AF. So far, she doesn't seem fazed by anything. Cars, children, horses, the mail carrier. Nothing freaks her out.

But I think she is still sad sometimes. She likes to bulldoze her way onto my bed at night via the mini staircase I bought for her, so it's really my fault. But could tell she wanted to snuggle, and I love it as well, so no regrets. I think we've both been lonely for too long to stand on ceremony.

I'm lost in thought as Queenie lifts her head and lets out a big, low 'WOOF.' That's all the warning I get before a black and white bullet hurtles across my lap and launches itself at my dog, yapping excitably as the end of its wayward leash smacks me on the face.

"Oh, shit! Dude, I'm so freaking sorry! Are you okay?"

I blink and look toward the voice. Then I blink again and wonder how hard I just got whipped.

Am I hallucinating?

The guy jogging up to me under the shade of the mighty oak tree has got to be at least six-five, and with the shorts and tight tank he's wearing, it's very easy to see how muscular he is. Like a real-life superhero with tree-trunk thighs and bulging biceps. His red hair is thick and cut short around the back and sides. There are pretty freckles all over his nose, cheeks and shoulders. Even as he grapples for the leash attached to the black and white blur, his smile is goofy, and his carefree laugh files up all the cracks in my heart.

"Rocky, no! Play nice, little man!"

I realize the blur is actually a Dalmatian puppy that's currently hopping all over and around Queenie. But Queenie seems to be watching with interest as the pup dances about, occasionally woofing her feelings regarding the youngster.

"It's okay," I say when I finally unstick my tongue from the roof of my mouth. This guy might be gorgeous, but he's also only human, and he doesn't even seem that scary. Aside from him being impossibly attractive, of course. "They're just playing. She'll tell him if she's had enough."

The guy puffs his cheeks out and rubs the back of his neck with one of his hands…which only serves to show off his insane biceps even more. "Sorry, man. I still have no clue what I'm doing with any of this. We're actually here to go to a class so this little monster can learn some manners."

"You're doing Big Bark Bootcamp?" I ask before my brain can catch up with my mouth. The embarrassing squeak to my voice probably betrays how excited I am by the idea, but almost immediately, reality catches up with me. A guy like this would never be interested in being anything other than polite with a scrawny nerd like me.

Except…his face lights up. "We sure are! Is that why you guys are here? You doing it, too?"

"Um, yes," I say shyly. "I just adopted my dog, and I wanted some help making sure she's adjusting properly."

I expect him to make his excuses and wait somewhere else so he doesn't have to talk to me anymore. But instead, he plops on the ground beside me and raises his eyebrows.

"No way! I pulled Rocky here out of a burning building. I'm a firefighter," he adds for clarification. He's not doing much to refute my theory that he's a superhero. Then he shoves his huge hand my way. "Lochlan Bell."

In something of a daze, I lift my hand and shake his. His grip is firm but not tight in that asshole 'I'm in charge' sort of way. "Dario Garcia-Perez," I say, then immediately regret it.

It's not just that I feel like a fraud telling him I'm Dario. That's what everyone at my new job calls me, after all. But Shane always warned me to drop the 'Perez' part because he reckoned it was too much of a mouthful. Also, that people didn't always like it being pointed out that I'm Hispanic—like the Garcia alone wouldn't make that obvious. He used to tell me I could pass for white like it was some great compliment, and said having just one surname would make that easier.

I hate that people might have a bad reaction to realizing my heritage when I'm nothing but proud of it. But I'm also just so tired of second-guessing everything and unnecessary drama.

And...*shit!* I need to be more careful about telling random people my surname, for crying out loud! This guy doesn't look dangerous, but then neither did Shane. I'd actually considered using a completely different name in public just for a little extra security. But that idea obviously completely flew out of my head when faced with Lochlan's gorgeous smile and cheery disposition.

Despite my misgivings—both about racism and security—Lochlan doesn't bat an eyelid or pause or anything. He just finishes the shake and juts his chin toward our scrapping dogs. "She's a rescue? She's got a lotta balls already! Uh, I mean..."

My laugh startles me. Not only does it melt my previous worries away, but I realize I'm actually laughing with someone I just met. It's so normal, but that in itself makes it so *not* normal.

I feel lighter all of a sudden.

"It's okay, I know what you mean." I regain my composure and look fondly at my girl. "She's a fighter."

Lochlan punches my arm. "That's why Rocky got his name! He's a fighter, too!"

I'm sure Lochlan only uses a fraction of the strength he possesses, but it's more just the touch itself that catches me by surprise. I'm pretty positive he's straight and doesn't mean anything by it. But having a hot guy put his hand on me—no matter how briefly or innocently—isn't something I was sure I wanted again.

However, it's like warmth blossoms from that small spot where our skin connected. My heart has felt shriveled and cold for so long. Yet in that moment, it flutters, like a butterfly emerging from its cocoon and unfurling its wings.

I cast around for something to say, trying to remember how to behave like a regular human being. "Queenie already had her name when I picked her up," I explain. "But I think it suits her."

Lochlan gives her an appraising look as she bats her paw at Rocky's head, trying to calm the pup down, or so it seems to me. "Oh, yeah. She's definitely got something regal about her. She gets shit done."

I chuckle again. There's still a part of me that's nervous to have this Adonis giving me attention. But there's also something so relaxing about his company that's helping me forget to be anxious. No one's making him talk to me, after all. Certainly not me. If he wants to sit here until the class starts, that's his choice.

The fact that he's not making an excuse to get away from me gives me the kind of confidence boost I haven't felt in forever.

"So, you're a firefighter?" I find myself asking. Talking about jobs seems like a safe enough topic for many reasons.

He nods, splitting his attention between me and making sure his puppy isn't beating up my dog. "With the One-Thirteen. This guy was hiding out in an old warehouse." He swallows, and something serious flickers over his face. "Shit, I keep imagining, like, what if we didn't get the call? What if I didn't find him in time? What if I never heard him and I left him behind? I don't—"

His anxiety is palpable, and before I can stop myself, I realize I'm reaching out and placing my hand on his forearm. His skin is warm against mine, and he instantly calms. His eyes flick to meet mine, and I nod reassuringly, suddenly feeling like the expert in the room—or the park, I guess. But that's because I *am* the expert at this particular thing.

"They're called intrusive thoughts," I say gently, repeating what my therapist has drilled into me. "Sometimes our brain likes to cope with trauma by playing out worse-case scenarios so it can try and feel prepared in case those situations actually happen." Embarrassment flies through me and I withdraw my hand quickly. "But you probably know all about that, being a first responder."

Lochlan is frowning in thought, however. He sniffs and reaches over to squeeze my knee, like he's reciprocating my brief touch. "No, thank you. I mean, yeah, we talk about that kind of stuff a lot. But no one's actually called it…what did you say?"

"Intrusive thoughts," I offer him.

He nods. "Yeah. It's like they're bullying their way through my regular, sane thoughts. That's good if I know it's like a stress response kinda deal. We have a shrink that looks out for us, so I can talk to her more about that now I know it has a name."

He bumps shoulders with me then lets go of my knee. I miss his touch immediately, but I'm so wowed that he's listening to the advice silly little me has to offer, I don't really mind.

"No big deal," I say, trying not to get flustered.

"Naw, man. I appreciate it."

He flashes me that smile again, and I'm glad I'm sitting down. Otherwise, I think my jelly legs would have betrayed me. But then he keeps talking and it somehow gets worse… or better, I suppose, depending on how you're looking at it.

"I'm happy we're going to be doing this class together," he says. "We can be buddies!" However, he then lifts his eyebrows and looks awkward. "Oh, unless you'd rather be left alone. I'm sorry, dude. I don't always know when to back off. My friend Lili says *I'm* the puppy, not Rocky. If I'm stepping on your peace and quiet, just tell me and I'll skedaddle. I—"

"No!" I blurt out, my face instantly flushing. "I mean, um, you're not bothering me at all. I'm new in town, actually. The whole reason I adopted was because I didn't want to be alone. So it's nice to talk to someone. Especially about this stuff." I gesture to Rocky and Queenie. Queenie has managed to somehow subdue the puppy and is now aggressively cleaning behind his ears. "Being a dog dad is quickly becoming my only personality trait."

Lochlan laughs and looks relieved, but then he squints at me. "Wait, you don't know anyone at all in Redwood Bay?"

I shake my head. "I moved here for work. My family's in San Diago, so they're not a million miles away. But it's not the same as seeing them every day and talking face to face. My colleagues are okay, but they're also IT nerds like me, so their social skills aren't amazing. And…" I wince. "Unlike me, who just monologued at you for five whole minutes."

Lochlan looks like he takes a second to realize what I said before he shakes himself. "Huh? No! You're fine, dude. Great, actually! I was worried people were going to judge the shit out of me in this class for being hopeless. I'm so glad we met first. And now you can say you know at least one person in town. Hey!" His eyes light up. "Let's swap numbers! We can walk these little monsters together. I—oh—haha."

He tilts his head, and I turn to also watch as Queenie throws herself against Rocky, wrapping him in her arms and cuddling him close…apparently whether he likes it or not. He wriggles a bit but then seems to give up and snuggle as well.

"I think they like each other," Lochlan says, sounding awed.

I swallow and try not to think of the litters Queenie supposedly had. Did she get a chance to even be a mom to them? Is that what she's doing to this wayward, orphaned pup now?

I was prepared to tell Lochlan that he didn't need to take pity on me and offer to hang out. I bet he has a million cooler friends than me. But if it's more about our dogs spending time together than us…then I guess it would be selfish to say no. Right?

"I think Queenie would love to go for a walk with Rocky," I say softly.

"Hell, yeah," Lochlan agrees cheerfully, pulling his phone out of his shorts. "Digit me up, bro! Then we can organize a puppy playdate."

It looks like more people are approaching from across the park for the class. So before I can change my mind or get distracted, I rattle off my number for Lochlan to input. He fires me a text and…that's it.

I've made my first friend in Redwood Bay.

The fact that he's insanely hot is probably going to come back to haunt me soon enough. But for now, I just enjoy the feeling of acceptance, wrapping myself up in it like a blanket.

I've made a friend.

And I *really* like him.

CHAPTER 5

Lochlan

It's not like I don't already have a lot of friends. The One-Thirteen are more like family than buddies, but then I also see my bros from high school kinda regularly and a few of the guys from the academy. I always seem to have a birthday or a cookout coming up, and if I want to watch a game or shoot some shit, there's always a bunch of people I can hit up.

So I'm not sure why I'm this excited to see Dario again, but I am. We agreed to meet after he finishes work, which leaves me at a loose end for most of the day. Normally I have plenty of stuff to get on with after I've been on for twenty-four hours, like chores and going to the gym. Except I've been useless since I got off shift this morning. We didn't get any major calls last night, so I actually slept at the station, and that means I couldn't even waste time napping the hours away today.

There's something about Dario that I find fascinating. I guess most of my friends are loud mouths, like myself. Dario is quiet, but when he does talk, he's so smart and funny. I dunno, man. I just want to see him again so bad.

I decide to head over to the beach early with Rocky and get some fish tacos. He's still sleeping a lot, so I figure he can get excited on the ride over there, sniff and run around for a bit, then chill out while I have my food.

Once I'm in motion, I feel better. I'm mad I've wasted the day and regret not doing the laundry like I should have, but I can make up for it tomorrow. Maybe I'm just excited about sharing my new pet parent era with someone going through the same sort of thing. The guys at work are already kinda over me quoting puppy training books at them all shift. Dario gets it, though.

We had so much fun at the class on Saturday. Cuz of my shift pattern, I'll have to miss next week, but Dario already promised me he'd take notes and meet with me to go over what Rocky and I are gonna miss. See? That's another reason to like the guy. He's kind, and people aren't always kind these days. My momma taught me that was the most important thing you could be in life. People are born smart or rich or whatever. But anyone can choose to be nice if they want to be, and that's important.

I park my truck and make sure Rocky's leash is secure before getting out at the seafront. Even though I've lived my whole life in Redwood Bay, the sight of the greeny-blue Pacific Ocean still gets me all the time. It's just so frigging beautiful. I inhale the salt air deeply, feeling the afternoon sun on my skin and warm breeze through my air, grateful that this is the place I get to call home.

The taco stand is always busy, but I manage to snag a picnic table for Rocky and I. With a few crunchy, tasty tacos in my belly, I relax. Dario texted to say he was leaving work, so he should be here soon with his big mutt, Queenie. I like her a lot, too. She's a real boss lady and doesn't take any shit from my poorly mannered son. I love that Dario rescued her as well. Not quite the same way I got Rocky, but a rescue nonetheless.

"Oh my god!" a young woman cries. I look up to see her and her friend pointing at Rocky. "Is that your puppy?"

"Sure is!" I tell them proudly. "You wanna pet him? He's real friendly."

I notice the women are both really cute, and I like how careful they are when crouching down and fussing over my little man. He's straining on his leash and doing his best to escape, but I've got a tight hold of the other end. The ladies coo over him, calling him adorable and precious and asking me questions about him.

I'm not that dumb. I can tell the first gal in particular is flirting with me. Body language is like fire to me. I might not be able to always explain it, but I can usually read it no trouble. Usually, I'd be excited and maybe ask for her number. But instead, I find my attention drifting back toward the small parking lot, watching out for Dario.

I guess it would be rude, right? If we agreed to meet up and he found me paying attention to some girls. They are very nice and there's two of them, so in theory we could have made a foursome of it. But my body language skills include a damn good gaydar, as they used to say back in the nineties. I'm almost certain that Dario's queer in some way, so for whatever reason it just doesn't feel right for me to try and score a date when we're supposed to be hanging. I'd be upset if he was looking all starry-eyed at some guy when I arrived, I reckon.

"Oh, there's my buddy!" I say excitedly as soon as I see Dario pull into the parking lot in a dark blue Toyota Corolla.

The ladies seem to get the hint without any hard feelings. "Enjoy your evening," the first gal says with a wink. They tell Rocky goodbye and walk on their way.

I gather my trash to dump in the can, then stroll over to

meet Dario as he and Queenie are walking over. "You made it!" I say, even though it's obvious that he did.

I'm just happy he's here. Maybe a part of me was worried that he wouldn't show. It's funny how I'm worried about impressing him, like he's one of the cool kids from school. He's got that 'I have my shit together in life' vibe that I'm still working toward.

"I'm starting to find my way about," Dario says with a little smile, glancing down as Queenie and Rocky sniff each other's butts with wagging tails.

It's probably weird of me and this is something I'd never admit out loud in case it made anyone else feel weird…but Dario is like kinda really pretty. Is it okay to say a dude is pretty? He has these sharp cheekbones and super long eyelashes. His smile is shy, but it's so nice. Pretty just feels like the right word.

Rather than say any of that, though, I indicate the beach and grin. "You'll be a local in no time. Redwood Bay is the best. So chill, but not snooty like other towns round here. And slap bang in between LA and San Diego. Actually, scratch that. Way more important is that it's equal distance between Disneyland and Legoland!"

Dario chuckles, and we naturally start walking together. The taco truck and parking lot are up higher than the beach, like most of the coastline around here. So we head down the steps set in the grassy verge.

"Isn't there a small amusement park around here as well?" Dario asks.

I nod, keeping my focus on the wooden boards. My feet are like boats and I don't wanna slip in front of my new friend and embarrass myself. "Critter Canyon Park. It's got this cute frontier vibe to it. Technically closer to San Clemente, but it doesn't really fit with their upmarket scene, so they let us claim it."

"Sounds fun," Dario says as we reach the sand.

"It is," I agree, watching as he lets Queenie off her leash. Rocky's not old enough to trust him like that yet, but she's a good girl. After just one class together I can tell she's not the kind to bolt off. "I haven't been in forever. Hey! If you felt like checking it out, I'd totally be up for going with."

He blinks at me. "Really?"

I shrug. "Absolutely. Oh, only if you'd want to, though. Sorry, I keep barging my way into your life," I say a little sheepishly. I don't want him to feel like he has to put up with me.

But he shakes his head with that small but pretty smile again. "Honestly, I think if you don't bully me into being friends, I'll never make any. So, um, thank you."

I puff out my chest, so happy he's okay with me being a pain in his ass. "Awesome. Maybe we can go when it's a little closer to the holidays. Obviously, we don't get snow around here, but they decorate it all for Christmas and that at least *looks* cold. A lot of the rides are a few decades old now, but they have this damn cool runaway train coaster if you're into that sort of thing."

He gives me a look I can't quite read. But before I can worry about it, he nods. "I love that sort of thing, actually. If you don't think it's, um, too childish or anything."

I frown, wondering why he'd be worried about something like that. "I think if you enjoy something and it's not hurting nobody else, who cares if other people think it's childish or dumb? Life's too short, man. We have to live in the moment. Catch that fish."

"Hm?" He raises his eyebrows questioningly at me.

"You know," I say as we idle along the beach. "Seize the day. Carp diem."

His smile goes from shy to kilowatt in a second. "Carp… carpe," he says with a laugh. "Clever."

I thought it was a particularly stupid joke, so the fact that he thinks it's smart makes me beam.

"So did you know much about Redwood Bay before you moved here?" I ask, curious to hear an outsider's perspective on the town I've lived my whole life in.

"I'd never heard of it until I got the job interview," Dario admits with a gentle laugh. "I was back living with my folks in San Diego, so it was nice to see how easy the drive between the two was right away. But when I got here, I just felt sort of immediately relaxed. It's peaceful, but there's still a thrum of liveliness running through it."

"I've never lived in a city," I say. "I don't know if it would be my jam. I create enough of my own chaos to be surrounded by it as well." He laughs at my silly joke again. I don't know why his opinion is so important to me, but I love cracking that shy exterior and seeing him happy. "Plus," I continue, "I don't think I could ever move somewhere the ocean wasn't on my doorstep, so I guess I never even tried anywhere else. Is that lame?"

Dario quickly shakes his head. "I love traveling and I do think it's great to experience other cultures and ways of living if you're fortunate enough to have the means to do so. But home is where the heart is. If your heart is happy, why leave your home?"

"That's some deep philosophical shit right there, dude," I say in awe, shaking my head and grinning.

Damn. This guy could be friends with anyone, yet he was worried he was putting a meathead like me out of my way. I'm the lucky one here.

"How long were you in San Diego?" I ask. I hope I'm not bugging him, but I want to find out what makes him tick.

He chews his lip, and his shoulders hunch very slightly. Huh. I've definitely touched a nerve. Damn it, that's the last thing I want to do. I'm about to tell him he doesn't have to answer any of my dumb questions if he doesn't want to, when he starts talking.

"I grew up there. Well, in the suburbs, so I think I'm probably more of a small-town guy in my soul as well. That's why I like it here. But I went to college in Arizona and lived in Phoenix for a few years."

I'm about to ask what prompted the change, but I don't like the tension he's carrying. Something tells me Phoenix wasn't the best place for him.

Thankfully, he gives me an opportunity to change the subject and hopefully bring back that big smile again. "Did you always want to be a firefighter?"

"Oh, hell no," I inform him with a wink. "I was gonna be Batman. When my pa told me that probably wasn't gonna happen, I sulked for like a month. Then I was gonna be an astronaut, until I realized it's mostly about math, and Martians aren't real. Then I was gonna be an archeologist, but I figured Indiana Jones probably found all the cool booby-trapped places already. Finally, in high school, I seriously committed to becoming a Charger. Worked my ass off on that field for it."

"What happened?" Dario asks.

I shrug. "I wasn't good enough."

"To be Batman?"

I drop my head back and laugh so hard it makes Rocky and Queenie come running to my feet so they can bark at me. When I look back down, Dario is grinning at me. Damn, I love that.

"To be fair," I say once I stop wheezing, "Batman is mostly about all his fancy toys, and considering my family aren't billionaires, that would have always put a dent in that particular plan." I shake my head. "I really loved football, but I had a couple of close calls with injuries that already rattled me and scared the shit out of my mom. We had a college scout come watch us, but it was mostly to see this other kid, Cassius Garda, who really did go off and play for the Seahawks for like a decade. When the scout wasn't interested in me, that was basically the end of the line."

"I'm sorry," Dario says sympathetically, but I shake my head.

"You know, I wasn't as heartbroken as I thought I was going to be. Yeah, I was kinda lost for a while. I had okay grades, but I wasn't sure if college was going to be right for me, especially after my folks had already helped pay for my sister. She got a partial scholarship and worked jobs alongside studying, but still. They said they'd do whatever they could, but I wasn't convinced enough to get into all that debt. Then we had this career fair at school, and as soon as I saw the firefighter's booth, it was like a lightbulb went off in my head."

"That's amazing," Dario says, sounding totally sincere. "Were your parents okay with that?"

"Well, my momma still loves to fret," I say with a laugh. "But her and Pa are damn proud, yeah. They like to tell stories about some of the crazy shit I've done. But the truth is, we rescue a lot of cats out of trees and clean up after a lot of fender benders."

Dario shrugs. "I bet the cats and their owners are still very grateful."

"Yeah, they are," I say warmly. "How about you? You always know you wanted to work in IT?"

He scoffs. "After the *second* family computer I pulled apart then couldn't put back together, my dad gave in and bought me my own one to mess around with. I broke it a lot still, but I learned a hell of a lot at the same time. So yeah, when it came to college, I knew I wanted to keep studying coding and all that. I figured I'd end up in Silicon Valley, but…"

He's thoughtful for a few seconds, and I can feel the weight of Arizona on him again. But then he shakes himself.

"I'm actually glad to be down south, closer to home. The start-up I'm working for is really exciting. It's nice to be on the ground level while the company is just beginning to spread its wings."

I love the way his eyes shine when he talks about his job. It's how I feel about the One-Thirteen. Even when I'm bone tired and stink of soot, even when it's been a bad call where we weren't able to save everyone, I know that I was put on this earth to help people.

Dario looks like he feels the same way about making computers run. And—hey—everyone uses computers. So he's also helping people in a way, right?

We arrive at the small pier and turn around. I could have walked all the way down to Mexico, but the sun is already going down, and besides, Rocky can't go too far before it wipes him out.

We talk more about work. I tell Dario about some of the more unusual calls we been on, and he tries to explain what it is he actually does with computers. I don't really follow it other than he speaks a couple of different coding languages and that his company provides some kind of data storage solutions…or something. Hell, I barely passed Spanish even though I knew it was really important to try, so if he can understand not one but *two* different languages, color me impressed.

As we get closer to the parking lot, though, I can feel myself getting distracted. It seems like we only just got here, and I'm not ready for it to be over yet. I don't have any plans tonight. I suppose I could do that laundry, but…

"Have you eaten?" I blurt out.

He blinks at me, probably confused as we were just

talking about how paperwork is annoying in any job. "Uh, no, actually. I picked Queenie up straight from the office."

"Would you wanna grab something together?" I ask.

I know I just had those tacos, but they barely touched the sides. I'd have no problem with more food if it meant our time together doesn't have to end so soon.

And there I go again, barging in his life. "Unless you have plans or whatever."

He swallows and looks away, and I'm absolutely certain I've overstepped this time. But then he takes a breath and smiles back at me. "Would you want to be my first house-guest? I was going to make pizza."

"Make it?" I ask.

He shrugs one arm, and I can't quite tell if he's embarrassed or proud. "I prepare the dough in batches to freeze and got some out this morning to defrost. If that's too much effort, though—"

"Are you kidding?" I can't stop myself from interrupting. "So we can stretch it ourselves and you've got toppings and stuff?"

"That's the idea," he says, his smile growing.

"Dude, that sounds so fun!" I cry.

I'm aware I'm probably acting like a kindergartener right now, but I don't care. I can't say I'm particularly talented, but I've always had a blast getting messy with arts and crafts. My sister has a toddler that I can sometimes join in with baking and painting eggs and anything involving glitter. But I've always thought that would be fun to do with buddies or on a date.

"Do you have beer?" I ask, thinking I can stop by the store if not.

But he nods. "And wine and spirits. My tias' idea of housewarming gifts was to stock up my non-existent bar for my non-existent friends."

I slap his shoulder, careful that it's not so hard I knock him over. "I exist!" I remind him happily. "And I'd be proud to be your first visitor. And Rocky, too, if he's invited?"

"Of course," he says, reaching down to pet my tired-out puppy. "They can play in the yard."

He has a *yard.* See? I knew he had his shit together. My apartment is tiny. "Damn, he'll love that," I say genuinely.

For a second, we just smile at each other. His dark eyes are so warm, and I've definitely not changed my mind about the long lashes that frame them being pretty.

Then I realize I'm being weird again, and laugh. We've stopped by the parking lot, so I jut my chin toward my truck. "Shall I just follow you there?"

"Yeah, sure," he says. "It's not far."

Nowhere in this town is. Heck, if I have one too many beers, Rocky and I could probably walk home if necessary.

"All right, bro. See you there!"

I'm so excited you'd think this was a date. Except I can't remember the last time I looked forward to seeing a girl compared to how hyped I am to be the first person to visit Dario's place. Even if I wasn't the first, I still want to check out where he lives and get to know him better.

Making new friends is *awesome.*

CHAPTER 6

Dario

THIS IS A BAD, *BAD* IDEA. 'WHAT WAS I THINKING?' FEELS LIKE it should be my motto these days.

The drive back to my place seems to pass in a flash, but I still manage to spend the entire time questioning my sanity. I promised I wouldn't tell anyone outside of my family my new address, let alone invite an almost stranger over.

But there's something about Lochlan that puts me so at ease, and I can't explain it. It's not that he's a firefighter, although I suppose that helps. It's that he seems to really *see* me and, more to the point, he's not put off by that. It's like when I talk, he hangs on my every word. I've spent so long feeling insignificant, or worse, a burden. However, on both the occasions I've hung out with Lochlan, he seems delighted by my company.

It makes me nervous. Like I'm constantly waiting for the other shoe to drop. But I'm not strong enough to resist a little compassion from a hot guy. Until he proves me wrong, I'm going to do my best to try and keep trusting him.

I just hope I'm not going to ruin how *he* feels about *me* by letting him into my home. I've told him again and again that

I just moved here, but surely he's going to expect a grown man to have *something* to show for his adult life. I think he's a bit older than me, and I'd hate for him to think of me as some immature college kid still.

I'd hate it even more if he ghosted me. I know we've hardly known each other a hot minute. However, I'm pretty sure I'd still be crushed.

Well, there's no going back now. As I swing into my driveway, I take a deep breath and reason with myself. Much like when he sat down with me under the oak tree before class began, no one forced him to ask if we could have dinner together. And he certainly didn't mean in a date way. I saw the way those girls were flirting with him when I got to the beach. So that makes him coming over much safer. He's just being my friend.

I need all the friends I can get right now.

His truck pulls up behind me, so I quit dawdling and get out of my car with Queenie right behind me. It's amazing how fast she's slipped into her new routine. "We're home," I tell her like I do every time we return. I want her to learn the word and know that this is where she belongs. That she's safe here.

But it's also kind of for my benefit as well. I've never had a place of my own. I love my family, but growing up with them was kind of a lot. I was pretty desperate to spread my wings and get to college. My roommate was okay, but we didn't exactly become friends.

And then I met Shane.

I shake my head, refusing to think about him right now. Instead, I look at my little house like Lochlan might be seeing it. It's an L shape with a cute set of semi-circle stairs leading to the awning and the front door in the middle. The steps make me think of mille feuille cake layers.

The left side of the house is two stories with a covered

balcony attached to my bedroom, and the right side is a single story. Like most architecture around here, the walls are white and the roof tiles terracotta. The patio out front isn't large and neither is the lawn out back. But I love that thanks to all the foliage it feels secluded from the neighboring houses. Palm trees sway around the edges and there's even a little fountain nestled in the shrubbery where birds like to play, much to Queenie's annoyance.

It might not look like a palace, but it feels like one to me. More importantly, it's all mine, and when I close the door on the world, I feel at peace and secure.

Lochlan's parked his truck on the street, and I watch as he and Rocky hop down onto the sidewalk, expecting to feel a sense of trepidation at him breaching my sanctuary. I am nervous, for sure. But I'm also hoping that I haven't made a terrible mistake. This might be okay.

"Um, so this is me," I say, trying not to cringe at my own lameness as I wave in the general direction of my house. He's going to realize where we are, duh.

However, he's grinning as he and Rocky jog up beside my car. "Dude, this is neat!" He cranes his neck and really takes it all in. "Yeah, if I were your folks, I'd be hella proud that you landed on your feet like this. Can we go inside?"

He walks past me toward the door, apparently oblivious as to how his words—no—his effortlessly given *compliments* shake me to my core. He can't mean it when he says things like that, can he? Like when he calls me smart and cool and all those other unlikely things.

But as he turns and waits expectantly for me to open the door, I can't help but feel like every bone in his body is genuine. This big golden retriever of a man doesn't know how to bullshit, I'm sure.

Or maybe I'm still reeling from so many years with a guy

who lied to me like it was breathing that I can't tell honesty from deceit anymore.

Catching myself before I can spiral down that rabbit hole, I head up the steps and unlock the door. "It's still pretty empty," I warn him again. "I saved up every penny for the deposit and that hasn't left much for anything else yet. I wasn't able to bring any furniture from my old place, so anything I have right now is from thrift stores or donated from my family, bless them."

As soon as he steps over the threshold, Lochlan automatically kicks off his sandy flip flops and looks around my small entrance hall. Someday, I'd love to have art on the walls, a nice coat rack, and a fancy lampshade. But at the moment, I'm grateful to have a rickety table to leave my keys on and a hook on the wall for Queenie's leash.

The whole place is tiled, so I want to invest in some rugs to stop it being so echoey. As it is, our bare feet slap as we walk toward the kitchen. I can feel Lochlan looking around as we enter the room.

"Oh, I can see your family knows what's important," he comments, and I chuckle, agreeing. I've got all the kitchen appliances I could need on the counter as well as a very healthy spice rack.

"You haven't even seen the cupboards yet," I joke. "My mom and tias keep sending me grocery deliveries and care packages. I might not have a dining table, but I'm certainly not going to starve."

Lochlan crosses his impressive arms and nods. "There aren't many problems that can't be solved by decent food. Your family sound like good people."

My heart flutters and I remind myself that he's just being nice. Although it's cool of him to acknowledge and appreciate my family. They mean a lot to me.

I'm sure he'd say that to any of his friends. Still, I can feel him *not* judging my space, and that's such a relief I can't stop myself from feeling grateful.

I open the back door and let the dogs out to play. "It's very secure," I assure him. "I've checked a hundred times. No one's making a jailbreak."

"Excellent," he says, then claps his hands together. "Come on then! Give me the tour."

"It won't take long," I assure him.

He shrugs and winks at me, turning the flutters I was experiencing into full blown tremors. "Then we can get to making pizza quicker."

"Oh," I say with a jolt, dashing over to the fridge.

I take the defrosted dough out as it'll need to rest for half an hour. But I also grab two beers before closing the door, then make short work of using the bottle opener and tipping some chips into a bowl to show that I don't intend to leave him hungry for long.

When I hand him his drink, he holds his bottle up. "Sláinte! Cheers to your new place, dude!" I let him tap the glass together. "May you have many happy years here."

A wistful smile tugs at my mouth. That feels like tempting fate to me, but it's a nice thought. "Salud to my first guest," I say, repeating the tap. We both take a drink, and for a second, I get lost in watching how his throat bobs as he swallows.

Get it together! I scold myself. No perving on my new (hot) straight friend, for crying out loud.

"Tour, yes," I splutter, spinning around in the open space I've yet to fill. "Well, as you can tell, this is the kitchen and then this side will be the dining room."

"In the meantime, it's a killer dance floor," he jokes, running into the middle of the sparse room and pulling some truly hideous moves. But it makes me laugh, which he seems to do a lot.

I love it.

The living room doesn't have much in it aside from an old couch and a medium-sized TV. But it works and the sofa is pretty comfortable, so I really can't complain. Even if it takes months and months, I'm going to slowly make this place my own and invest in furniture that brings me joy.

For now, it's got lots of potential, which I tell Lochlan.

"Oh, for real," he says, nodding and looking around like he's mentally decorating. "Good bones. You could have book-cases and sideboards and all sorts in here."

"I want a big potted plant on the floor in that corner there," I say tentatively, so used to my ideas being laughed at.

Lochlan, of course, just nods and lifts his eyebrows. "Yes, great idea! What kind of colors do you like? Warm? Cool?"

I shrug and move toward the stairs. "I'm not sure, really. I guess I'll have to figure that out as I go."

"Yeah, totally," he says cheerfully. "You can really make it your own that way."

"I hope so," I say as we go upward.

He can't see my bashful smile, but it's there. I'm sure—again—that he's just being nice. However, it's validating that he gets how important it is to me that this place is stamped with my personality…even if I'm not entirely sure what that looks like just yet.

It's only as I open my bedroom door that I realize how intimate showing him in here is. I try not to blush and fumble over my words as I tell him the mattress is one of the only new things I did splurge on this month because the idea of a used one was too gross for me. He notices Queenie's mini staircase immediately and admits that Rocky's been sleeping on his bed too.

I let him look in the bathroom as I glance at the closed office door. I hadn't thought through that he might see it, but as it's shut, I hope I can get away with it.

"And that's just full of junk," I say dismissively, waving my beer bottle at it, already moving toward the stairs again. "I've barely been able to fit my desk and computer in it."

"I still want to see, though," Lochlan cries, reaching for the door handle.

"Oh, it's tiny, you won't—"

I'm not even sure what I was going to say. I just wanted to stop him from looking inside.

Too late.

He flings the door open to reveal that the office is indeed small…but it's also the only room in the house I've been able to properly decorate. My cheeks really do flame as horror creeps over me. "See, it's just junk," I say, trying to will him to come back out of the room.

But he's turning slowly and looking absolutely enchanted.

"Oh, man," he gushes. "Is this all yours? Sorry, dumb question, it must be because it's here."

I lick my lips and edge over the threshold, looking around at all my posters, figurines, and general nerdy paraphernalia. The only shelves I have so far are in here, bursting with the evidence of my childhood obsession that doesn't seem to have died yet.

"I told you I was a geek," I mumble.

I'm sure there are cool things that cool people collect. But ever since I was a kid, I've been tech driven and fascinated by what the human race will invent in years, decades, centuries to come.

So it's probably no surprise that my biggest passion is science fiction.

Star Wars. Star Trek. Stargate. Battlestar Galactica. If it's got 'star' in the title, I probably have some sort of collectible from it. Not to mention Doctor Who, Aliens, Predator, The Expanse, Terminator, Firefly, and even more niche franchises that a lot of people won't have heard of.

I cringe, waiting for Lochlan to laugh at me. I knew

bringing him to my pathetic, empty house was a mistake. But I *never* expected him to see my secret stash. Especially when I've been parted from it for so long. Getting it all out of storage and displaying it has brought me so much joy. But seeing it from an outsider's perspective, it's so clear to me in that moment that I should just have left it all in boxes. What kind of adult has toys like this? Not sexy, attractive ones, that's for sure. He's going to think I'm a fucking child. I should just—

"Holy shit!" Lochlan cries. I realize his gaze has traveled upward and he's pointing at the top of my cluttered bookcase. "Is that the Millennium Falcon made out of *Legos?*"

"Uh…yeah," I utter, then it's like my nerves take over and I can't stop talking. "I worked every summer job I could when I was thirteen to buy it myself. It took about six months to make in between schoolwork. I can't believe it's survived all this time but, um, yeah. It's just some silly kid thing."

Lochlan scowls at me. Like full on frowns and shakes his head. "No it's not. Don't say things like that, okay? You worked hard for it, and I bet it took a shit ton of patience to make it. Han Solo was my *man* growing up. In fact, this whole room is like a wet dream."

I blink, not sure I heard him right. "You…like sci-fi?"

He scoffs and starts inspecting my daleks and xenomorphs more closely. "Remember which dorky kid wanted to be an astronaut?" he asks, jerking his thumb at his chest. "What I really wanted was to be Han or James T. Kirk or Malcom Reynolds." He rubs his chin. "Fuck it. I'd have been Ellen Ripley in a heartbeat, too."

For a second, I can't breathe. My throat has thickened so much, it's difficult to swallow.

Shane mocked the *shit* out of me for 'believing in little green men.' I'd already figured that out by the time we moved in together, so I kept this whole collection in my parents' basement. Which was a smart move, because the one time I dared to bring a 'Live long and prosper' mug into the apartment, it mysteriously smashed within a few days.

I dread to think what might have happened to the Falcon.

I clear my throat and try to find my voice. "Ripley and Sarah Connor were the eighties sci-fi queens," I manage to say without squeaking too much.

Lochlan doesn't seem to have noticed my minor breakdown. He clicks his fingers and nods, his gaze still devouring all my trinkets. "Those mothers be *mothering,*" he quips. "Hey, we should watch something super classic after we make pizza. Like Demolition Man or Fifth Element. You know, something where the colors and costumes are off the chain."

A laugh bubbles out of me. It feels like more than relief. The joy of not only being accepted and not judged...but *embraced* and celebrated is almost too much. "I'd love that," I say, not caring that I do squeak this time. It's that or burst into tears. "I've got a few different subscriptions, so chances are we'll be able to find whatever we want."

"Something cheesy to go with our cheese pizzas!" Lochlan cries. He finishes his beer and raises his eyebrows at me. "As much as I'd love to spend all night here, shall we go make food and get our geek on?"

I nod, unable to speak for a moment. "Sounds great," I say after a beat.

Sounds perfect. Because Lochlan is perfect.

If only he wasn't straight...but asking for that really would be too much.

Right now, I'll take all of him I can get.

CHAPTER 7

Lochlan

It's quiet in the house.

Or rather, it's been a slow shift so far. The One-Thirteen is never quiet.

"You're a cheat!" Sawyer yells for the seventh or eighth time.

Anton rolls his eyes, gesturing to the board laid out between them. "How do you even cheat at Chutes and Ladders?"

"Then how come you keep winning?" Sawyer demands.

Anton flashes a grin made up of movie-star perfect teeth at him. "I'm just that talented."

Lili huffs and turns the volume up on the British baking show she's put on the TV. "It's literally a game of chance. You can't cheat and there's no skill to it. That's why it's a *kids'* game."

Anton and Sawyer frown at her until Sawyer snaps his head back to the board. "Another round?"

"Hell, yeah!" Anton cries as they reset the board.

I chuckle from one of the sofas. I'm not really paying attention to Lili's TV show, but it seemed safer to sit here rather than anywhere near the dining table where Sawyer and Anton are duking it out.

They make unlikely best friends. Sawyer has a different man, woman, or person-in-between in his bed almost every week, and Anton's a single dad who I don't think has even dated since he finally admitted he was gay and amicably divorced his lovely ex-wife. But the two of them just go together like peanut butter and jelly.

Kinda like me and Dario, I guess.

We're so different, but he's quickly becoming my favorite person to hang out with. We had such a blast the other night, making pizzas and geeking out over old sci-fi movies. We watched Starship Troopers and talked non-stop about all our favorite characters in various franchises. I only went home because he had to get up early for work the next day, but honestly, I could have stayed all night.

Luckily, I only had to wait a few days to see him again, when we met on Sunday so he could help me catch up on what I missed at the doggy training class. Speaking of which, Rocky's currently asleep at my feet, behaving like an angel. But we had to go out for several hours during our last shift, and this time was at night, so Nancy wasn't here to keep an eye on him. I was worried sick for the whole call that he might get himself in trouble and I wouldn't be there to help him.

As if reading my mind, Captain Valentine chooses that moment to come down from his office. Great. I can catch him and run my idea by him. "Something smells good," he says in the direction of the kitchen.

Del, one of our paramedics, looks up and gives him a little salute. "I'm making tagine. Lamb and veggie."

It's always tricky cooking for the house. We could get called at any second, so you want something that can be covered and reheated or shoved in the fridge. Most of us have favorite dishes we make when it's our turn, not to mention how Mrs. Bloom likes to surprise us. She always says, 'An army can't march on an empty stomach' and I think there's a lot of wisdom in that.

Speaking of being called out at any second, I better not miss my chance for a chat. So I wave my hand, not wanting to move my feet and disturb Rocky. "Cap! You got a sec?"

He nods and wanders over. "Where's everyone else?" he asks before I can get a word in.

"Rico and Teddy are in the gym," Lili supplies, not taking her eyes off the pear tarts the contestants are making on the TV.

Yara, our other paramedic, looks up from the coloring book she was working on. It's the kind that has lots of flowers and butterflies around slogans like 'Fuck the Patriarchy' and 'Eat the Rich.'

"I think Gene's in his bunk, doing his French lessons," she says sweetly.

I'm not the only one who chuckles. Our grumpy driver has been promising to take his wife to Paris their entire marriage. Little does she know, he's actually booked it for their anniversary this year. We've been giving him shit about his terrible attempts to learn the language, but I secretly I think it's super cute he's putting in all this effort for her.

"Cap?" I say, calling his attention back to me.

He raises his eyebrows. "Yes, Bell?"

Suddenly, I'm aware of everyone watching me. Fine. They all know I'm an annoying dog daddy by now. I've got no reason to be embarrassed.

"I was thinking how I'd like to keep an eye on Rocky when we go on calls when Nancy's not around," I explain.

Cap folds his arms and arches an eyebrow at me. "Go on."

"Well, my friend said he could fix a camera for me that I can check on my phone. If we set Rocky up in the meeting room with his bed and puppy pads and stuff like we did last time, that wouldn't bother anyone else, would it? Then if I get a down moment during the call, I can check him in seconds."

I didn't want Cap to think I was intending on slacking off. But at the same time, I'd work better and harder if I wasn't distracted worrying that Rocky was okay.

Okay, I was also worried about him getting up to mischief, which Cap would probably care about more. But as his dad, first and foremost I wanted a damn baby monitor on my son.

Valentine sighs. "You want to put cameras in the station?" he clarifies wearily.

I shake my head. "Just one. Okay, maybe two. But just in the meeting room, and I'd only turn them on when we go out at night. I could deactivate them the rest of the time, at least that's what Dario says."

"Oooh, *Dario*," Lili says, actually pausing her show to flutter her eyelashes at me. "The mysterious new friend."

I roll my eyes at her. "There's nothing mysterious about him. I told you—we met at the dog training class."

"Sure, buddy," Anton says with a scoff.

"But…we did meet there?" I say in confusion.

"Dario, Dario, Dario," Sawyer adds in a high-pitched dreamy voice.

"Oh fuck off, all of you," I grumble without any heat. All right, there's maybe a little heat. "I'm allowed to make friends outside of this house."

"Frieeeeends," Lili says, nodding with wide eyes.

I frown at her. "Yeah, friends. I can have a friend that's smart and stuff."

She softens and reaches out to squeeze my knee. "Dude. That was so not my point."

"Good," I say, still bristling. "I'm not some dumb meat-head, you know."

"That's not what I was getting at, babe." She huffs. "I don't doubt that if he's spending all this time with you and helping you out like you say, that he likes you just as much as you like him."

"Yeah, *likes*," Sawyer says and punches Anton's shoulder.

I'm still confused. "Why don't you think I'm good enough to be Dario's friend?" To be honest, I'm a little hurt by the way they're acting.

"Bell," Captain says in his 'patient' tone. But when I glance at him, his expression is sympathetic. "I don't think that's what they're implying."

"Then what?"

Lili smacks my thigh and laughs. "You *like* this guy, Beast! Like...*like* like him."

Oh, is *that* what they think? I laugh in relief. "Huh? No, guys, you know I'm straight. I can have a new friend and it just be that, okay? I mean, I think he's gay, but he might not be. And that's not here nor there anyway. Don't make it weird."

"The only thing weird here is you, bro," Sawyer says, shaking his head.

I feel myself getting hot under the collar. "No, it's not like that! You know I support all of you. I'm just not...that's not... he's my *friend,* all right? Please don't be dicks."

Rocky's woken up and is pawing at me, clearly sensing my distress. I've learned dogs are pretty amazing at stuff like that. Way more empathetic than my so-called buddies.

Lili sighs and reaches over to pet him. "We're not trying to be dicks," she says fondly.

"Sawyer is," Anton quips.

Lili hums and nods. "True."

"Don't listen to any of them," Del says in his calm,

melodic voice. I look over to see he's moving food to the dining table. Suddenly there's a scramble for everyone to grab a seat. Chutes and Ladders gets hastily shoved back in its box, winning apparently not as important as eating.

"Thanks, man," I say sincerely to Del for sticking up for me.

He shrugs as people start attacking the bowls of tagine and the buttered rolls. "I'm sure we'd all be excited if you met someone special. But sometimes toxic masculinity makes us forget that men are allowed to have close friendships they're enthralled by."

"Enthralled," Sawyer says with a snort. Lili smacks the back of his head.

"Ahh, dude," she says sounding genuinely sorry. "My bad if we made you feel shit. I'm happy you met someone cool."

"He *is* cool," I agree, poking at my chickpeas. "So, Cap, is it okay if he does his tech thing? He's got the same set up for his dog as his house when he's working from his office."

Luckily, he gets to work from home a fair bit. But I like that he still wanted to make sure Queenie was okay when he's out. His office is close to his place, so he can even walk her in his lunch breaks. He's such a responsible dog daddy.

Valentine sighs and considers me a moment. "We can give it a trial run. But!" he holds up his fork before I can say anything. "I reserve the right to pull the plug if it gets weird of freaky or whatever. I don't want anyone to feel like they're being spied on."

I shake my head. "No, absolutely not," I agree. "Thanks, Cap! I'll work it out with Nancy when he can come over and install it."

Judging by how the rest of the team are grinning at me like hyenas about to attack, I have a feeling that the best time for Dario to come over will be when the second or third watch are on shift.

Cap hums like he's still not convinced, but he said yes, and for now, that's good enough for me.

As usual, Rocky is sitting expectantly at my feet, so I sneak him some lamb. I think about how I can't wait to tell Dario about this.

Because yeah, these guys can suck it. He *is* a great friend.

They're just jealous, I'm sure.

CHAPTER 8
Dario

I wouldn't say I'm a natural gardener, but my yard isn't big and I'm giving it my best go.

The sun is dipping in the sky. As I worked from home today, I was able to wrap up on time and get straight out here, making the most of the daylight I had left. I also gave Queenie a good walk during my lunch break, and I fed her at the usual time, so she's taken care of. Mostly. She still keeps trying to 'help' me by digging holes wherever I'm weeding.

I'd be lying if I said I really minded. Seeing her coming out of her shell more and more as the days go by brings me immense joy. It's like she's remembering how to play, almost like being a puppy again.

Unfortunately, that means she keeps trying to start up a round of tug with my gardening gloves if I slip them off. I've got several of her toys scattered around me as I work on the dilapidated flowerbed, but nothing is as appealing as the gloves, apparently.

"Queenie, no!" I cry as she runs off with one of them for the third time. If she could cackle, I know in that moment, she would.

But that's when my phone rings, just as I'm trying to scramble to my feet. I sigh and watch her scamper into the corner by the back door, slobbering all over my glove. It's getting dark anyway, so I should probably call it a night. Hopefully I can ease the damn thing out of her mouth before she chews any holes in it.

I brush my hands and, seeing as it's my mom, I quickly hit the green button to accept. "Mamá," I say happily.

"Mijo," she cries. "I just wanted to check in, but please tell me if I'm disturbing you with your friends or anything."

I smile at the obvious attempt to pry into my social life and do my best to quash the sad pang in my chest. She means well, obviously. But it's not like I've turned into a party animal in the month since I moved out.

"You're not disturbing me at all," I promise, tidying up my fork and trowel as well as the bucket of weeds I've pulled up. "I've been out in my yard. You'd be proud."

"Oh, yes!" she squeals. "You remember what I said about mulch? You call me before you buy anything because I have spare, and I don't want you putting the wrong thing down."

I chuckle and throw the weeds into my trash. "I promise, Mamá. It's just a little yard, though. Not like yours. I'll be happy if I can just keep it tidy, that's all."

"Of course, of course," she says quickly.

However, I doubt that'll be the last I hear about mulching or composting or the right time to plant what flowers or what slug pellets to buy. I don't really want to risk anything poisonous with Queenie around, but I guess I can worry about that in spring when we'll both be more settled in the house and things will need planting and so on.

"How's work?" she asks as I put the tools back into my small shed. "Are you eating enough? How's Queenie?"

I laugh and shake my head, cataloguing all the questions. "Work is good. I feel like I've settled in now and don't need to check what I'm doing with my supervisor every five minutes. My team went out for drinks on Friday night."

"Oh, wonderful!" my mom enthuses.

I don't have the heart to tell her it was a bit awkward, and I only stuck it out for two beers before making my excuses to head out. Actually, having Queenie was the perfect way to escape because several people made 'aww' noises when I said I had to get home to my dog, so I didn't feel too guilty.

Perhaps over time I'll get along better with them. They don't seem terrible, after all.

Actually, it wasn't really them so much as the bar we were at. I still find crowded places exhausting. It's like I have to be on high alert and try and pay attention to every conversation, sudden movement, and loud noise, so I can never fully relax.

I can relax with Lochlan, though.

It's a good thing I'm not on video with my mom, as I can feel myself blush just thinking about my super hot firefighter buddy. I wouldn't want Mamá getting the wrong idea. So I hastily move the conversation along.

"And Queenie is good, although right now she's stolen one of my gloves, so I'm trying to get it back." I lock eyes with my bulldog and try and project an alpha vibe. "Queenie. Drop it."

She shakes the glove before spitting it out and flopping onto her back, her tongue lolling and her tail wagging. I roll my eyes and rub her belly.

"Good girl," I grumble, even though she isn't really.

Oh, who am I kidding. Yes, she is.

"So the doggy training classes are paying off?" my mom asks.

"Yeah," I say cheerfully. "But honestly, I think it's more the socializing that's doing her the most good. And she's slowly realizing that she can trust me, and this is her forever home. At least, *I'm* her forever home."

Who knows how long I'll stay in this house, after all. If the last year has taught me anything, it's that nothing is guaranteed, and anything can change on a dime.

But not Queenie. She's mine now and I'm hers. We're a little family of two. I'd never abandon her. She can rely on me if nothing else.

"How about food?" my mom barrels on. "Did you get the groceries I sent? You better be making the time to cook, mijo, and not getting takeout every night."

Picking up the slightly soggy glove, I laugh and head inside, dropping both gloves by the back door and making my way to the living room where I can collapse on the sofa.

"I can't afford takeout any night, Mamá, let alone *every* night," I assure her.

She knows every penny I make is going into the house or into savings. If I keep my life frugal now, by next year, maybe I can relax knowing I have back-ups in place and a chunk of my mortgage interest paid.

"And you need to stop sending me deliveries," I add. "I'm fine, I swear."

She hums, and I don't think I'm going to win that battle anytime soon. If it makes her feel better, I guess I don't mind. But…I'm also aware that I really, *really* need to be standing on my own two feet again. There's a fine line between letting someone fuss and be kind, and feeling like I'm helpless and can't manage anything by myself.

"I made your red pozole recipe the other night," I say to stop her from fretting too much. "It wasn't quite as good as yours, but it was pretty close."

"Oh, that makes me so happy," she says warmly. "Did you add avocado?"

"Yes, and sour cream because my friend…I mean, uh, it was slightly too spicy."

Shit. The silence at the end of the line tells me she didn't miss my slip up. I didn't want to tell her about Lochlan in case she gets the wrong idea. But sure enough…

"Friend?" she squeaks hopefully.

I chew my lip, a familiar fear crawling through my chest. It's not my mom I'm wary of. She's never been anything other than supportive, not even blinking an eyelid when I came out. But allowing myself to be vulnerable with *anyone* is still difficult.

"Uh, yeah," I say, forcing myself to try and sound cheerful. "Just someone I met at the dog training class. Queenie loves this guy's puppy, so we've been doing some extra work together. And he just happened to be here the other day around dinnertime, so…"

"Mijo, that's wonderful," she says with far too much excitement. "Dinner with a nice young man? Is he handsome? What does he do?"

"Mamá," I say in a warning tone. "He's just a friend. He…"

I should tell her he's straight. That would be the easiest way to shut down any unreasonable expectations fast. But there's a pathetic part of me that doesn't want to admit it out loud and close that door for myself. Not just yet. I've been so unhappy for so long. I want to cling to a silly daydream for a little longer, even if it's tragic and probably only going to hurt my own feelings in the long run.

"He's a firefighter," I say instead, wincing at my own cowardliness.

"Ohhhh, a *firefighter,*" she says breathlessly. I'm not sure if I want to laugh or cringe at my mother lusting after Lochlan when she has no idea what he looks like or even anything about him.

I mean, she's not wrong. He's got an insane body, a

gorgeous smile, and sparkling eyes. More than that, though… he's just so kind. And goofy. And fun. And earnest.

Urgh. My chest squeezes with desperate longing. Despite swearing off all men for good after Shane, it's like my stupid heart skipped the memo. Logically, I know he's off limits in a dozen different ways. But emotionally, physically, I can't stop fantasizing about what it would feel like between those tree-trunk thighs. What his pretty pink lips would taste like. What—

"Send me a picture of him," my mom interrupts my spiraling thoughts. She giggles through the phone and I sigh.

"I don't have any," I say truthfully.

"Then what's his name?" she asks. "I'll find him on the Instagram or the TikToks."

"Ma-*má*," I beg, willing her to behave. "You're not allowed to stalk my friend, okay? He's a nice guy, but he's just a friend, I swear. We talk about trimming claws and home-made dog treat recipes and, well, he likes sci-fi as well, so I showed him my collection." That's not quite how it happened, of course, but my mom doesn't need to know that.

I expect her to tease me more, but her voice softens. "He sounds like a nice boy."

"He is," I assure her.

"Oh!" she cries, excitable again. "If he's a special friend, you should bring him home for Thanksgiving."

I scoff and shake my head, rocking off the sofa and heading back to the kitchen. I think I need a glass of wine to go with dinner after this conversation. "I'm sure he's got his own family to spend the holiday with, Mamá."

"You don't know that," she says scornfully. "You be polite and ask him, okay? You know we always welcome everyone in our home. Well…almost everyone," she adds darkly.

I definitely don't want to go down that road again right now. She tried so hard to get along with Shane, but he always had this difficult air about him when we visited. I told myself he was just a bit awkward, but the truth is, we'd leave and then he'd spend the entire trip back to Phoenix complaining about my family. He'd frame it in a way that he was just worried about me and how they treated me. Stupidly, I listened to him.

I let him drive a wedge between us.

Not anymore, though. I still don't want to hash over all that again, however. So I rally and force myself to smile, even if my mom can't see it.

"Of course I'll check if Lochlan has somewhere to spend Thanksgiving. But he might even be working. Fires don't stop for the holidays, you know."

"Lochlan?" she repeats, and I curse myself, jamming the phone between my shoulder and ear so I can open a bottle of red. "That's a pretty name," she comments.

"Hmm," I respond, knowing full well she's probably already using her Google-Foo to search the internet for a Redwood Bay firefighter called Lochlan. It's an unusual name, so she most likely won't even need his surname.

Honestly, it probably won't take her long to find him, and perhaps I should stop resisting the inevitable. Lochlan *is* special to me. Even if it's in a purely platonic way. He's done so much to restore my confidence and make me feel at home here in town.

"I'll ask him, Mamá," I promise softly. "You're right. I'd hate for him to be alone over the holidays."

I know that she just really, *really* wants me to be happy. After everything I went through, in her mind the best thing for me would be to meet a 'lovely, handsome man,' as she says frequently, bless her. She doesn't understand that for me, the best thing is to thrive on my own, at least for the time being.

So I'm not convinced she's really hearing me when I say

he's just a friend. If I told her he was straight she might back down, but as I'm talking to her in that moment, I realize that's only an assumption on my part. We've never discussed our orientations, so who knows? Perhaps I'm wrong.

That's almost certainly wishful thinking. But if it enables me to cling to the Schrödinger's cat of Lochlan's sexuality and my pathetic crush for a little longer, I don't have the strength to resist.

However, she does have a point. I would genuinely hate for him to be alone over Thanksgiving or at any time. Because someone like him should never be lonely. His family is here in town and he's close with his firefighter buddies, so I'm sure he absolutely does not need my help.

It can't hurt to ask, though, right?

And, I might be twenty-eight, but there's still a part of me that can't disappoint my mom. If she's telling me I have to do this, for her as much as me, then it gives me an excuse to do something silly. I'm sure Lochlan and I will laugh about it when I bring it up.

So that's what I decide to do. I'll honor my word and make the offer, but with an eye roll and a fond 'Moms, am I right?' attitude.

We chat a little more before we both need to make food, so I tell her I love her and end the call. As I prepare some chicken, I sip my wine and feel the warmth spreading through me. Lochlan has been so kind to me. It'll actually be nice to offer him something in return. Installing the puppy cams at the firehouse and his apartment doesn't count. That's like regular work for me. Inviting him to San Diego might be a token gesture of sorts, but it'll still be from the heart.

Because as the wine thrums through my veins, I can admit to myself that in an alternate reality, I'd love nothing more than to bring Lochlan home to meet my family as my boyfriend. For a few hours, I let my imagination take the wheel as I picture introducing him to my abuelas, parents, cousins, tias and tios. How he'd charm the pants off them but never make me feel like I'd been forgotten about.

I bet Lochlan Bell would make a great boyfriend. I try not to be jealous of whichever lucky girl gets to find that out for herself.

For now, what's the harm in dreaming?

CHAPTER 9

Lochlan

"I KNOW THESE AREN'T PROPER REDWOODS LIKE UP NORTH," Dario is saying as we walk along the forest path. "But holy fucking shit."

I drop my head back and laugh. "I know, right? I grew up here and it still gets me. Like…some of these bad boys are a couple hundred feet tall."

It's true that actual coastal redwoods aren't native to SoCal. The air is too dry for them. But back in the seventies or something there was this tourist and environmental campaign where they just went nuts and decided they were going to try planting them anyway. Apparently, they use some kinda drip watering system to make sure the trees get the moisture they need.

The town popped up not long after that. I think those guys were so proud of what they'd done, they just needed somewhere to name after the forest to prove what they'd done. Not to mention somewhere for folks to stay if they were going to make it into any kind of sightseeing spot. And that's how Redwood Bay came to be. It's pretty cool, really. I love having this on our doorstep.

"It's kind of humbling. Or I feel so, anyway," Dario adds, shaking his head.

I nod. "No, I get it. Sometimes I get so up in my own feelings or whatever. Then you come here and realize how small your problems are most of the time and you should probably just chill."

We continue down the track between the enormous trees with our dogs, enjoying the peace and quiet. I love that we're texting each other most days to see if we can coordinate walks together. This is the first time I've thought to bring Dario up to this particular route, though. Queenie and Rocky love the beach and the park so much, we've spent a lot of time there. But from the way their tails are wagging furiously as they sniff every inch we walk past, the woods are just as exciting to explore, maybe more so.

It strikes me that maybe I was nervous to come here because it feels like it's just us alone in the world right now. I'm sure there are plenty of other folks around, but unlike at the beach or park, we can't see them. I didn't want Dario to feel…I dunno. Pressured maybe? I've barreled my way into his business over and over again, I didn't want to be all 'Come up to the forest in the middle of nowhere with me!' you know?

But then he asked about different places we could try and when I suggested up here, he didn't seem bothered at all. Now, he keeps looking around at the towering giants surrounding us in awe, smiling and stopping every once in a while to take deep breaths. He's gone over and touched the bark a couple of times as well, like he's really connecting with nature.

It makes me feel calm and settled just watching him. I'm so happy he feels okay being 'alone' with me. I never want to make him uncomfortable or anything like that.

Yet again I think about Phoenix and whatever the hell

could have gone on there to make him so skittish. Nothing good, I'm sure.

I try my best not to dwell on it, though. If he wants to tell me, he will. "Did you know that the redwood bark is like a foot thick, so it makes them pretty damn fireproof?" I ask. He's always sharing cool facts with me, so it's nice to have something to offer him back for a change.

"That's good," he says, nodding. "They must be so old. It would be really sad to see them taken out by a wildfire."

"Some of them are over a thousand years old," I say excitably. "Can you believe that?"

He shakes his head. "I'm not even thirty yet and some days I feel so old," he says with a laugh. It's funny that he's younger than me when he's so smart and stuff. He's so worldly, and I know he likes to read up on random things just for fun.

"Naw, you're not old," I say. "Just wise. Like an owl."

He laughs and looks up at the canopy. "Which tree should I live in if I'm an owl?" he asks. "I'll need a good one."

"A sturdy one," I agree. "Hey—did you know we have a walkway experience thing here? It's in a different part of the woods, but there are these rope bridges like a hundred feet off the ground." I bump shoulders with him. "I like to pretend I'm on Endor with the Ewoks."

He grins that amazing sparkly way he does whenever I make a sci-fi reference. Honestly, I swear seeing his spare bedroom was the best thing ever. I've got buddies who like watching those kinds of things, but they'd never, I dunno, collect sonic screwdrivers or memorize the blueprints for the Enterprise or whatever. It's like Dario and I have our own special language. I don't have to explain that Ewoks are from Star Wars. He just knows.

"I'll take you there," I say, aware I'm stomping into his life and making plans for us again. But the way he's grinning tells me he doesn't hate the idea. "We can bring our lightsabers and pretend we're fending off the empire."

He looks at me all warm and glowy and it makes my stomach feel all light and bubbly. Damn, I know I need to be careful I'm not overwhelming him, but it's so easy to make plans together. We could see each other every day, and I bet I wouldn't get bored. It's funny that in all this time, I've had so many different kinds of friends, but never one like Dario.

"I'm not sure how good I'd be with the heights," he says with a chuckle. "But, yeah. I'd love to go there. Um…" He takes a deep breath and frowns, like he's building up to something. "Actually, speaking of making plans, I've got a silly thing to ask you. You're going to laugh."

"Oh?" I say, immediately interested. But he seems nervous, so I do my best to reassure him that it's a good kind of interested. "You can ask me anything. I bet it's not silly."

"It is," he says quickly, rubbing the back of his neck. "But, um, thank you. Anyway, it's just that my mom and I were talking about Thanksgiving, and she wanted me to invite you. To our Thanksgiving at her house, I mean. In case you were at a loose end. I told her that was ridiculous, and you have your own family, and you might be working or whatever. But she made me promise that I'd mention it. I think she's happy I made a friend here in town."

He's still looking awkward as all hell, so he's probably completely unaware that I've puffed up like a damn bullfrog with pride. "Your mom wants to invite me to your Thanksgiving?" I repeat, feeling like I've won the lottery or something. I don't know why, but the fact that his mom knows who I am tickles me pink.

"I told you it's silly," he says, peeking over at me. "You have plans, right?"

"Uh, I guess," I say, struggling to remember what they are in that moment. Oh, that's right. "I was supposed to be going to see my folks, and my sister and her family are coming over, but we do that every year. Besides, I can see them on the Friday if I want. So I'd be honored if your mom really means it."

Slowly, Dario stops walking and blinks at me. "Lochlan, no. I'd never pull you away from your family."

I blow a raspberry. "I see them all the time, they'd be fine with it. If your mom insisted on including me, then I'm super touched."

He's waving his hands, and I'm a bit confused. He wouldn't have mentioned it if *he* didn't want me to come, would he?

"I think she might think that, um, we're dating or something," Dario says, looking mortified. "Or thinking about dating. She got a bit overexcited. She's just hopeful that..." He shakes his head and laughs nervously. "Nothing. She just wants me to be happy."

"Of course," I say, still not quite following. "And seeing you bring a date home for the holiday would make her think you're happy?"

He blinks at me. "You're straight, right?"

"Uh-huh," I say. "But I've got loads of buddies who are LGBTQRS...you know, the whole alphabet." I make him laugh again, not as nervous as before, and I'm glad. I'm not sure why he's so tense. "Are your family nagging you to settle down?"

"No, nothing like that," he says quickly, then nibbles on his lip. It's so cute, but I'm worried *he's* worried, and I want to fix that. "They just..." he continues, seeming unsure. "I wasn't very happy in Phoenix. They want what's best for me, and I think seeing me in a relationship would make them fret less. That's why my mom pushed me to ask you, in case I was hiding a secret boyfriend or something." He rolls his eyes, but his expression is fond. "Plus, she really does care that no one's left alone when she and my tias will be cooking enough to feed a thousand. But you have plans with your own family, so—"

"No, hold up," I say, wagging my finger as my brain whirs. The dogs are still sniffing around us, so I can give myself a second to sort out what I'm thinking. "Do you *want* them to worry less about you?"

He studies me for a second before shrugging. "I mean, yeah, for sure. I don't want them to love me any less!" he clarifies quickly. "It's just…I want to show them—and myself —that I'm okay. To me, that's proving my independence. But to them, I think they want to try and convince me that I'm a catch and deserve to have a nice boyfriend."

Yet again, I'm not sure what happened in Phoenix that's got his whole family so concerned, but that's not really the issue right now. I can't do anything about what happened before, but I can see a really obvious way to help in the present.

"So, like, what if you *did* rock up with a hot boyfriend that thought you were totally awesome?" I ask him.

He scoffs and rolls his eyes, like that's a crazy idea. It makes me bristle because he's my new amazing friend and I wish he could see himself like that. But I keep my mouth shut, wanting to hear his answer.

"I'm pretty sure they'd have a holiday on top of the holiday we were already celebrating."

"Perfect!" I cry, jerking my thumbs toward my chest. "Then that's me! I'm the hot boyfriend who thinks you're awesome!"

Dario splutters and looks at me like I've grown a second head. "W-what?"

"Think about it," I continue excitedly. "We just bend the truth a little bit and say we met in class, which is true. Then we hung out loads, also true. But *then* we say we started dating, so it's all new. I can go, tell your folks how cool and cute I think you are, and they'll stop all that fretting and give you a bit of breathing room. Sound good?"

Now, I'm not the IT guy here. However, he's looking at me in a way that makes me want to turn him off and on again. "But…you're straight?" he says eventually.

"Pft," I tell him with a grin. "I'd make a damn fine bisexual for a day, I'm sure." He's still looking shocked and maybe kind of anxious, though, so I quit playing around. "Hey, it's just an idea. If it's going to make you even more stressed, though, then just—"

"No!" he cries, rubbing his hands against his hips and glancing away before meeting my eyes again. "I'm not stressed, I promise. Just a little taken aback. But also…really touched you'd even think about doing something so crazy."

Relief floods through me. "Naw, I run into burning buildings for a living. That's crazy. Pretending to be your honey for a hot minute'll just be fun. Besides, how much pretending will we really need to do if we say we've only just started dating? Maybe hold hands? I'm cool with that if you are."

Dario shakes his head. Even though he's still smiling faintly, my heart drops a bit. But then he speaks. "I don't deserve a friend like you, Lochlan, I swear."

"Of course you do," I say hotly. "It's me who can't believe someone as smart and cool as you likes hanging with a dipshit like me."

He takes a deep breath and narrows his eyes at me. "How about from now on…neither of us are allowed to put ourselves down, and we both have to accept the other really enjoys being their friend."

I bark out a laugh and raise my hand. "High five to that, my dude!" He lifts his arm kinda shyly, but I crack our palms together so loudly the dogs both come running and yapping.

When everyone calms down, Dario takes another big

breath, looking like he's considering everything we've said. "This might not actually be an insane idea," he says, glancing at me as if he's checking I'm going to tell him he's wrong.

But he's *so* right. "You bet your ass!" I cry. "You'll make your family happy which will make them chill, so you get to chill, plus we get to spend the day together *and* I get to eat a shit ton of tasty food. It's win-win-win!"

He looks like he's got about one percent resistance left in him, but then he shakes his head and beams at me. "It's only a little, tiny white lie, right? And a road trip sounds fun, even if it's only a hour away."

"I've driven farther for good steak," I assure him. "Now! Let's practice."

He swallows. "Practice?" he repeats weakly.

I nod and stick my hand out, wiggling my fingers. "Come on, *boyfriend.* Let's walk some more."

For a moment, he looks at my hand as if he's deciding whether or not it's a bomb. But then, carefully, he slides his palm against mine.

A shiver runs up my spine. I guess it's been a long time since I held anyone's hand. It doesn't matter that it's a guy. It's nice! I swing our arms between us.

"Easy-peasy," I declare. "I'm a natural bisexual!"

He bites his lip and shakes his head, like I'm as much of a naughty puppy as Rocky. I'm okay with that, though.

"You certainly are something," he murmurs, catching my eye as we carry on down the trail. I feel like I'm a hot air balloon, ready to lift off with all the excitement brewing in me.

This is going to be fun!

CHAPTER 10
Dario

YET AGAIN I FIND MYSELF BEGGING THE QUESTION, 'WHAT WAS I thinking?'

In the moment, I let Lochlan convince me that this insanity might actually be a good idea. He was so convincing when he was talking about how a little white lie could go a long way to helping my family believe that I'm doing okay now, and they don't need to keep smothering me with their anxiety. I'm all for that.

But now Lochlan and his dog are in my car with my dog as I drive us all to my parents' house, and it's hit me that this whole scheme is, in fact, horrendous.

There's no way I'm going to get through this without anyone figuring out we're just faking it. More importantly, there's no way I'm going to get through this without Lochlan realizing that I'm absolutely bananas about him. Like, I couldn't stop thinking about him and fantasizing about him before. Now he's pretending to be my boyfriend and going to be holding my hand in front of my whole damn family?

Not to mention that I don't trust anyone to remember to call me Dario. Why should they? It's my own stupidity that led to me having to change my name. But when Lochlan discovers I've been lying to him this whole time…

Yeah. Titanic-level disaster waiting to happen on so many levels.

Lochlan might say he's cool with me being gay and has a lot of queer friends and all that, but how is he going to react when he figures out I'm lusting after him like a teenager with his first crush? It feels like such a betrayal, especially after he's been so incredibly kind to me. He's giving up his *own* Thanksgiving, for crying out loud. In his mind, he's just being a good friend. He has no idea how I really feel.

Because to be honest, I've got very little clue, either. I know I like him a hell of a lot. But after Shane, the idea of dating anyone scares the shit out of me, no matter how nice they appear. I don't know if I'll ever feel able to let another man close to me like that again.

Except when I imagine Lochlan Bell stripping my clothes off and sucking my cock, nothing else seems to matter.

"Shit!" I'm so lost in my thoughts that I almost miss the light turning red. Luckily, I notice just in time and slam on the brakes. "Sorry, sorry! Is everyone okay?"

I glance at Lochlan in my passenger seat, then in the rearview mirror where Rocky and Queenie are both on their hind legs, looking up over the back seat from the trunk.

"We're fine," Lochlan says with a chuckle. "Are *you* okay?"

"Yeah, I'm fine," I reply automatically with a tight smile.

Lochlan, the bastard, unfortunately continues showing what a great friend he is by sympathetically reaching out and squeezing my knee. It's a really sweet gesture, but at the same time, the touch makes my skin feel like it's on fire and my cock aches in my jeans, imagining him sliding his hand up higher.

Christ, it's been too long since I had sex. The prospect of a random Grindr hookup isn't appealing at all to me. The idea of trusting someone I know with my body is terrifying, let alone a stranger. But maybe it'll be necessary if I'm going to prevent myself doing something monumentally stupid in front of Lochlan.

He breaks the spell that's fallen over me by removing his hand, thank goodness. "Are you *sure* you're okay?" he asks, his tone gentle. "You seem tense. Are you worried about seeing your family?"

I am, but not in the way he's thinking. I'm worried how they're going to react to him. If I'm going to break my mom's heart when she realizes I tricked everybody. Or if by some miracle she doesn't sus it out, will I upset her when Lochlan and I 'break up'?

The light goes green, and I pull off, paying better attention to the road this time. We're not too far from the house. I just need to get us there in one piece.

"Not worried," I say truthfully. "They can just be a bit overwhelming. Hopefully when we get there, they'll see I'm doing okay and stop stressing over me, so that will chill me out as well."

"You're doing better than okay," Lochlan says fiercely, and my heart melts for him a little more. He leaps to my defense all the time without even thinking about it. It's so adorable. "You're doing awesome, and they'll realize that in no time. You just concentrate on getting us there and then we can relax."

If only. I'm driving us back this evening, so I won't be able to have a drink to stop my brain from whirring. But perhaps I'll stand a better chance of not confessing all my dirty thoughts to Lochlan if I'm stone cold sober. So that's a silver lining, I guess.

I've also just realized that I can maybe wave off any confusion about my name by saying that I decided to start going by my middle name in college or something, and no one ever remembers that at home. Yeah. That could work. No big deal.

Okay, that's one disaster possibly averted.

"Thank you again for doing this," I say quietly. "I know it's a bit weird, but I do think it could actually help."

He scoffs. "Of course, dude! I wouldn't have suggested it if I didn't seriously think it could ease things up for you. Just think of me a social lubricant."

I bite the inside of my cheek to stop myself from having an aneurysm. I don't need to be picturing anything easing up with lube right now.

"Not many people would be open to a scheme like this," I manage to say without choking on my own spit. "If it works, I'll owe you big time."

"Naw," he says, shaking his head. "I'm sure a day filled with home cooking and good company will even us out just fine. Although maybe you should let me know if there are any relatives I should avoid for whatever reason."

I laugh, wondering if 'all of them' is an acceptable answer and if I should simply turn the car around right now. Honestly, I'm not sure what I'm more concerned about. If they're all going to be suspicious of him...or that they're all going to love the crap out of him and get too attached.

"Nobody has extreme politics or bad body odor that I'm aware of," I say, pulling into a street a few blocks away from the house. "My tio Miguel might try and talk you into investing in Bitcoin, but my abuela can usually distract him when he gets bad with her chocolate chip and peanut butter cookies."

"Duly noted," Lochlan says, sounding like he's taking his role very seriously. Of course he is. I suspect that Lochlan is physically incapable of letting anyone down, ever. "Hoping I can also get in on that cookie action, though, if I'm charming enough."

He arches a questioning eyebrow at me, making me laugh and temporarily forget all my worries. He's got such a talent for that, I swear. "Don't be surprised if we're greeted at the door with baked goods, iced tea, and about a hundred hugs."

"Oh no, how terrible," Lochlan deadpans, making me snort.

When we near my parents' place, I can see that the driveway is already overflowing with cars, and I groan slightly as I envision who's already arrived. *It's going to be fine,* I remind myself sternly. I *love* my family. I only agreed to this harebrained scheme because I thought it might give them some comfort. And we only have to stay a few hours. I'll soon be back in my quiet little house.

Alone.

No, not alone. I'll have Queenie. She's also here to assure my family that I'm not all by myself and that I'm moving on with my life in all kinds of good ways.

After I find a space to park along the sidewalk, I look in the rearview mirror at the excitable pups watching us. "Are you guys ready for the carnage?" I ask in the same tone of voice I use when asking if Queenie wants a walk or a treat. In other words, I'm hyping her up to distract myself from all my niggling worries.

It sort of works. Kind of.

The sounds of barking and whining and paws hitting against the window of my trunk certainly leave little room for contemplating anything else. Plus, Lochlan's booming laugh warms my insides from top to toe.

"Easy, guys!" he says with a grin as he unbuckles and opens the passenger side door. "Remember all those manners you've been learning in class, please! We're on a mission to impress everyone today."

I hover on the sidewalk, watching as he opens the trunk

and gets both dogs to wait, sit, and give him their paws in exchange for treats, just like we learned from our training sessions. I know I'm trying to keep a lid on my crush here, but it's impossible for my heart not to ache with longing as I watch this big, muscular firefighter use baby talk as he gently lifts each dog down to place them on the ground, holding their leashes delicately so they don't strain and choke themselves.

"Thanks," I say softly as I take Queenie from him and lock the car.

This silly infatuation will fade, I'm sure. And when it does, I'll be grateful that this kind and handsome man chose to spend today with me. I want to enjoy the moment and not get lost in all my trivial woes, and that starts now.

Or at least, it'll start once the initial introductions are done. I give myself permission to fret until then. But after that, I promise myself that I'll appreciate getting to spend time with my family as well as Lochlan.

We don't have much stuff with us, but he did insist that we stop at a gas station so he could pick up a bunch of flowers for my mom, because 'that's just what you do,' apparently. So, he cradles them in his arm like a baby, Rocky's leash in the other hand, then follows me as we approach the house. Queenie's corkscrew tail is wagging, and I smile down at her before pressing the bell.

"Good girl," I murmur soothingly. To think, a few weeks ago, she was sad and alone in that shelter cage. Now she's about to meet a whole bunch of slightly crazy people.

The door swings open, and you'd think from the way my mom almost bursts into tears that I'd been deployed for two years rather than only moved out last month.

"Mijo!" she cries, dragging me into a hug. "I was getting worried! Was the drive okay? Come in, come in!" She ushers me over the threshold then clasps her hands to her chest.

"And this handsome young man must be Lochlan. We're delighted to have you here."

"The honor's all mine, ma'am," Lochlan says brightly, holding out the flowers. "These are for you."

Mamá lets out a soft sound as she takes them carefully from him. "Oh, Dario. What a gentleman your friend is. Lochlan, these are beautiful. And please, call me Alicia."

Okay, so Mamá does seem to have remembered to use my new name. That's a good start.

"Dario said freesias are your favorite," Lochlan tells her bashfully, clearly pleased that my mom likes him already. "And that you're a keen gardener."

"They are, and I am!" she says gleefully, closing the door behind him. "Let's put these in some water and I can show you outside. Dinner isn't ready just yet, so we have some time. Dario's father is in charge of the kitchen today."

"So it's a good thing we have a firefighter in the house," a new voice says, and I turn happily to see my tia Gaby sashaying down the hall to meet us. In each hand she has a lime green drink in glasses with salted rims. "Julio's sure to burn the house down any second."

"Oh, hush," Mamá says with a laugh. "Lochlan, this is my baby sister, Gabriella. Gaby, this is *Dario's* friend, Lochlan."

My tia presses one of the drinks into Lochlan's free hand, her kohl-lined eyes dragging up and down his body very obviously. "Hot stuff, kid," she practically purrs at me.

"Aww, thank you," Lochlan says, clearly not bothered by my outrageous aunt ogling him.

"Gaby," I groan, mortified. "Please be nice."

"I'm always nice, *Dario*," she says with a smirk, giving me the second drink. Well, she could be more subtle about it. But so far, I'm two-for-two on the name.

"Oh, no thanks, I'm driving," I say, assuming it's one of the deceptively strong margaritas she likes to make at family gatherings.

Mamá frowns at me. "No," she says firmly, wagging a finger. "You're not going to sneak off after a couple of hours. You're staying the night. I've already made up all the guest beds. Otherwise, I'll have washed the sheets for nothing!"

Panic grips me and I glance at Lochlan. But I should have known he'd take this all in his stride. I guess a man who faces danger every time he clocks in for work wouldn't be fazed by a family who struggles to remember what boundaries are.

"Aww, you shouldn't have gone to all that trouble, Alicia," he says warmly.

"It was no trouble," she tells him before looking back at me. "But it *will* be if nobody sleeps in them."

"You're not escaping," Gaby says to me with an arched eyebrow. "So you might as well accept it."

"We haven't packed to stay overnight," I protest weakly.

Again, Mamá waves off my concerns. "We have spare toothbrushes. Please, Mig-mijo. We've missed you. I promise, you can head home after breakfast tomorrow."

I bite my lower lip and look to Lochlan for guidance. He gives me an easy one-armed shrug and sips his drink. He doesn't seem to have noticed my mom's almost slip-up, either.

"As long as you've got something for the dogs to eat as well as the humans, Alicia, I don't see a problem with it."

"Yes, yes, lots of tasty chicken for these babies," Mamá assures him, crouching down to fuss over Rocky, who immediately explodes at the attention, jumping and licking and barking. "Aww, aren't you a darling. And this must be Queenie!" she says, extending her hand to fuss my dog as well. "Such gorgeous babies. Yes, you are!"

I take a second and weigh everything up. The whole point

of this rouse was to prove to my family that they don't need to worry so much. Maybe if I run off like I'd planned, they'll keep fretting. But if we give them all day and tomorrow morning, they might really believe that I'm in a stable relationship with a nice guy who can take care of me when they can't.

Despite all my protests about how I just want my independence, that does actually sound so nice. But we're not dating for real, so I shove that thought down and try to forget about it.

Practically speaking, I know I've got a charger in my car that is compatible with both my phone and Lochlan's. What else do we really need? We can wear the same clothes for the drive back without it being too much of an issue.

And Mamá said she'd made up the *beds*. Plural. It's not that my mom is prudish, it's more that she's respectful. Separating us when we've only just started dating (as far as she thinks) not only makes sense in her eyes, but it works in our favor since we're very much not dating, and it would probably be super weird for Lochlan to sleep next to another guy.

To make sure, I catch his gaze and raise my eyebrows questioningly at him while my mom and tia coo at our dogs. He nods but also quirks his eyebrows back at me, asking the same question.

It appears that he's okay with it if I am. That's settled then. Go big or go home, I guess. Literally. Time to perform the hell out of this charade.

At least it won't be hard for me to fake being besotted. Hopefully, Lochlan will just think I'm a great actor.

I sigh. "Okay, then," I concede, taking a sip of the margarita that is indeed rocket fuel. I do my best not to splutter as the first taste of tequila goes down. "You win. We'll stay."

"Perfect!" Mamá cries, clapping her hands as she stands

back up, making both the dogs bark. "Everyone's in the yard. We should join them."

"Is it escape proof?" I immediately ask in concern. But then I shake my hand as well as my head. "It's okay, I'll go check. I know what to look for. Queenie probably won't try anything, but Rocky's a wannabe Houdini. We can keep them on their leashes until I've done an inspection."

"Good thinking, baby!" Lochlan says, the term of endearment rolling so naturally off his tongue my heart flips before I can remember it's only make-believe.

My mom loops her arm through mine and sweeps me off to the back yard via the kitchen. I notice Gaby hanging back with Lochlan, but that's okay. I trust him, and despite her over-the-top nature, Gaby is actually great. He's going to be talking with plenty of my relatives, I'm sure, so I need to relax and trust that I don't need to hover.

Like *he'd* need *my* protection from anything.

Regardless, I tell myself that the hard part is done. We're here, and no one is instantly pointing fingers and yelling that we're frauds. Mamá isn't even telling people that Lochlan is my boyfriend. Sure, the way she says *'friend'* has heavy implications, but it's technically the truth. It won't hurt if people jump to the slightly wrong conclusion. In fact, that's kind of exactly the plan.

So that's it. The rest of the visit should get easier from here.

Right?

CHAPTER 11

Lochlan

I'M HAVING SUCH A GREAT TIME.

Dario's family is super nice. He was right to warn me that some of them have seriously big personalities, but a lot are more reserved as well, like him. One thing is for sure, and that's they know how to host. Even though Dario's dad is cooking a big ass turkey dinner, there are plates of homemade nibbles on every surface, and I'm certainly never left without a drink in hand.

Everyone seems to want to talk to me. They make me feel like I'm a celebrity. Aunts, uncles and cousins all have stories about Dario that they want to share with me. Although it appears like he used to go by Miguel when he was younger or something, as people seem to be using both. Some of them hastily correct themselves, so I don't ask about it in case it's a sensitive topic. I always know who they're talking about, anyway, which is all that really matters. I'm here to be his boyfriend and big him up, so I want to laugh and sigh happily at their tall tales.

It cracks me up when someone thinks they're going to embarrass him by showing me photos of old Halloween costumes, but all I do is get impressed at how accurate his Starfleet uniform was or excited by the full body make-up from when he was an Avatar alien. One time he made himself an actual Dalek outfit, complete with light-up accessories.

And when I gush about how awesome Dario is—how clever and inventive and funny—whoever I'm talking to blinks in surprise at me.

Then they agree.

It's so *easy* to be Dario's hype man. I tell various people how we've not only been training our dogs together, but how Dario helped me and Rocky catch up when I had to miss a session thanks to work, and how Dario's been researching extra training techniques for us to try. I tell them how he set up the puppy cams for us both and how now we both check in for each other when one of us is at work.

"I'd never look unless Dario asked me to," I assure his grandma on his mom's side as I hold out my phone. I want to show her the app to give her an idea of the setup. "And he has to turn the cameras on for them to work in the first place. But if he gets stuck in a meeting, I can take a peek and make sure Queenie is okay. See?"

"Ohh," she says, raising her eyebrows before beckoning over the man I think is her husband and firing off some rapid Spanish, pointing at the screen. "Very good," she then tells me with a nod.

"You think Dario could do this for our cats?" the gentleman asks.

I nod vigorously. "I bet he'd be delighted to."

When we're settled down to eat at the three tables that have been pushed together and surrounded by a wild mismatch of chairs, I find myself with Dario on one side, and a mischievous looking Aunt Gaby on the other.

One of her crazy strong margaritas was enough, so after I

finished the glass she gave me, I had some water then switched to a beer that one of Dario's uncles had ready and waiting to shove into my hand.

I've been so busy talking, and Dario was out in the garden with his mom making sure the dogs don't have any escape routes, so I haven't really seen him since we arrived. I can see that he's also abandoned the margaritas and is drinking red wine. I love that I know that's his drink of choice. It's cool to feel close with someone in that way, especially as we didn't meet all that long ago.

I'm glad he decided to stay. I would have done anything he wanted, but part of me was worried that he wanted to leave so early because he's hiding from something or afraid. The way he's relaxing now makes me think that it's not his family he's worried about. For a hot minute I was dead certain there was going to be a homophobic asshole or a creepy groper he was trying to avoid.

But that's not it.

Maybe I'm way off base…but I think what he was concerned about was letting them be *nice* to him. During dinner, I catch him flinching a couple of times when someone tells him he's looking good, or they congratulate him on his new job and home and shit.

I, for one, can't help but beam when he's getting compliments. I know we haven't known each other ages, but damn it if I'm not still proud as punch for him. Whatever happened in Phoenix, it doesn't take a genius to figure out that he had to have had a lot of guts to start over in a new place.

Perhaps he thinks that it's no big deal and he doesn't deserve their praise. Or that they're over-exaggerating. But they're not, so I join in with bigging him up, slinging my arm around him and giving him a good squeeze when I tell whoever's listening that he's the best.

And, yeah, maybe my next beer needs to be a water,

because at one point I definitely drag him against me where we're sitting and kiss his temple.

I do that to everyone, so it's really not a big deal to me. But afterward, Dario blinks at me with those pretty eyes of his like I did something remarkable. Hopefully it was okay. I know that no one's talking about it out loud cuz they're being all polite and stuff, but we *are* trying to leave them with the impression that Dario has himself a big ol' firefighter taking care of him now, so they can worry less.

Dario grins at me a few seconds after the kiss, though, and leans into my side. I've still got my arm around his shoulders, so I give him a squeeze and kiss the top of his hair again like I do with Lili when we're tipsy.

Dario isn't Lili, though, that's for sure. And yet, he feels so right here, like a baby bird tucked under my wing. I try not to snort as I picture myself as a momma bird, pecking anyone with my sharp beak if they dare to come near the nest I've made to protect Dario.

I haven't had so many beers I forget that no one here appears to be a threat. But Dario is certainly haunted by whatever has them fussing over him, and that's what—or who—I'd like to peck in the face.

Instead, I settle for giving his mom a wink when I catch her staring sweetly at us. I've still got my arm around her boy's back, and out of his sightline I see her place her hand on her heart and sigh wistfully. It's so cute. I think my mom would really like her. Hell, I think my family and this family would get on like a house on fire, one that I wouldn't have to worry about putting out.

When the meal is done and my belly feels the way Rocky's does when he panic eats his food, I insist on helping clear the dishes. That's the way my momma raised me, and I won't take no for an answer.

So I end up in the kitchen, loading the dishwasher while

most everybody else lounges around in the yard, cranking up the music and playing a noisy game, no doubt in an attempt to stop them all from falling into Thanksgiving food comas.

"I like you," a confident voice announces from behind me. I turn and see Gaby grinning at me like she knows a secret.

"Why, thank you, ma'am," I say bashfully. The dishwasher won't take much more, so I grab a towel and dry my hands before looking more closely at the machine. "Oh, uh, do you know how to turn this on?"

"Sure do!"

Gaby darts over, and in the blink of an eye, she's fished a tablet out of a small metal tub, programmed a setting, then closed the door of the machine with a solid click. In a couple of seconds, it starts whirring, telling us that it's begun its cycle.

"Come, sit," Gaby says, dragging me across to the now empty dining table.

The sounds coming from outside are comforting as Gaby fetches me a fresh beer and sits me down in the end seat. She positions herself at the head of the table, so the corner is between us. Once we're both settled, she picks up her margarita in one hand, then lays her free one on top of mine.

"You really like Dario, don't you?" she says. Her voice is warm but there's something else there. That anxiety that Dario's been so aware of.

"Yes, I do," I tell her truthfully. Even if it's not in a boyfriend way, I do think he's a blast. "He's quickly become my favorite person," I assure her.

She nods. "I can tell. You respect him. You think he's wonderful, don't you?"

"Yes, ma'am."

"Good," she says firmly. "Because he is. He's a little diamond. After what that fucker put him through, he deserves a guy who looks at him the way you do. Like he's a prince in a goddamned Disney movie."

I only catch some of her last few words because my brain immediately latched onto two words in particular. "I'm sorry, Gaby. But do you mind if I ask what you mean by 'that fucker'? Who are you talking about?"

Her expression drops. "Oh, no," she says, sounding kinda guilty. "I just assumed…I thought you knew. Shit."

Okay, so that makes me torn. I don't want to go snooping around in Dario's life. Lord knows I've barged my way into so much of it already. But now I'm the one with worry writhing in his gut like a snake.

"It's all right if you don't want to say anything more," I assure her. "But is it something to do with Phoenix? I get the feeling something bad happened there and he left his whole life behind because of it."

Her eyes go wide. "That's *exactly* what happened," she hisses and pokes my chest before scooting her chair closer to mine. For a few moments, she just stares at me, as if weighing up what to say next. "If Dario didn't tell you, it might be because he feels ashamed. But he has *nothing* to be ashamed of. So…okay, I'm going to give you the CliffsNotes version, not because I want to gossip, but because he deserves to be treated like a fucking king. I think you know that, too. But I want you to understand *why* as well."

As far as I'm concerned, Dario deserves that because he's the best. However, I'm getting the impression that Tia Gaby is about to drop a more specific bombshell on me.

I nod. "I promise I'll be discreet."

She bites her glossy lip and takes another sip of her cocktail before speaking again. "Dario dated a guy called Shane in college. They seemed so happy together at the start. Alicia was proud of her boy for spreading his wings, but I could tell that she had this…doubt about Shane. Like a shadow lurking in the corner of your eye."

I swallow, not liking how ominous that sounds. "Okay," I prompt her tentatively.

"It wasn't too bad until they moved in together after graduation," Gaby continues. "Dario got a job he was really excited about, so to begin with, it made sense that he was coming home less and less. He was busy, you know?"

She crooks her eyebrow in a way that makes me think that it wasn't work keeping Dario from his family. My stomach sinks. Sure enough, she's got more to say.

"He wasn't calling much and only visiting during the holidays." She waves her hand around to indicate where he was missed during those times. "It's not a long drive, you know? But the way Dario and Shane acted, you'd think they were in Australia, dios mío."

She sighs and I squeeze her hand where she's still holding onto me. This was obviously very hard on Dario's parents and the rest of his family. But in that moment my heart is breaking, guessing what Dario was probably going through back then and hating it just as much in the present day.

Gaby continues. "Fourth of July last year, so like eighteen months ago, was the breaking point. Julio—that's Dario's dad—says he's had enough so he and Alicia get in the car, saying if Dario won't come to them, they'll go to *him*." She sniffs and looks at me through her thick lashes. "They surprised him. Luckily, Shane was out, but Dario was very keen to get them to leave before he came back. It didn't take a genius to see he was scared. That's when I got involved."

"Yeah?" I say, leaning in closer, completely engrossed in her awful tale.

She nods. "Alicia learned everything she knows about internet sleuthing from me. When she and Julio confessed how worried they were, I started poking around Dario's socials and reaching out to friends from college. They all said the same thing."

I know what's coming, but my guts are still in knots anyway.

"Nobody had seen Dario or heard from him in months. Some of them years, since even before graduation. They told me enough little throwaway comments about what Shane 'didn't allow' for me to put it together. I found out afterwards I was right and then some. Shane was good, he did it slowly, always framing everything as doing what was best for Dario. But he was picking out his clothes, not letting him wear anything he thought was too provocative. He convinced Dario that all his friends were jealous and controlling when—"

"That's actually what he was," I cry in horror.

"Bingo," Gaby says. "He convinced Dario that we—his family—were trying to break them up. Shane persuaded Dario to start putting his salary into Shane's bank account. Shane started giving Dario an *allowance*, then bitched when Dario tried to explain it wasn't enough for basic groceries."

There are tears in her eyes now, but she blinks them back furiously. I've long put my beer down, sick to my stomach with what I'm hearing.

"This took ages for Dario to confess to us," she says, her voice thick with emotion. "So I'm not surprised he hasn't blurted it out to you or anything. But, Lochlan, you need to understand, okay? This pathetic little fucker, he got in our sweet boy's head. He convinced Dario that he couldn't do anything on his own. That all his ideas were embarrassing and laughable. That…that he was so useless, no one else would ever love him. He twisted Dario's thoughts so much, he really believed that he should be grateful for Shane's 'love.'"

I can hear the air quotes in her anguished tone. I scrub my free hand down my face. "Fuck," I say heavily.

I've done training on how to recognize domestic abuse on the job. It's devastating to see how often it rears its ugly head, sometimes where you'd least expect it. These predators are so damn smart about hiding it. There isn't a single part of me that blames Dario for finding himself in that situation. But I already hate this Shane guy more than is probably reasonable considering we've never met.

For his sake, I hope we never do.

"How did Dario escape?" I ask in hushed tones.

I'd hate for him to think we were talking about him behind his back, but I gotta know. Sure, I thought he was shy when we first met, but in a cute, nerdy way. I had no idea he's been through so much trauma, and I feel guilty for it. I should have seen or guessed or somehow known…

Not that it would change the past in any way. But still, there's a part of my big, dumb caveman brain that's convinced I should have done something different. Well, I can certainly do whatever I can to help Dario now, that's for damn sure.

Gaby looks like she's torn between letting the shimmering tears collecting on her lashes fall and screaming the house down in rage. Both would probably be quite cathartic.

"Shane hit Dario," she whispers.

My blood runs cold and a buzzing rings in my ears. That big dumb caveman brain of mine is seriously unhappy. The urge to track down Dario right that second and wrap him protectively in my arms is almost overwhelming. But I need to know how this story ends before I can do anything.

"Of course," Gaby says with a sneer, "Shane was all 'It was an accident! I'll never do it again! I love you, baby!' But thank *God* Dario still had enough fight in him to realize the line had finally been crossed. He knew his family loved him no matter what, and he had to get out."

"So they broke up?" I say with relief.

Sadly, Gaby shakes her head. "It was like Dario had a blindfold lifted from his eyes. He could suddenly see that he had to leave, but he knew that Shane wouldn't *let* him leave. Our boy is so fucking smart, though." Her expression is one of fierce pride, and I agree with her completely. "He acted like everything was fine, but he knew that Shane was watching him all the time. Checking his phone and computer and all that. That's when fate stepped in, and he got a crazy bonus from work as well as a pay rise. He was able to convince them to send the extra money to a new bank account he opened, so Shane never saw it. That HR lady was like a dragon." Gaby shakes her head in admiration. "She understood completely when Dario explained the situation. She had so many genius ideas about how to help him escape safely and make sure Shane couldn't find him again."

"And he did escape?" I ask, even though I've known him for a few weeks now, so of course he did. But I don't know if I've ever felt like this before. So furious and devastated and anxious all at once.

Holy shit. No wonder his family is so protective.

Gaby nods and takes a deep breath. "Shane went on a work trip. Once we'd confirmed he was on the plane, me, Alicia, Julio, and Julio's brothers were at Dario's place within the hour, packing him up and getting him the hell out of there. Shane had visited here a lot." She indicates Dario's folks' lovely home. "So we moved him in with me to begin with. He didn't have much stuff as he'd left everything Shane had ever bought for him or made him buy, so he was easy to hide. Then Dario blocked his number, closed all his socials down, and waited for Shane to come home and find the note he'd left saying it was over and not to try and find him."

Despite all the horror I'm feeling right now, I'm also proud, so proud. I knew my dude was brave AF, no matter what he's said to me. He's got a backbone that I saw right from the start.

"And that's when he changed his name?" I ask. Gaby looks at me in alarm, but I wave my hand. "I'm just putting two and two together. Some of his relatives I've been talking to this afternoon called him Miguel."

She slumps and sighs. "Yeah, you've got it. You're the first person they've met from his new life, so I don't think they really get how important it is for him that he maintains this new identity. I told him he should really change his surname as well and get it all legalized, but he was furious at the idea of Shane taking his connection to his family away like that. So Dario is only a change, socially. But seeing as he never posts on anything like Instagram anymore, I guess it doesn't matter. His work knows not to ever publish his name or picture as well."

"Wow," I say, exhaling and rubbing my forehead. "Did Shane ever come looking for him?"

"Once," Gaby says gravely. "Here. But Alicia made it very clear that Dario didn't want to see him, and if he ever came around again, he'd be violating the restraining order they had put out on him."

"No way," I say in awe. I knew I liked his mom. "Is there really a restraining order?"

"You bet your ass there is," Gaby says with a scoff before taking a big gulp of margarita and shaking herself all over, like she's trying to rid herself of any trace of that scumbag. "It covers this house and mine, but not Dario's new place as including there would mean informing Shane of the address, which nobody wants. But Dario is clever. I doubt Shane will ever find him, so Shane won't be popping over for a visit any time soon. Unlike me! I'm dying to see it, but he won't let us help furnish it! Can you talk to him, please?"

And just like that, the conversation shifts. I explain to her that Dario really wants to stand on his own two feet by picking out and buying all that stuff himself, and she does seem to listen to me.

Probably because I now understand on a whole new level what he's been through and want to support him with my whole chest. That's probably coming across in everything I'm saying to her. By the way she's smiling at me, I think she gets it.

Dario is a warrior. He survived a terrible situation where he was made to feel worthless and helpless, but he's neither of those things. Now his need to be independent makes total sense to me.

I might not be his boyfriend, but I think I might be his *best* friend. And I'm going to work my ass off to show him he's supported and brilliant and can furnish his own home with his own money in his own style, no matter how long it takes.

When I'm done hype-manning the shit out of my new best bro, he's not even going to *remember* that asshole Shane's name.

CHAPTER 12
Dario

LOCHLAN HAS BEEN ALONE WITH MY TIA FOR AN AWFULLY LONG time, I realize. It's not like I don't trust Gaby. She's always been awesome, and she was also there for me big time when I needed help the most.

It's just…there are certain things about my past that I'd prefer my new friend doesn't find out. It's a miracle he doesn't think I'm a loser yet. However, if he finds out how stupid, how weak I've been, he's bound to ghost me in disgust.

I know he's straight and this whole boyfriend thing is only pretend. But I'd still prefer it if he wasn't aware of the worst moments in my life to judge me by them. I'd rather be friends and suffer pining after him than not have him at all.

Just as I'm contemplating getting up from the fire pit and seeing where they've gotten to, they both emerge out into the yard, holding drinks and laughing.

"Look, all I'm saying is that the Billy bookcases are the favorite for a reason," Lochlan is telling Gaby, waving his hands about so much that his beer is in danger of sloshing out.

"Yeah," Gaby scoffs. "Because they're *basic* for basic *bitches*. If you want something sophisticated, you go with an Idanäs. What the fuck are they teaching kids these days?"

I wince and look around, but it seems like most of my younger cousins have already gone to bed, thankfully. They were probably tired out by running after Rocky and Queenie all day.

Lochlan chuckles and gives Gaby a very light push. "I bet I'm not even ten years younger than you."

"Young enough," Gaby says with a wink as she shoves him back before wandering off to give one of my tios a hard time.

I grin at hearing their banter, relaxing. Lochlan doesn't *look* appalled as he sits down beside me in the chair I kept vacant for him. In fact, he scoots closer and immediately reaches out to take my hand, giving it a squeeze.

My heart flutters. I know he's just pretending, but I cut myself some slack. The fact that he's committing this seriously to the role is touching in its own way. Seeing him interacting with my family is amazing but surreal as well.

After doing a number of puppy training classes together, I know he's got a way with people that mystifies me. But witnessing him happily chatting to some of the most important people in my life, I can finally say once and for all that it seems completely genuine. He means it when he asks people questions and he really listens to their replies.

Obviously, I've been fooled before. I'd like to think that I'm a little older and wiser now. I'm so much more aware of what red flags to look out for, and one of the biggest ones is about *myself*.

If my family raises serious concerns about someone in my life, I'm never going to ignore them ever again.

That doesn't seem to be an issue here today, thankfully. As if to illustrate my point, when Gaby next walks behind me, she pauses to place her hands on my shoulders and lean in so she can whisper in my ear.

"This one's a keeper."

I blush, but she moves on before I can fumble for a reply, so I don't have to come up with one. Just smile bashfully as she grins at me from over the fire pit.

I know he is, I think privately, where my secrets are safe. *I just wish he was mine to keep.*

After a couple of glasses of wine, though, it's a little difficult to remind myself of this fact. Especially when Lochlan resolutely keeps his hand clasped around mine long after it's necessary to keep up our rouse. More than that, when he's talking with my dad about fishing, he keeps rubbing his thumb over the back of my hand. I'm not even sure he's aware he's doing it.

I'm sure it means nothing. I've noticed he likes hugging people hello and goodbye, and he's a human golden retriever in so many other ways. I bet he just finds touch comforting.

Like I used to before it was weaponized against me and withdrawn as a form of punishment. Damn, I'd kind of forgotten how much I missed simply holding hands with a nice guy. Since we first tried in the woods the other day, I've been craving more. Lochlan does it so naturally.

When he finally lets me go to play tug with Rocky and a stick the pup found somewhere, I try not to feel the absence of his skin against mine too keenly. I do trace my fingers over where his thumb has been caressing, though, chasing the ghost of his presence.

The evening passes in a happy blur of games, laughter, and good conversation. I discover that Lochlan isn't very good at performing charades but he's ridiculously enthusiastic about it, and he's actually pretty great at guessing what our other teammates are doing. In fact, when it's my go, he's so quick at blurting out answers that one of my tios good-naturedly accuses us of cheating.

Having a special bond with Lochlan like that makes me feel all warm and fuzzy inside, even if it is just for a game. But the way his eyes meet with mine and light up when he guesses correctly is nothing short of beautiful.

He's beautiful.

Gah.

I switch to herbal tea for the last couple of hours, not wanting to overdo it and embarrass myself—either by confessing to my family that Lochlan isn't really my boyfriend or by confessing to Lochlan that I wish he was. I notice that he swaps between beer, water, and soda, which reassures me. Not that I'm policing his drinking or anything. I'd still like him if he was a party animal.

It's just that Shane was a spiteful drunk. I hate that I keep comparing Lochlan to him, but the fact that he's not getting wasted in front of my folks then being snippy is another green flag to me.

He's tipsy enough that as we decide to hit the hay, I have to practically drag him away from complimenting my dad on the turkey dinner, and both him and my mom on their beautiful house…and equally beautiful son.

"You're a nightmare," I mutter as we head back inside the house. To my surprise, he takes my hand again, despite the fact that no one's really watching us. Before I can tell him that he doesn't have to impress anyone, a voice calls from behind us.

"I'll show you where you are for the night!" Gaby says. We stop and let her catch up, and I can't help but notice a sparkle in her eye that usually means she's up to trouble.

She's always up to trouble, though, so I try not to put too much weight into it.

"Come on, you two," Lochlan says, whistling for the dogs to follow us.

"Oh, is Mamá okay with them sleeping with us?" I ask Gaby.

Gaby snorts. "I think the general vibe is that if they pee on the bed, you guys have to clean it up. But yeah."

"That's fair," Lochlan says sagely.

"Are most people staying over?" I ask as Gaby leads us upstairs. Some of my relatives come from a fair distance and more people than usual joined us for the day. I assumed a few families might have organized motels, but now I'm not so certain.

Sure enough, Gaby nods. "It's okay, though. Your mom's worked her magic and made room for everyone. Don't worry, you're back in your room."

She winks at me again and scampers ahead to the door of my childhood bedroom. Mercifully, Mamá and I redecorated it before I went off to college precisely because she does like to host as much of the family as she can during the holidays. I didn't want anyone to feel uncomfortable sleeping there.

Mind you, while a lot of my relatives would probably find it intimidating to have a Klingon Bird of Prey ship looming over the bed as they slept, I bet Lochlan would have gotten a kick out of it.

Not that he's going to be sleeping here tonight.

"Cool," I say as we approach a proud looking Gaby. She's swung the door open and is presenting the room like a gameshow assistant displaying a fabulous prize. "And where's Lochlan?"

She laughs and lightly slaps my chest. "Oh, no one gives a shit about that, babe. If you can't resist the urge to fuck, just keep it quiet so the kids don't hear. Hell, so *I* don't hear."

"W-what?" I splutter. My feet feel like they've rooted to

the spot and my heart is suddenly racing a million miles an hour. "Mamá said she made up two beds?"

Gaby snorts and pats my chest before releasing me. "No, she said she made up *lots* of beds. I was there, I heard her. I also helped make them all." She pinches my cheek, but I'm too stunned to react. "I made sure you got the best sheets and fluffiest pillows. Now say 'Thank you, Tia Gaby.'"

I blink, too full of dread to play along with her joke. But my mind is also whirring. If I want my family to believe we're a couple, I'm not going to get very far by refusing to share a bed. In fact, I should be acting relieved and excited right now.

Doing my best to smile and look coy, I rub the back of my neck. "If you're sure Mamá and Papá won't mind?"

She claps Lochlan's shoulder in a friendly manner and winks at me. "I promise you, mijo, they're thrilled."

With that, she wiggles her fingers at us and strolls away. Which means I no longer have an excuse not to look at Lochlan.

I wince, peeking over at him. "Oh my god, I'm so sorry," I whisper.

"Ah, it's fine," Lochlan says with a shrug as he wanders into the room, looking around appreciatively. I hurry after him and the dogs come as well, sniffy everything they can shove their noses into. "I'm used to sharing sleeping space when I'm on shift."

"Yes, but not…" My words die in my throat as I realize Gaby's given me the duvet cover and pillows from when I was five. The set with cartoon trucks, diggers, and cars all over it. "Not that," I say, indicating the source of my mortification. Why couldn't they at least have been the ones with the Toy Story aliens on? "Honestly, I didn't think we even still had those sheets."

Lochlan just shakes his head. Even though I'm dying

inside at the thought of sharing a room with him, let alone a bed, I kind of assumed that he'd be cracking jokes to lighten the mood.

"Seriously, dude, I don't mind," he smiles but it looks heavy, like now that we're alone he's…sad about something. Awkward, I'd understand. Amused or even pissed off. But sad? I'm not quite sure what's going on. But before I can ask, he points at the bed. "Look, new toothbrushes. Just like your mom promised. Do you mind if I freshen up?"

I'm so thrown by his attitude that I simply nod as he grabs one of the packages. "Uh, sure. Why don't you take my en suite, and I'll use the bathroom in the hall."

That gets a slightly happier smile out of him, which makes me a little less nervous. But I'm still feeling confused as I take myself out into the hall again. Then confusion morphs into something uglier.

All my old fears crawl back up my chest and into my throat like they've never left. I barely register brushing my teeth as I start worrying that I've upset him somehow. That I'm going to walk back into that room and find him *disappointed* in me, which is so much worse than just being plain old mad.

Except Lochlan isn't Shane and I really need to get a grip on myself.

When I do return, there *is* a shock waiting for me. Just not the kind I was expecting.

"Oh, hey!" Lochlan says brightly, as if he's not standing in my old bedroom wearing nothing but his goddamned briefs. The way they cling to his ass, thighs and…*bulge*…leave nothing to the imagination. I quickly avert my eyes, but he doesn't seem to notice or be bashful at all. Like he always parades his muscular body around in his gay friend's childhood homes.

"Hey," I manage to say in a strangled voice. He's busy

folding his clothes into a neat pile on top of my dresser, so I get a second to see that his chest is sprinkled with freckles and soft red hair, just the way I'd imagined.

Oh, god. This is how I die.

"Do you have a side?" he asks. He lifts Queenie then Rocky onto the bed where they start running around and sniffing the bedding. *Please don't pee now,* I beg silently. This moment is awkward enough.

"Hmm?" I blink and drag my gaze up to meet his, desperately hoping he didn't catch me drinking in all six foot five inches of golden skin and thick, juicy muscles. Dios mío, I'm having fantasies about being crushed by those legs again.

Lochlan points at the bed. "A side that you prefer to sleep on."

"Oh," I say, understanding but absolutely not caring. "Um, no. You?" I'm lying, of course. My side is the one he's on. But the thought of him coming any closer to me in this state is making my brain short circuit.

"I'm good here," he says thankfully, and pulls back the covers, getting comfy in the bed where I jerked off nonstop when I was a teenager.

This is fine, I tell myself as both dogs rush to lick his face, their tails wagging furiously.

Now what? The idea of stripping down and sharing a mattress is terrifying. But at the same time, I'm never going to get comfy enough to sleep in jeans. It's not a long drive I have to do tomorrow, but I still don't want to be awake all night. It's the same reason I'm not doing the noble thing and offering to sleep on the floor. This whole charade has exhausted me in the past few days leading up to it, plus all the memories I've been stirring up about Shane. I suddenly just want to sleep so badly I could cry. I just want my brain to *stop.*

After a few torturous moments of deliberation, I pull off

my pants and socks, staying in my underwear and T-shirt. There, that should be both comfortable and modest.

"Okay, settle," Lochlan says firmly to the dogs and points to his feet. Queenie trots down to lie at the end of the bed right away, but Rocky takes a little more encouraging, giving me a few extra seconds to think.

All I have to do now is get into a bed with the ridiculously hot straight man that I'm head over heels for. No big deal.

He doesn't seem to have gotten the memo that we're supposed to be stressed, though. By the way he's got his hands under his head, he looks completely relaxed. Or maybe not relaxed…but lost in thought. He certainly seems oblivious to the turmoil I'm going through, which is probably a blessing. But how is this not wildly uncomfortable for him?

Perhaps he just doesn't see me as sexual in the slightest. That thought is depressing enough that it strangely quiets some of my nerves. I finally pull back the covers and get under them before he can notice my hovering and ask why I'm being weird.

Even though he's the one being weird, in my opinion.

As soon as I lie down, he flips on his side, frowning at me and biting his lower lip. The lamp is still on behind him, but since I closed the door to the landing, we're now mostly in shadow. I was hoping the low lighting might have hidden my skinny body, but let's be real. I'd need some serious CGI to turn me from Steve Rogers into Captain America.

"Hey," Lochlan says softly, pulling me from the anxious, random thoughts that were no doubt doing their best to distract me from the situation I've found myself in.

"Hey," I say back. Maybe if we talk a little, it'll somehow be miraculously less awkward when we try and sleep without accidentally kicking each other. "Again, I'm so sorry about all this. You agreed to do me this ridiculous favor, and now–"

"Gaby told me about Shane," he blurts out, his expression pinched.

"Oh," I say softly. Well, at least he's succeeded in distracting me from my previous worries. But now my brain is scrambled with a whole load of new anxieties.

"I'm so sorry, dude," Lochlan says in distress. "She thought you'd already mentioned it to me, then she was determined to give me the scoop because she was worried you wouldn't tell me because you were ashamed—which you definitely *shouldn't* be—and, well, she was basically like 'this is what he's been through, so if you hurt him, I'll kick your ass.' I understand if you're mad."

When it's clear he's finished speaking, I take a deep breath and attempt to assess how I'm really feeling. Because, yeah, I really didn't want him to hear how weak and stupid I was.

But he's not looking at me like that's what he thinks at all. In fact, he seems upset. Like…actual tears pooling in his eyes.

I can't stand that he's fretting about what my reaction is going to be. He hasn't done anything wrong, not really.

"I'm not mad," I assure him genuinely. Before I can think better of it, I reach out and cover his big hand with one of my smaller ones. "I was afraid of what you'd think of me if you found out. But I know Gaby was just trying to protect me from doing something so stupid again."

His frown depends. "Stupid?" he repeats.

I sigh and look away from him into the gloom. "Letting myself get fooled like that. Manipulated."

Lochlan's face morphs into something…incredulous. "You're not stupid or foolish or anything like that!" he cries. "You're brave! Dario, I'm so proud of you!"

For a second, I'm speechless. "Proud? I was a complete idiot!" My throat is getting tight and hot tears sting my eyes, but I do my best to choke the words out. "I believed the lies he fed me about my old friends! My *family.* I had to escape my old house when he was away with the help of a *police escort."*

Lochlan shifts and grabs my hand between both of his, eyes blazing. "Exactly. That must have been so scary. But you did it. You got out and you've already built yourself a whole new life!"

He's got it all wrong and I shake my head, clenching my jaw before I speak. "I should never have gotten into that situation in the first place. If I had any sense, I wouldn't have."

Lochlan's brow knits as he stares at me. "It's not about sense. You're a nice guy and he was an asshole. That's not your fault."

"It *is* my fault!"

I shout so loudly the dogs lift their heads and whimper. I don't want to upset them or for any of my family to hear me, though. So I take a breath and at least lower my voice if I can't control my emotions.

"I stayed so long and pushed everyone else away," I choke out, tears spilling down my face. "I told them *they* were the crazy ones. I was a coward. I should have—"

In a sudden flurry of movement, Lochlan has dragged me against his chest, wrapping his arms tightly around me. I'm so stunned that I just freeze, but he presses his temple against mine and makes a keening noise.

"Dario," he rasps. "A lot of people never escape. You know that, right? I've seen it so many times in my job. People stay or...or worse. So much worse. I think this is why Gaby told me the whole story. Because if you really think you were a coward or stupid or any of those things you just said, maybe you *do* need your boyfriend to convince you otherwise." He lets out a puff of air and a small chuckle. "Or at least your pretend boyfriend."

After a few seconds, I remember how to breathe again.

My head is swimming and I'm overwhelmed by the feeling of Lochlan's strong body encircling me as well as his warm, woodsy, spicy sent. I'm not strong enough to resist. I tuck my face against his neck and my entire body shudders for a moment.

"I know it could have ended much worse," I mumble after a while. His embrace tightens around me. "It doesn't stop me from feeling weak and foolish but…thank you, Lochlan. It means a lot to me that you care."

"Of course I care," he says, sounding relieved. "And I promise that you'll never have to go through anything like that again."

"I know," I agree, feeling a little of that relief myself. "My family has been incredible throughout it all."

"No doubt," he says fondly. "But I meant you have *me* now. If anybody even thinks about trying something like that with you again, I'll kick their ass back into the last century."

I laugh weakly, but my appreciation runs true and deep. I don't doubt he means that. My golden retriever friend, who has no idea what cradling me in bed while we're both mostly naked is doing to me. My body is going haywire.

But my heart feels like one of the jagged fissures that's been there for so long has just been superglued back together.

I realize I'm drifting off to sleep in his arms, but I don't fight it. Lochlan Bell might not be my boyfriend, but he's the best pretend boyfriend I could ever ask for.

It's not much. However, after everything I've been through, I'll take it.

CHAPTER 13

Lochlan

"THIS ASSHOLE WOULDN'T EVEN LET DARIO HAVE A TREKKIE *mug* in the house," I continue to rant, aware that I'm sounding like a broken record. But it's been six days, and I'm just as pissed about everything I learned over Thanksgiving as ever. "Like, he totally got a kick out of making Dario feel small. After I found out, Dario called himself stupid so many times. He's the smartest person I know!"

Lili sighs and puts her weights down. We were supposed to be working out in between calls, but it's like my brain can't focus on anything else right now. I feel bad for distracting her, but she's my best friend and I really, really need help sorting this out. Because my other, new best friend is already beating himself up enough about it all, so I can't talk to him again.

"Sorry for being a pain in the ass," I mumble, dropping down to sit on the rowing machine.

"Yeah, you are," she says, rolling her eyes. But she also reaches out and grabs my arm. "You know why? Because finding out someone you care about was in an abusive relationship is a total mindfuck. I get that you feel completely helpless right now because unless you find yourself a Delorean, you're not going back in time to stop it."

I perk up with a little smile. It always tickles me when she says something dorky to get me out of my feelings. Normally she deliberately confuses Star Wars and Star Trek just to piss me off, but she's right about this one. I'd love Doc Brown's time machine to scare that jerk Shane into switching colleges before he could ever meet Dario.

But then he'd just have found some other sweet guy to terrorize, no doubt. That bums me out again.

"I can't stand that this guy is still living rent free in Dario's head," I say. "Dario should be proud that he was able to get himself away safely. But he still feels like it was his fault. Like he was asking for it."

Lili tugs my hand and pulls me to come sit on the workout bench next to her. "That's what these people do," she says, wrapping her arm around my back. "They gaslight and manipulate their victims so they can control their every move. It's how they get their sick kicks. Then they isolate the person they supposedly love so their friends and family can't make them see how awful the situation is."

"'Love,'" I scoff, feeling my blood rush as I clench my fists. "What Shane did is nothing like love. It's the *opposite* of love."

"I know, hon," Lili says sympathetically, patting my shoulder. She takes a breath and holds it long enough that I look at her and frown. She narrows her eyes at me and exhales, seeming like she's deciding what she wants to say next. "I think you know all about the right kind of love."

Oh. Why was she worried about saying that? "Damn straight I do," I grumble. "When you love someone, you do everything you can to lift them up and support them."

"No, not 'damn straight,'" she says with a tired laugh, shaking her head. "Damn *not* straight. Beast, buddy. You know you've been doing nothing but lifting up and supporting Dario since you met him, right?"

I'm really not following her. "Yeah, cuz he's my friend. I love my friends like I love my family. We've been over this! Please don't make it weird. I'm straight."

She covers her eyes with her hand for a second and makes a little squeaking sound before looking at me again. "Are you, though? And before you say 'yes' I want you to really, *really* think about it. Did it feel uncomfortable pretending to be this guy's boyfriend for two whole days?"

"No, it was easy," I say with a shrug. "Even when his mom made us up his old bed to share for the night. Dario's just so cool to be around. It didn't bother me."

She blinks slowly at me. "You're only telling me now that you *slept* together?"

"Yeah, as in *sleeping*," I fire back at her. "There weren't enough beds and, besides, it would have made his family suspicious if we'd freaked out. They think we're dating, remember?"

"Did you even think about offering to sleep on the floor?" she asks.

"No," I tell her, then my insides run cold. "Oh, shit. Do you think *Dario* was uncomfortable?"

She holds her hands up. "I don't know. Did *he* say anything about sleeping on the floor?"

I shake my head. "No. He was only worried that I'd be uncomfortable, but honestly, I was already so upset about Shane, the bed thing didn't seem important. And he was totally cool when we snuggled, so—"

Lili goes all floppy and slides to the floor, the back of her hand pressed to her forehead, as if she's having a fainting fit. "There was *snuggling,* too?" she demands from by my knee.

"Dario was crying about Shane," I explain. "I didn't know

what else to do to calm him down and make him see sense. It was, um, nice, though."

My skin prickles and I feel a bit hot remembering just *how* nice and right it had felt to finally shield Dario with my body like I'd wanted to since the moment Gaby had spilled the beans. It was like I'd been all consumed with the idea that if I could just stand between Dario and all the bad things in the world, I could protect him in a way he hadn't been protected before. As soon as I'd pulled him against me, it was like that momma bird finally chilled out and stopped trying to peck everyone else. We'd fallen asleep like that.

I'd spent every night since then falling asleep while hugging a pillow and thinking about it. Thinking about him. Which…okay, maybe was a little out of the ordinary.

I open and close my mouth a couple of times, trying to organize my thoughts. "I just wanted to protect him," I say weakly, aware I'm becoming repetitive.

Lili puts her hands on my thigh then rests her chin on her knuckles. "You want to protect everyone," she says softly. "You do it every day, and not just at work. I reckon you'd step in front of a moving train if you thought it would save someone's life. But here's my question: Do you think you'd snuggle with any of the guys here at the One-Thirteen?"

"Um…maybe?" I say. It's hard to picture, but if any of my guys were crying, then I'm sure I'd hug them.

But would I hug them *in bed*? Wearing only my briefs? Again, I hadn't even thought about that with Dario, but would I do that with Rico? Sawyer? Del?

Lili sighs again and heaves herself to her feet. "Come on," she says, taking my hand and pulling me up as well. "Let's go do some science."

I don't protest as she leads me into the common area where most of the guys are chilling or cleaning the rigs. It looks like Teddy has just come back from giving Rocky a quick run around the block like he said he was going to while Lili and I were in the gym. Now they're playing tug with a rainbow-colored knotted rope.

"Uh, quick question!" Lili shouts by way of an announcement. I'm suddenly nervous what she's going to do as everyone looks our way. "When you have a friend who is very upset about something, what do you do?"

"Invite myself over with beer and nachos to watch the game," Sawyer says from the sofa without missing a beat. "Unless they're more of a pink wine, ice cream, and rom com type of person. I'm flexible like that."

He grins as Anton snorts. "Yeah, we've all heard about how *flexible* you are. Personally, I find art therapy works on all ages."

Del looks up from his paperback. "Be a good listener," he says sincerely.

"Bake them their favorite treat," Yara says from the kitchen where she is indeed baking.

"Flowers," Gene chips in with a haunted look in his eyes. "Doesn't matter what happened or who's fault it really was. Just go with flowers."

Lili tilts her head to look at me like some kind of owl. "Interesting. Okay, gang, how do we feel about hugs?"

"Depends who we're hugging," Teddy say with a slight frown before scooping a wriggling Rocky up. "Puppies get ALL the hugs! Don't they, Rocky? Yes, they do."

Sawyer's nodding, though. "Yeah. A good hug can go a long way."

"Seems a little extreme to me," Gene grumbles, crossing his arms.

Lili licks her lips and taps her chin. "So that probably means snuggling in bed for the night is a step too far, hmm?"

She's met with a general air of confusion that makes me nervous again. No one's asking why she's got all these questions, but it probably won't take them long to figure stuff out. I want to defend myself and clarify the circumstances, but Anton speaks before I can. "For a friend?" he asks.

Lili laughs. "Oh, no, sorry. That would be for a significant other."

The whole room seems to let out a breath and laugh. "Oh, yeah," Sawyer says with a dismissive wave of his hand. "Then snuggling is basically the first thing you do."

"A great number of studies show that being held is extremely therapeutic," Del says sagely.

"That doesn't seem like anybody else's business," Gene mutters, easing farther down in his armchair, the tips of his ears tinged pink.

"Who's upset, anyway?" Rico asks, coming closer to us with his coffee mug in hand.

I get the feeling that if anyone's worked it all out, it's him. Because I've been yapping about Dario's shitty ex all this shift and the previous one as well, and he's the kind of guy that pays attention. Del has most likely put it together as well, but he's too polite to call me out on my shit like Rico would.

Lili shakes her head at him, though. "Oh, it's just a hypothetical, Lieutenant. Proving a point to this egghead here. I think Gene's right. The answer is probably flowers. Thanks, guys!"

Gene gives us a salute and appears relieved that we're not going to make him talk about his feelings anymore. Lili ushers me back toward the bunk room. My head is spinning so much that I don't resist.

"Okay, so, I'm weird," I say dejectedly as she pushes me to sit on the bed I consider mine. Obviously, I share it with people on the other shifts. But when I'm here, it gives me a little familiar comfort. "Message received."

"What? No! Urgh." Lili plops beside me and cups either side of my face. "Please listen to me as your bisexual elder."

"You're like…six years younger than me," I point out.

She scowls at me. "Yeah, but I'm really, *really* bisexual, so shut up and listen. I know it might be kind of scary to discover something new about yourself, but just because it's a surprise doesn't make it not true."

"What's not true? Or…true?"

She rubs her thumbs against my cheeks. "That you are crazy about Dario and it's not platonic. And before you hit me with all that 'I'm straight!' stuff, just sit with that thought for a second. What would it mean if you had feelings for this guy? Would it be so terrible?"

"I never said it would be terrible," I argue hotly. But then the fight blows out of me almost immediately. "It's just not who I am."

She lets go of my face and takes my hands in hers instead. "But what if it *is?* Can you just let your imagination run free for a second and see how it makes you feel? Like, you said sharing a bed was nice. Is there anything else you can think of that was nice in a more close and personal way?"

It feels like there's a horse in my chest that wants to buck at everything she's saying. But I trust her, so I do what she says and just sit for a second with the idea.

Sharing a bed *was* nice. Cuddling was nice. And… "I liked holding hands," I say, unable to stop myself smiling at the memory. "I figured that was just because it had been a while since I did that with anyone, but…maybe it was because it was Dario."

Whoa. It's almost like I can feel something blossoming inside me. It's light and bright and kinda sparkly.

Do I have a crush on my friend? On a guy?

Lili seems to be watching me have all these thoughts. Her

eyebrows raise when I meet her gaze again. "Dario is special, right?"

"But…" I say, still very much wrestling with all of this. "But if I was…if I am…*bi*…surely I'd have figured that out by now, right? I'm thirty-three, for god's sake."

She shrugs. "I mean, what took me ages to work out that not *everyone* is bi. It always seemed natural to me. But sexuality, like a lot of things, is on a scale. Maybe you're just a little bit bi. Maybe you're Dario-sexual. It doesn't really matter. You can label it however you want or not at all. All that matters is how you feel about him."

I chew on my lip. "How do I know if it's a crush or if it's just friendship, though?"

Lili tilts her head like an owl again. "How do you normally tell with a lady?"

Honestly, I don't seem to crush on all the many girls, not like other guys I know or in movies. I have to really get to know them first, so it's not just that I think they're pretty. I need to like their personality as well.

But…wasn't one of my first thoughts about Dario that he was pretty? It was, I remember, because I was worried that was creepy or strange. But maybe it was just…bisexual?

"Um," I say to fill the silence all my whirling thoughts have created. "I normally ask a girl out because I can't get her off my mind and I just want to spend more time with her. I like girls who are smart and cool and funny and got a bit of spunk, you know? They're…"

"Brave?" Lili suggests, her expression warm and her tone hopeful.

I slump back and drag my hand down my face, blinking a couple of times as I stare at nothing in particular.

Brave. Dario is brave. And everything else I just said. I do think about him all the time and we've been hanging out as much as possible already.

I still love all my friends here and outside of work and my family as well. But haven't I been saying for weeks that Dario's quickly become my favorite person of them all?

Shit.

It hits me all of a sudden that this has quite possibly been in front of my face the entire time. I was just too afraid of such a huge change in my life to admit it.

"Do I have romantic feelings for Dario?" I whisper. "Am I bisexual?"

I look back to see her smiling. "I think those are questions worth asking, my friend." She pats my shoulder and stands up. "Here's another one. I think you need to spend some serious time thinking about whether or not you'd like to do more than hold hands and snuggle with Dario."

"Like what?" I say, my brain too mushy to get what she's saying.

Her expression is kind, though. "Like kissing, perhaps?"

That makes me gulp. Kissing is such a leap from hugging. However, it doesn't make me freak out like I thought it might. In fact…didn't I kiss him on the head at Thanksgiving? I'm pretty sure I did. Would it be so different to try it on the lips?

"What if he doesn't want to kiss me back?" I ask.

Her smile turns into a beaming grin. "That sounds like a question you need to ask Dario, don't you think?"

I puff out my cheeks. She's probably right. But of course that's the moment the alarm goes and we have to sprint into action. As always, my focus from then on is laser sharp on the call and the ones that come after it.

However, I spend the in-between times pondering all of Lili's questions and more. By the time morning comes, I feel more confused than ever. There's one thing I know for certain, though, and that is that I need to speak to Dario in person. As soon as possible.

Even if it's going to be ten times scarier than all the burning buildings I just ran into.

CHAPTER 14

Dario

Life has been suspiciously calm since the Thanksgiving trip. I'm not used to calm. Instinctively, I'm waiting for the other shoe to drop.

So when my doorbell sounds on Wednesday evening, I'm kind of not surprised that I jump three feet off the ground and scare the pants off Queenie, even though I know I'm being ridiculous.

"People are allowed to ring the doorbell," I mutter to myself as I make my way to the front of the house. "Otherwise, how would I know anyone's outside?"

By the time I reach for the handle, I've convinced myself it's simply a delivery for something I've ordered online and forgotten about. I'm holding off purchasing big things like furniture until I'm more financially stable, but there are still plenty of little bits and pieces I'm slowly getting together. Off the top of my head, I can't think of what this could be, but perhaps it's just taken the package a while to make its way to me. It could be a nice surprise.

When I open the door, I get a surprise all right. I've got a polite smile on my face to greet the driver...except it's not a delivery. It's Lochlan. And he looks extremely stressed out.

"I'm sorry I didn't text or call or whatever to ask if I could come over," he blurts out before I've even fully got the door open. Rocky's at his feet on his leash and immediately strains at the sight of Queen as she rushes over to say hello. "Is it okay if I come in? Are you busy? You're probably busy. This is a bad idea. I should just go. I'm sorry, I just—"

"Lochlan," I cry with a nervous laugh. "Are you okay? No, I'm not busy. Yes, you can come in."

He looks at me sheepishly and slips his hands into his jeans pockets, despite the way Rocky's leash is tugging at his wrist. "Are you sure you're not making dinner or anything?"

I shake my head. "I was thinking about it but haven't started yet. You'd be more than welcome to stay and join me, if you like? I was considering throwing together a stir fry, but I could be talked into something covered in cheese if you need comfort food."

He genuinely doesn't look great. The entire time we've been friends, he's usually the cool and collected one, always ready to crack a joke. But now he's all worked up again. Like…

Oh. Like the state he was in at my parents' house after he found out what happened between Shane and I. By the morning and our drive back, I really thought he was okay with it all. Hell, *I* felt the best I ever had since I'd gotten away from that bastard. Has Lochlan gone down another rabbit hole fretting over me?

If I hadn't been so weak in the first place, he wouldn't be so consumed about avenging my honor or whatever, I'm sure. A fresh wave of shame rushes through me as I step aside and let him and Rocky inside my house.

"Uh, dinner sounds nice," he says as he toes his shoes off. "Great, actually. Thank you. But can we talk first?"

"Of course," I say, sincerely worried what this conversation is going to entail. But I don't think there's going to be any putting it off with Lochlan in this condition, so it's probably best to get it over and done with as soon as possible. "Shall I get us some drinks?"

Lochlan releases Rocky and he and Queenie run off to play. "Yes, please," he says with a small smile. "Just water or iced tea, though. Whatever you have open."

So this isn't a 'crack a beer and chat' sort of situation. I don't know if that makes things better or worse. Probably worse.

Rather than dwell on it, I nod and head to the kitchen to fetch a couple of glasses of water with ice and—because my mother's voice is echoing in my ears—some chips and dip in case he needs something to nibble on. My stomach is in knots, and I can't even think about taking a bite of anything right now. But remembering my manners helps give me a tiny sense of control, at least.

Lochlan is wringing his hands by the time I set everything on the coffee table and settle myself on the other end of the sofa. I'm so used to his rambunctious personality that I'm at a loss of how to console him when he seems completely tongue-tied. Then I remember that he finished a shift this morning, and inspiration hits me.

"Did something happen at work?" I ask.

I'd never want him to be traumatized after a bad call or for anyone to get hurt. But at least if he is troubled by something that he witnessed on the job, I'd like to be there for him. In fact, I'd be honored if he turned to me for comfort or advice, especially after how fiercely he defended me on Thanksgiving.

He blinks and seems to register what I said. "Oh, no," he says, shaking his head before he frowns. "I mean, yeah, it happened at work. But it was a conversation, not a car wreck or anything."

"Okay, good," I say, genuinely relieved. "Is it something I can help with, or do you just need space to rant?"

"It's, um, about you," he says.

All the times I expected him to be awkward at my parents' house and he wasn't, yet now he looks like he wants to crawl out of his skin.

I know the feeling.

Holy fuck. What have I done to piss him off this badly?

"I'm sorry," I blurt automatically, my mind immediately racing through all our recent calls and texts. Nothing comes to mind that could have unsettled him like this, but what if I've been wrapped up in my own feelings and worries and didn't notice saying something insensitive? I'll be so distraught if I've been that selfish.

My words seem to shake something loose in him, though. He refocuses and meets my gaze with blazing eyes. "What? No! You haven't done anything wrong or bad or...Jesus, Mary and Joseph, I'm already fucking this all up."

"You're not fucking anything up," I assure him softly, worry eating me up inside.

He drags his hand down his face and then rubs the reddish stubble on his chin. He's so gorgeous even when he's sad. But I don't deserve to be ogling him right now when I've clearly done something awful.

Then I take a deep breath and remember this is Lochlan I'm talking to, not Shane. Spiraling isn't going to help anyone, especially not him if that's what he's come here for. I should be honored I'm the one he wants to trust like that.

I am worthy, I repeat silently. *I am strong. I am loved.*

Lochlan isn't going to bite my head off, I'm sure of it. I need to be honest with how I'm feeling. That's what my therapist has been drilling into me lately, anyway.

"You are kind of freaking me out, though," I admit with a wince. "Are you sure I didn't miss your birthday or something?"

Thankfully, that gets a small laugh out of him. "Naw, you're good. My birthday's not till March. I mean it, you haven't done anything wrong. This freak out is all on me and my dumb ass. I just…dude, my head is swimming. I want to say so many things, but I have no clue where to start, and I'm worried that if I say the wrong thing you're gonna hate me and I'm going to ruin everything."

My jaw drops open as I try and process all he's said. "I don't think I could ever hate you," is what comes out of my mouth first. "What would you ruin?"

"Our friendship," he says immediately. That does make my guts twist. His friendship is so important to me.

Oh…god. He couldn't have found out how I really feel about him, could he? Is he going to accuse me right now of being a creep and tell me to back off? Shame rinses through me like acid and my mouth is suddenly dry.

I reach for my water and take a gulp, focusing on the bobbing ice cubes instead of facing him, like a coward.

"If I've ever done anything to make you uncomfortable, I'm so sorry," I say breathlessly, tears pricking at my eyes.

"You haven't," he says, sounding like he's pleading. The next thing I know is he's plucking the glass from my hand, setting it back on its coaster, then…wrapping his hands around mine.

My breath hitches. There's no one here to impress. Why's he touching me like this?

"I'm doing this all wrong," he says woefully. "I can't get the words out, so you're making up ones to fill the blank spaces and they're all the opposite of how I'm feeling and what I'm completely failing to say. Dario…I…"

He sounds so anguished, I dare to lift my gaze and look

into his beautiful green eyes. There's something about them that makes me think of Queenie at the shelter, desperately begging me to notice her, to love her. The feeling is so strong and sudden that a lump rises in my throat, and I lose the battle with the tears that have been clinging to my lashes.

"No, don't cry," he says, reaching up to brush them away. "I never want to make you cry, ever."

"I never want to make you upset like this," I counter him. "Please—please tell what's wrong so I can fix it."

He inhales then lets it out slowly and shakily. "There's nothing *wrong*…or at least *you* haven't done anything wrong. And I don't want you to feel you have to *fix* anything. But if I stop dragging my feet and explain myself already, we can both, like, take a step back and see how we feel, right?"

My nerves are still off the chart, but I still nod. Anything is better than this suspense.

"Absolutely," I say, shifting my hands so we're holding onto each other now. "You can always talk to me."

He nods back at me, but it still takes him several moments to open his mouth again. "Dario…I…I like you," he manages to utter. "I'm actually kind of obsessed with you. Not in a stalker way!" he practically yells, squeezing my hands. "I just mean…you're who I think about all the time. When I wake up and when I go to sleep. I want to tell you every single thing I'm doing just to talk to you. You have no idea how much I've stopped myself from narrating all the boring shit I do, like you need to know whenever I walk Rocky or brush my teeth or what I'm watching on the damn TV."

He rolls his eyes and laughs. However, it seems like I've stopped breathing. I'm not quite sure what's going on here.

"But that's how I feel," he continues. "Like everything is so exciting now because I want to tell you about it. And…and I can't stop thinking about what you went through with Shane. I'm so angry with nowhere to put all that energy. I can't bear that he crushed you like that. I don't even know what he looks like, but I've probably punched his face a million times in my mind already. But then I remember how you got away from him and started a whole new life—here! In my little town! And that meant we got to be buddies, and I don't want you to ever call yourself weak or stupid or a coward ever again because you're none of those things! You're amazing and I always thought it was wild you even wanted to be my friend so…"

He bites his lip and flinches.

"Fuck. I've barged my way into your life over and over again, and here I am, word vomiting without even asking you how you're feeling or if you'd be interested in me at all like that. I'm sorry. I don't mean to be a jerk. I'd never, *ever* want to make you feel pressured or trapped. I want the opposite! I want to give you all the support and freedom you deserve. So, um, what do you think?"

"What do I think…about you?" I say, trying to pick through the many threads of consciousness he just threw out in less than two minutes. "Lochlan, you're amazing," I say with every ounce of conviction I possess. "I know we've covered this several times before, but I still can't work out in what timeline you'd want to be *my* friend. I'm just glad it's this one. And the way you went above and beyond to support me with my family was next level." I laugh and try and break the tension with a joke. "How could I ever hate my fake boyfriend?"

He swallows, looking dead serious still. "What if it wasn't fake?"

A shiver runs all over my body. "What?" I croak.

"Being your boyfriend," he says, his voice small but his gaze locked with mine. "What if I didn't want that to be fake?"

I look down at where he's still clinging to my hands, then

back up at him. My ears are ringing, and my heart is suddenly racing a million miles an hour. He can't be saying what I think he's saying.

Can he?

"But…you're straight?" I rasp.

A nervous smile tweaks one corner of his mouth, and he gives a lopsided shrug. "What if I'm not?"

No. This isn't happening. It's got to be some sort of sick joke. "Then you could date any guy you wanted," I say. The 'duh' is left unsaid but it's heavily implied.

He closes his eyes and inhales deeply. "I don't want to date any guy," he says softly. "I've never wanted to date a guy before. But…I think I want to date you, Dario."

Words fail me. My skin is prickling all over and I can't seem to get enough air into my lungs. "D-date me?" I stutter.

He peeks through his rose gold lashes at me. "I mean, we're kind of already dating, right? We spend so much time together and I met your family. I just thought…only if it would be something you'd want…that we could try, um, other stuff, too."

"Like what?" I ask, terrified of what I want the answer to be. *This can't be really happening.*

"Like, uh, kissing…maybe?" Lochlan says with a grimace, as if he's just as terrified as I am.

Because as much as I've been crushing on Lochlan since we met, I think I only did that because him being straight made it feel safe. Shane broke me in ways I've been afraid I'll never recover from. So I'd be a fool if I wasn't afraid of getting into anything with another guy. But Lochlan isn't just some random guy. I trust him. And clearly this is an enormous deal for him. He wouldn't be telling me this now if he wasn't sure about how he was feeling, right?

Besides…nothing could ever hurt me the way Shane did,

I'm sure. If I don't take this chance right now, I think I'll regret it for the rest of my life.

"You want to kiss me?" I ask in complete disbelief.

If this turns out to be a fever dream, I'm going to be so mad. Because I've pictured so many insane scenarios where Lochlan Bell asks me that very question, but they mostly involved us being on a spaceship that's about to crash, forcing him to confess his true feelings before we possibly die.

If I die now, I'm going to be even *more* pissed.

"Yes," he says with conviction, making my head spin. "I've thought a lot about it and it's obviously brand-new territory for me, but I'd really like to try. But *only* if you'd like that as well, because you're not some sort of experiment! You're my friend and I respect you. But I also think I'd really like to try touching you like a boyfriend might if that's something you—"

He would have probably kept rambling on like that, tying himself in knots over my consent all night if I let him. So I don't.

Before he can worry himself into oblivion and change his mind, I take him up on his offer of a scientific experiment to see how he might feel about kissing me.

By grabbing the front of his T-shirt and crashing my mouth against his.

CHAPTER 15

Lochlan

It takes my brain about zero point five seconds to work out what's happening. He leans back as quickly as he leaned in, and we both blink at each other.

Then I grab Dario on either side of his face and kiss the ever-loving shit out of him.

I've been doing what Lili suggested since we had our chat and really imagining what this might feel like. How leaning in cautiously could send chills up my spine. Thinking that Dario's lips would be soft and sweet.

I was wrong. He's an absolute fucking firecracker.

Before I can even process that the kiss I've been agonizing over is happening in 4K technicolor surround sound, Dario is scrambling into my lap, straddling my hips, and rubbing…

Whoa!

That…that feels really fucking amazing. His cock is, like, so solid against mine as he grinds on top of me, pinning me down as our lips and tongues tousle like wild dogs. I thought my little buddy was shy. And I'm sure he still is about a ton of things.

But not this, apparently.

I dig my fingers into his ribs and moan, jerking my hips to chase that delicious friction. I've never really thought about what rubbing my cock against another cock might feel like. Whenever I've watched gay porn (because who isn't curious, right?) it's always been about the blow jobs and penetration. But this is exciting and primal in a way I wouldn't have guessed.

Unfortunately, oxygen becomes an issue far sooner than I would have liked. Dario jerks back, gasping for air, and even though I don't really want to, it allows me to do the same. I figure the more O2, the more kissing, so I'll allow it.

Dario's lips are already beautifully red and swollen, slick with our spit. That caveman part of my brain rears up again, thrilled to have marked what's mine. But Dario's eyes are wide as they search mine.

"Is this okay?" he rasps.

I crook an eyebrow at him. "The fact that we've stopped kissing? No." I grin and thread my fingers through his thick, dark hair, pulling him down to devour his mouth once more. He lets out this happy little moan that makes my dick throb in my pants.

Yesterday, I would have sworn blind that I was as straight as an arrow. But now, here I am, slipping my hands under Dario's shirt, wondering how fast we can get naked.

However, the sensible, firefighter part of my brain finally takes the wheel from the caveman, and this time it's me that pulls back and takes a breath.

"Are *you* okay?" I ask between pants, moving my hands from under his shirt to rest on his hips. "We kinda went from zero to sixty there. I'm not complaining! In fact, the last thing I want to do is pump the brakes. But we've both been wrestling with some shit recently and I wanna make sure we're actually in the right head space."

He groans and drops his head on my shoulder. "How are you so fucking perfect?" he mumbles.

I laugh and run my hands up and down his back. Damn, that feels so natural.

I've thought a lot about Lili's words. How she said that labels don't matter. It only matters how I feel and how Dario feels. But I thought I'd be more afraid of touching him like this. These feelings have made me question so many fundamental things I thought I knew about myself.

But really...who cares? Maybe I'm bi? Maybe I'm something else? All I care about is that I think Dario is attracted to me like I'm attracted to him. And judging by what's going on in our pants right now, that attraction is *large*.

"So...does this mean you like me, too?" I ask tentatively. Dario starts laughing quietly, his whole chest shaking, before he lifts his head and looks into my eyes.

"Yes, Lochlan, I like you a ridiculous amount," he says warmly, tracing a finger down my cheek. It makes me shiver deliciously. "I really thought you were straight, though, so I'd resigned myself to a lot of pining."

I scoff. "I really thought I was straight, too. Lili practically had to bang my head against the wall to make me see sense." I release a breath, puffing out my cheeks. "I've been so dumb."

Dario cradles my face again, suddenly frowning. "No, Lochlan," he says firmly. "If I'm not allowed to call myself stupid or weak, you're not allowed to call yourself dumb."

"But I missed all the signs that were literally right in front of my face!" I protest.

He smiles and bobs his head from side to side. "I think you're incredibly in tune with your heart," he says, resting his hand over where mine is beating. "Sometimes, it just might take your head a little while to analyze what that means."

It doesn't seem so bad when he puts it like that. I'm probably not done beating myself up about it. A part of me is worried that I didn't notice something so important about myself because of internalized homophobia. I've heard the guys at work talking about that before. Like…did I not realize I was bi because I thought being queer was okay for other people but not for me?

Or is Lili right and I just genuinely haven't been attracted to a guy before the way I am to Dario? Am I being too hard on myself?

All I know is that he feels so insanely good in my arms right now. We naturally shift a little so we're chest to chest and he's resting his head on my shoulder. Then I have a thought that makes me worry about something slightly different.

"Did I string you along?" I ask.

He frowns and looks up at me. "What do you mean?"

"Well, you said that you, um, like me, but you thought I was straight. Was I out of line with the whole fake boyfriend thing? I'd never want to make you uncomfortable, Dario."

He hums and sets his palm over my heart again. God, I love him putting his hands on me so much, and we've only just started doing it. I want his hands all *kinds* of places.

"You weren't an insensitive dick, if that's what you're worrying about," Dario says with a warm chuckle. "You were incredibly sweet, actually. But you did kind of drive me insane, yeah. It was like you were so close yet so far away."

I card my fingers through his hair at the back of his head. "I'm sorry," I say sincerely.

"No, it's fine," he says, looking earnestly into my eyes. "It's not like you were leading me on purposefully, were you?"

"Absolutely not," I tell him hotly.

His smile is so sweet that the fire blows out of me right away. "Exactly. So don't worry that you've mistreated me in any way at all. In fact, you've never been anything but kind and thoughtful. Even if I thought we were just friends, you always made me feel important, Lochlan."

Warmth tingles through my whole body. "Good. Because you are important. Not just to me, but to the world. No one should ever make you feel otherwise." I swallow and place my hand over his where it's resting against my heart. "So…if you thought we were just friends before…does that mean we're something else now?"

His grin is shy but there's heat in his eyes as he looks up at me. "I think we're definitely something more now. But seeing as this is all new to you and I'm still getting back on my feet, we don't have to rush into anything or put any pressure on ourselves."

In principle, I agree that I want to go at whatever pace Dario needs. The abuse he went through was no joke and he deserves plenty of time and space to flourish now. On the other hand…

"I'll follow your lead, baby," I say, trying on the pet name and loving the way it feels, not to mention the way it makes Dario blush. "Though just so you know, I have no intention of seeing anybody else. And yeah, it's kinda nuts how I've fallen head over heels for a dude. But then again, is it really a big deal these days for a dude to catch feels for another dude?"

Dario sighs. "It is in some places for some people, yeah."

"Well, those people and those places are dumb," I declare. "I like you and you like me, it's that simple."

Dario shakes his head. "You're amazing, I mean it."

I also shake my head. "Naw, I'm just a big dumb jock," I say, winking so he knows that I'm deliberately trying to provoke him by using that word again. I like how he defended me earlier about that. "You know what was amazing, though? Kissing you. That freaking rocked. Can we do more of that?"

Dario licks his lips and squirms around so he's straddling my hips again. "You like this, huh?" he rasps.

Oof. If I thought he was confident before, that's nothing to what he's oozing now. Most of the girls I've been with were sweet and giggly, and I loved it. But there was this one chick who bossed me around and rode me like a cowgirl. That was fucking *epic.*

So the fact that's the vibe adorable Dario Garcia-Perez is giving me now makes me excited in a bunch of ways I can't quite even describe.

Other than hot. It's fucking hot. *He's* fucking hot.

"Oh, baby," I croak, my dick thickening in seconds. "Yeah, I like this a fuck ton. Can I touch you? I don't know what I'm doing, but I want to do it all."

Dario laughs and captures my mouth for a searing kiss. "I imagine it's not so different from touching a woman. Skin is skin."

I shake my head and glance between us. "I can assure you that it's already feeling pretty different. Why don't you tell me what you want? What you like. I just want to make you so happy, Dario."

His cheeks are flushed and he's already breathing heavily, but he looks at me with such wonder for a second. "You do make me happy," he says softly.

My heart sings.

Tentatively, he leans down to kiss me again. But this time, it's him who slips his hands under my T-shirt, his fingertips brushing against my stomach and making me jump in the best kind of way.

Of course, Dario notices. "Is this all right?" he mumbles against my lips.

"It's perfect," I promise him. "It's all perfect. Less talking, more kissing. I'll tell you if something freaks me out, but I doubt it will."

He laughs, the sound warm and golden. But he listens to me. As he takes hold of the bottom of my shirt, he just raises his eyebrows to check I'm okay. I simply lift my arms in response.

In a flash, my top is on the floor and his hot little hands skim down my chest. "You're like an Avenger," he says before leaning down and sucking one of my nipples hard, like it's a lollipop.

I cry out in shock. No one's ever done that to me before, which I'm immediately mad about. Holy fuck! This is great! I buck up from the sofa and thread my fingers through Dario's hair to keep him from moving. The last thing I want is for him to take my surprise as hesitation and stop what he's doing.

I meant what I said. I'll tell him if anything is too much for me. However, I'm pretty sure he can do anything he wants with me, and I'll love it.

"Oh, baby," I say with a gasp. My hands find their way under his T-shirt again, and he pulls back so I can remove it.

Obviously, this is one of the places where his body is significantly different to any woman's that I've been with. But I'm still drawn to the lovely expanse of smooth skin, the curve of his slim hips, and his dusky, pebbled nipples. It felt so good when he kissed and sucked me there, so I decide to try touching him there myself. He watches me as I slide my hands up his flanks and rub my thumbs over the tight buds, holding his sides as I do. He groans wantonly, and my cock aches.

Fuck! I want to do so many things with him, and I have no idea where to start.

"I want to make you come," I say. I don't care how. I just want to be as close to him as I can. I want to get naked and kiss him all over and maybe come as well.

Mostly, I want to take care of him in such a primal way. But I need him to show me the way.

"Yes," he hisses, his eyelids fluttering shut.

He captures my mouth with his own, kissing me fiercely and pressing our chests together. The skin-to-skin contact is electrifying, and I moan against his lips. My hands glide over his taut body, warm to my touch. But then he grabs my shoulders and tugs at me, pushing me to lie down the length of the sofa with him still straddling my hips. My heart's hammering in my chest but I'm not afraid. It's like I'm about to explode, excitement bubbling through me like a shaken soda can.

Looking up at him is awe-inspiring. His hair is kind of a mess, his lips are swollen, and he's breathing heavily, telling me he's losing his mind just as much as I am.

I don't care what he says. I was a total jackass for not realizing he had feelings for me earlier and then fucking with those feelings by pretending to be his boyfriend in front of his family. But I was even more of a dummy not to realize that I wasn't faking anything at all, not from the moment we met.

He's my favorite person in the world and right now, there's no place I'd rather be than under his hot, squirming body.

But I am going to lose my mind if we don't get back to the good stuff immediately. I respect that he doesn't want to push me in my first make-out session with a guy. However, I'm so over that fact already. There's nothing about this that's scaring me off. Just the opposite, in fact.

"I'm yours, Dario," I say, my voice coming out all raspy with lust. "You can do whatever you want with me."

It's quite possible that those words break something in him, judging by the stunned look on his face. That's okay, though.

He's got me now to put him back together.

139

CHAPTER 16
Dario

I can't have heard that right. This huge hunk of a man not only let me push him down to climb on top of him, but he's given me permission to do whatever I like with him?

My mouth goes dry, my thoughts frazzle in my brain, and my hands begin to shake. How can getting the thing I wanted the most in my wildest dreams scare me so much?

Well, I know why. Because it was drilled into me that I shouldn't want it.

It pains me to think about Shane yet again, but he always insisted on being in charge and on top when we had sex. As if he had to dominate me otherwise his fragile masculinity would shatter, no matter how it made me feel. I convinced myself that it was fine. That I loved him, so us being intimate was all that mattered.

Especially when he would withdraw his touch to punish me when I'd disappointed him. And he'd always make it crystal clear that I only had myself to blame. So I came to treat every time we'd fuck as some kind of sign that staying with him was worthwhile and that things would get better.

But that's all in the past now. Lochlan obviously senses

my hesitation as he reaches up to caress the side of my face. I melt against his palm, feeling like I'd just been free-falling and now my parachute has opened, catching me mid-air and keeping me safe.

"We don't have to do anything more than this," he assures me, his voice so warm and rumbly. I quiver all the way down to my toes. "We can kiss some more, or we can snuggle and watch some TV. I don't care, Dario. I just want to be here with you, and not in a friendly way." He frowns. "Well, I *am* still your friend. I just mean—"

I lean down and crash my mouth into his. "I know what you mean," I mumble against his lips. I'm smiling, loving how he naturally manages to fill me up with happiness again. Like sunshine parting the clouds on a cloudy day. "Thank you, Lochlan."

He grins back at me. "For what?"

"For being patient when my brain goes into overdrive." I laugh and shake my head. "And thank you about a million times over for being bisexual. I don't need anything for Christmas now. That's the best present I could have ever asked for."

"It's pretty awesome, right?" he cries in delight. He might be a redhead, but I can't stop thinking of him as my human golden retriever.

Could he really be mine? He said that's what he wanted. If he doesn't want to date anyone else (and I certainly don't have any other prospects) then…maybe he could be.

Maybe I could be *his*.

I still want to take our relationship slow. But that doesn't mean we can't be heading in a very exciting direction.

I inhale deeply then kiss him sensually for a bit, loving the feel of his huge body under me. He trusts me with this, and I trust him with just about everything. He's not going to flip on a dime and hurt me, I'm sure of it. I know I was fooled before, but this isn't the same.

He's nothing like Shane. And if I don't stop worrying that he secretly is, I might ruin the best thing that's ever happened in my life.

After all the times he's called me brave, I need to show him that I can be.

"How do you feel about getting naked?" I ask.

"Yes," he blurts the second I get the words out. "Fucking hell, yes. Do you need help? I can help. I want to rub against every inch of you right this damn second, baby."

I laugh and blush, loving how bold he is with this silly nickname already. It gives me that extra confidence boost I need.

"You just lie back," I tell him, unbuttoning his jeans and dragging down the zipper.

"Hell, yeah," he says breathlessly, automatically lifting his hips to enable me to push his jeans down.

I leave his boxer-briefs for now—we're still going slow, after all—but I get off the couch for a moment to yank his pants and socks completely off. I drop them to the floor and simply gape for a second as the sight of this Adonis sprawled out over my sofa.

"Dios mío," I croak.

He grins and flexes his bulging arms behind his head. "Oh, you like that, huh, baby?"

I snort and quickly strip down to my own underwear. "I like it a lot," I say as I crawl back over him, shivering at how much of our bodies are touching with almost nothing between them. I feel like I'm burning up, running the best kind of fever.

He slides his arms around my back as I lower myself, kissing him hard and grinding my crotch against his.

"Fucking *fuck*," he yelps into my mouth.

I chuckle in amusement and nuzzle my nose against his, giving us both a chance to catch our breath. I'm dizzy with lust, throwing caution to the wind. Getting laid was about a thousand miles off my radar today, and the endorphins are taking over my body as well as my mouth.

"Oh, you like rubbing yourself against my big cock do you, dirty boy?" I growl.

He makes a choking sound and covers his eyes with his hand for a second, squeezing his temples. "Yes, baby, yes," he says, his voice strained. "Don't stop. *Fuck!*"

I kiss along his jaw like I've been so desperate to for weeks now. His hands flutter over my back, like he doesn't know what to do with himself and is absolutely loving it.

Giving one last thrust, I decide to tease him and move down his body, leaving his hips jerking like a fish on a line. He whimpers and I laugh.

"Aww, don't worry, dirty boy. I'll give you something even better."

He nods frantically, threading his fingers through my hair as I start kissing down his gorgeous body. He tastes like sunshine and masculine muskiness. The soft ginger hairs across his pecs and down his abdomen tickle my nose as I trace my lips along his skin.

"Yes, yes, yes," he chants like a prayer. He's a puddle under me. I feel giddy with power and so incredibly privileged at the same time to be here with him like this when he could have anyone he wanted.

Anyone at all in the whole damn world, and he's picked me. I'm the one that's turned his head and made him challenge his sexuality. Even with all the doubts in my mind about my self-worth, that's pretty difficult to ignore.

When I reach his underwear, I don't hesitate to peel the elastic band down, letting his cock spring free. It's just as big and juicy as I'd been imagining it might be having seen him almost naked in my bedroom before. I glance up to see him watching me intently, and I hold his gaze as I slip my lips over the leaking head and swallow him down slowly. I wrap my hand around the base of his shaft and take my time.

"Fuuuuuck," he groans, gasping and screwing his eyes up. "That feels so amazing, baby. Don't stop. You're so perfect. So good."

If I wasn't trying my best to gag on his junk, his words would have taken my breath away. Warm gooeyness seeps through me to my core at his lovely praise. Being in charge has always been the thing that turned me on the most during sex. But Lochlan telling me I'm perfect as I use his body and make him feel amazing is a whole new level of pleasure.

The noises he makes as I take him all the way down to his root are so needy and delicious. He keeps calling me 'baby' and 'sweetheart' and telling me how flawless my dick-sucking skills are. I'm tempted to make him climax like this, but there's a voice in the back of my head that's urging me to make this experience special for him. Memorable.

I bet he's had a lot of women suck him off, after all.

But he's almost certainly never tasted a cock himself.

As I pop off and crawl back up to him, he whimpers in protest until I kiss his lips again. "Was that nice?" I ask.

"Fucking awesome," he mumbles without hesitation, kissing me desperately and rutting his cock against mine through my briefs. I love that he doesn't demand that I get back down there and make him come. I'm in charge, and he seems to be enjoying that just as much as I am.

"Do you want to try it, dirty boy?"

He blinks at me, apparently taking a second to work out what I'm asking. "Oh!" he suddenly blurts. "Sucking dick? Sucking *your* dick?"

I nod, wondering if I've gone too far. But he nods back, even though he's frowning slightly. He's skimming his fingers up and down my back in a soothing gesture, though, so I figure that's a good sign.

"Yes," he says firmly. "I really, really want to try that with you."

Relief rushes through me. "You've never done it before?" I guess, feeling a burst of pride when he shakes his head.

"I don't want to do it wrong," he says, sounding genuinely concerned. "I want to take care of you, baby."

Oh. *That* was his hesitation. How can he be this hot as well as this cute?

"You are taking care of me," I assure him with maybe a bit too much sincerity for the tone of the moment. But with the way he beams at me, I don't cringe at my words. I just continue. "You're being so good for me. *You're* perfect. If you like, you can just lie back and let me do all the work?"

He puffs out a breath of air, a goofy smile tugging at his mouth. "Is that what you'd enjoy?" he asks.

Visions of all the things I wasn't allowed to do and all the things I was denied in the bedroom with Shane flash before my eyes. The fact that Lochlan's concern is primarily my enjoyment and not his own is another level of attractiveness.

"I'd fucking love that," I say, emotion making my voice catch.

I don't know when the last time was that I felt this free. Lochlan looks at me reverently as I move up the sofa, and he wriggles down a little. Wordlessly, I pull my throbbing, leaking cock out from my boxer-briefs, and rub the tip against his swollen lips. I could have come from just that sight alone, but I squeeze the base of my shaft before pushing into the wet heat of his mouth.

We both moan, and I have to issue restraint to not immediately start fucking his face. I grip onto the back of the couch to help steady myself, then start gently thrusting deeper, not quite all the way back to his throat, but certainly enough that when he sucks and swallows me down, I'm wailing with no regard for my neighbors. Hopefully they can't hear us, although I really can't bring myself to care in that moment.

"Take it, dirty boy," I utter, loving how he digs his fingers into my ass cheeks and his eyes roll back in his head. When he said he wasn't fazed by being with a man and wanted to try anything, I guess he meant it.

I don't know if that's going to extend to swallowing spunk, however, and I don't want to grind everything to a halt to check. So I make an executive decision for us both and slip out of his mouth to move back down the sofa. He's panting when I kiss him again, tears clinging to his lashes, but he's also grinning like crazy.

"Holy…fucking…shit balls," he utters between kisses. "I loved that, Dario. You could have come like that, I mean it."

I tuck that information away for later, but right now, I have a different plan. "I want us to come together," I say, shifting so I can wrap my hand around both our lengths.

It's a bit of a struggle to get my fingers all the way around, but that doesn't stop Lochlan's eyes going comically wide. He snaps his gaze down between us, then up again.

"I didn't know guys could do that," he squeaks adorably before groaning in pleasure. Then he snakes his hand between our bodies on the other side and helps me encase us both, making a slippery channel for us to thrust into together.

"Lochlan," I moan, kissing his mouth before dropping my head and burying my face against his neck.

"Dario, baby," he cries as we rut hard and fast. "So perfect, so good, just like that, don't stop. Come for me, baby. *Come for me.*"

I scream as I let go, spilling my load all over our hands and his stomach. I'm not even finished before he's joining me, gnashing his teeth and digging the fingers from his other hand into my back.

I hope he leaves bruises. I want proof that this really happened.

Because as soon as I catch my breath, I feel the shame already starting to creep in. It crashes over me like one of those big waves the surfers ride down on the beach.

Oh…no.

Was I too much? Did I push him too far?

This is why I left our underwear on. I had a feeling one of us—or both—might want to preserve our dignity once the moment was over. I hastily tuck myself away, but before I can do much else, Lochlan is already wrapping his arms around me and crushing me against his chest. Apparently, he doesn't care about the mess cooling between us and is oblivious to my oncoming panic attack.

"Oh my fucking god," he says breathlessly, planting kisses on my damp hair. "Dario, I…oh. Are you okay? Was that okay? Was *I* okay?"

I gulp and try and take a breath to compose myself. He doesn't sound disgusted with me. "You were perfect. Are you sure I wasn't too much?" I ask in a tiny voice.

He yanks his head back to frown up at me, his expression immediately turning concerned, no doubt in response to seeing my almost tearful face.

"Hey, hey, no! Why are you upset? What do you mean 'too much'? That was completely and utterly spectacular. I'd go again for another round right now if I had any spunk left in my balls whatsoever. But…did I do something wrong?"

For a moment, I just stare at him. "No, you were beautiful," I murmur. Slowly…the panic is fading before it even really began. Because of this amazing man. "But I was…I called you names…I was bossy."

He blinks at me. "And it was super fucking hot, dude. I

had no idea you had that in you. Talk about the best surprise ever. That's *my* Christmas present sorted for the year."

I take a shaky breath. "Really?"

He nods. "But did *you* enjoy it? I thought you did, but…"

Before he can feel guilty over my messed-up bullshit, I gently press a finger to his lips. "I loved it," I say sincerely. "I just…I don't normally let loose like that."

His eyes flick over my face as understanding seems to dawn on him. For a second, he clenches his jaw, no doubt in anger the way I've been treated in the past. Then he relaxes and carefully pulls me back into a hug.

"Baby, listen to me. I want you to get as freaky as your heart desires with me. I loved you taking charge. People always think because I'm a big guy I like giving orders, but I really don't care about that. Seeing you be all commanding got me horny as fuck, all right? I never want you to be anything but yourself. Ever."

I keep my face tucked against his neck as a few tears escape down my cheeks. He just holds me as I sniffle for a little while. But then I let out a big breath, like I'm releasing so many of my problems. When I do, I realize how cold and sticky the mess between us has become.

"Eww," I say, making us both chuckle as I lean back and look at the grossness. "We should probably clean up."

"Can we shower together?" he asks hopefully. My heart leaps. I'm not used to that kind of aftercare.

"I'd love that," I tell him softly. "Then will you stay for dinner?"

He traces a finger along my jaw then pecks a little kiss to the top of my nose. "I'd love that," he echoes me.

I'm still not convinced this is really happening. But until I wake up, I'm going to enjoy this dream for as long as it lasts.

CHAPTER 17

Lochlan

I know I'm probably biased, but I swear I live in the most beautiful place in the world. And today, the stretch of shoreline that Redwood Bay took its name from seems particularly gorgeous, with the turquoise sea to my right, and the mountains rising beyond the town to my left. I take a deep breath in, letting the salty sea air fill my lungs, and grin.

Yup. Life is good. Plus, I have a triple cone of peanut butter, chocolate, and banana ice cream in my hand. What more could I want?

Well, obviously Dario. But I'm trying really hard not to overwhelm him, even though I'd happily see him twenty-four seven. It's enough knowing that we'll being hanging out tomorrow. I still don't really think of us meeting up as dates, because we're doing the same kind of fun stuff as we were doing before. Like tomorrow, we're going to try roller skating.

The difference is, though, when we go back to his place or mine afterward, now there are *orgasms*. Kissing, too. But we can do that out in public as well. In fact, Dario seemed really surprised the first time we went out and I wanted to hold hands and kiss him and stuff. I get that he was surprised when I came out to him—heck, it was a helluva surprise to me when I eventually realized. But I think it's more than that.

He's shocked that I want to be seen in public with him because, like, he doesn't think he's good enough for me. I feel like we've been having this same debate since we met and had agreed to stop it already. Cuz, yeah, if anyone's not worthy, it me being with him. But I don't care anymore. He said he wants to be with me, so I'm gonna tell the whole damn world that he's mine. I'll rent a plane and write it in the sky for the entire town to see if that's what it takes.

It makes sense to start smaller than that, however.

"You're quiet today," my mom comments as we amble down the beach. I've got my flip-flops dangling from the hand not managing the already dripping ice cream cone, and the warm sand feels so good between my toes.

"Yeah, but he's also smiling like a lunatic," my sister, Shelly, adds with a twinkle in her eyes. "Loch, you gotta secret you'd like to share? Is that why you suggested we all came out here today?"

I just grin more at them. Aside from the red hair and freckles Shelly and I both inherited from our dad, she and Mom are the dead spit of each other. Dad, on the other hand, is kind of average in height and size, unlike me. I glance over at him as he plays with Rocky and Shelly's toddler, Orson, in the shallow water. Apparently, I got my bulk from my grandpa on Mom's side, although he passed when I was a baby, so I never met him. I've heard lots of stories about him from various aunts and uncles, though.

For a moment, I feel fit to burst with happiness and gratitude that I got blessed with a damn good family. Lots of folks don't.

Shelly holds hands with her husband, Greg, and I give

thanks that she met such a nice, down-to-earth kindergarten teacher who treats her like a queen. My mom holds onto her sun hat, so the wind doesn't snatch it away, laughing at my dad as he throws a tennis ball for Rocky. Orson claps his tiny little hands in delight, yelling "Doggy! Doggy!"

"Jeeze," I say thickly, laughing and shaking my head at my sister. "I'm smiling because I just love you guys so damn much."

Shelly stops walking and lowers her pistachio cone. We all stop and look at her. "Lochlan Bell," she says, her eyes widening in horror. "Are you dying?"

"What?" I cry. "No! Oh my god, no. Can't I just be happy?"

She glares at me and takes a big lick of ice cream before starting to walk again.

"Of course you can be happy," my mom says, rolling her eyes. "Is there any reason he shouldn't be, Shells?"

Shelly is still frowning at me. "He's always a dopey fool. This is something else."

"Shelly, be nice," Greg mutters, making me laugh. "Hormones are an excuse that only gets you so far."

"It's fine," I assure him as my sister rubs her round belly. "Nothing can bring me down on this glorious day, I promise. And Shelly's right."

"That you're a dopey fool?" she prompts.

I would smack her arm like we've always done since we were kids. But she's cheating by being pregnant again, so I settle for a loud tut. *"I've got a secret,"* I tell them in a sing-song voice.

Shelly gasps, almost choking on her ice cream. "I knew it!"

"Can we guess?" my mom asks.

"Sure," I say playfully with a shrug. "I bet you won't get it, though. At least not all of it."

"You got a promotion at work?" Greg tries.

Shelly shakes her head before I can respond. "No way he could keep studying for the lieutenant's exam quiet. If he goes for it, we'll never hear the end of all that bitching and moaning until he passes. Right?"

I bob my head, still grinning. "Rude but correct. No studying, no exam, and no promotion. Rico's not going anywhere and I'm not sure I'd even want his job anyway." I wrinkle my nose. "Who wants all that extra paperwork?"

Shelly rolls her eyes but respectfully says nothing. She knows that she's the brainiac of the family and I'm the meathead. I've never been cut out for anything involving too many numbers and forms and all that.

"You met a girl?" she asks instead.

"Nope," I say smugly, my skin tingling all over.

If she'd said 'someone' instead of 'a girl' the game might have been over too quickly. I'm so excited, but I manage not to spill the tea as she and my mum look disappointed for a second but then rally themselves. I know they're keen for me to settle down. It's kinda like Dario's family in that they think that's the best way to find happiness. Mom and Dad have always drilled into us the importance of having a well-rounded life. But they're all romantics at heart.

"You won the lottery?" Greg guesses.

"I wish," I bark.

"You got Taylor Swift tickets?" Shelly asks eagerly, her eyes lighting up.

I scoff. "The Eras Tour is over, babe. Who's the fool now? You'll just have to wait until the next one."

"I'm not forgetting your promised to take me," she grumbles.

"There had been a lot of tequila before I made that promise," I remind her. "But sure. One day, me, you, and however many kids you have will go see Mother."

"And me," Greg says, sounding a little hurt he's been left out of our imaginary concert plans.

"Fine, fine," I say, waving my hands and losing a few droplets of ice cream. "When I win the lottery, I'll take you all. Keep guessing."

"Hmm…you're buying a house," my mom tries.

"Again, when I win the lottery," I reply. "So, no."

"Who won the lottery?" my dad asks as he jogs up to us with Orson on his hip and Rocky's leash in hand, my pup running eagerly beside him. Orson immediately reaches for Shelly, who transfers him to her hip where Greg gives their son a lick of his chocolate ice cream. I take Rocky from my dad as we continue heading toward the pier, managing to get his leash handle over my flip-flops without getting too much sand everywhere.

"Lochlan has a secret and we're trying to guess what it is," my mom explains.

"Oh," my dad says, his eyebrows raising. "Have you met someone special?"

"Yes," I say gleefully, just as Shelly says, "No."

Her head snaps toward me. "You said you hadn't met a girl?" she accuses.

"I did say that," I agree.

Greg laughs. "Oh, he's met a boy, then. Not a girl."

They all laugh but I don't say anything. I just keep smiling. The joke doesn't hurt. They wouldn't have any reason to suspect anything different, after all. It's not like *I* even knew.

Once again, it's Shelly who stops walking first, her face slack with shock. Everyone else slows to a halt as well, looking confused.

"Huh?" my big sister utters. "You…what?"

I do the best jazz hands I can without dropping the remaining ice cream from my cone, my flip-flops or Rocky's leash. All around us, people are walking by, flying kites, surfing, running, playing with dogs, doing yoga, sunbathing, and making sandcastles. But my little bubble of the universe has suddenly become very still, buzzing with uncertainty.

I feel so calm, though. Like this is exactly where I'm meant to be, at exactly the right time.

"I met someone special," I elaborate. "And that someone is a guy. His name is Dario and he's wonderful."

My dad blinks. "So you're telling us you're…"

"Bisexual," I confirm, my heart rate picking up a little. I'm sure they won't react badly, but it is kind of a huge deal to come out. I always knew that thanks to my many queer friends. But apparently there's a difference between knowing and appreciating something and experiencing it for yourself.

My mom screams. Like actually screams, then drops her ice cream to the ground, and dashes to throw her hands around me, smacking me with the sun hat still in her hand.

"Oh, sweetie! I'm so happy for you!" she squeals in my ear. Rocky has darted over to snuffle at her discarded cone, but I'll let him for now. Hopefully it won't make him sick.

"Yeah?" I rasp. "You don't seem all that surprised."

She chuckles and lets me go. "Let's just say I wondered from time to time."

"Really?"

How did she wonder when I never have?

She shrugs. "Mom's intuition," she says, like that's a reasonable explanation.

I'm too busy staring at her in disbelief to see Shelly raise her hand, so she gets in one of those hard smacks on my arm that I'm not allowed to give her. "Ow!" I cry indignantly, glaring at my sister. Orson then reaches over and bats my nose, copying his mom. "Ow," I say weakly again as Shelly guiltily spins her son away from me.

"Sorry," she says with a grimace before quickly scowling

at me. "But why didn't you ever tell me! Did you think I wouldn't be cool about it?"

She looks so hurt by that idea, so I quickly shake my head.

"I didn't know myself, I swear. I only met Dario a few weeks ago, and I knew I liked him a whole lot. But Lili sorta had to bang my head against the wall to make me see my feelings were actually more than that. Luckily, Dario feels the same way, so…yeah. We're taking things slow to start with, but we're dating and he's very special to me. Like *really* special."

I feel a hand clasp my shoulder and turn to see my dad looking at me, his eyes a little glassy. "That's wonderful, son," he says.

Greg grabs my flip-flop hand to awkwardly pump it a couple of times. "Congratulations, man. Maybe during Pride month next year, you could come and speak to the kids?"

"Greg!" Shelly cries. "The man literally just came out! Give him a break. Besides, doesn't someone from the One-Thirteen always speak?"

Her husband shrugs. "Yeah, but not *my* brother-in-law. I'd finally be contributing for once."

That's so cute of him to want to do something like that for his class. I feel so light, like I could drift away into the clouds.

"I'd be honored to come down to the school," I tell Greg, touched that his first thoughts were about inclusion and representation. Yeah, Captain Valentine does usually ask us to do all kinds of community events during Pride month as we're a particularly diverse team.

But this time I'd be the 'B' in LGBT. Not just an ally. The realization makes me giddy.

I still need to double check Shelly is okay with this, though. Sure, she was mad when she thought I'd kept something juicy from her. But now she knows what that secret is…how does she feel?

"We good?" I ask her.

My sister scowls again. "No. I reserve the right to pout over all the years I missed out on getting up to shenanigans with my *bisexual* brother. But…whatever. I'm happy for you, even if you're a jerk."

She beams at me, so sincere she's a little tearful, and the last worry leaves my shoulders. I knew it would be fine, deep down. Still, that was my first ever coming out experience, and even if it wasn't really too stressful, it was still important, and it couldn't have gone better all things considered.

"Biswexull!" Orson cries, waving his mucky hands around.

Oops. Apparently, he got a fistful of pistachio when Shelly wasn't looking. But while Greg leaps into action with a wet wipe he's produced from nowhere, my sister simply grins at her son.

"That's right, Orson! Uncle Lochlan is bisexual, and he has a boyfriend!" She suddenly snaps her head and looks at me with wide eyes. "Holy fff-udge." She glances at Orson, but he's apparently too busy getting his hands cleaned by his daddy to notice her almost swearing. Then Shelly is grinning between me and Mom. "This is the friend you spent Thanksgiving with, right? So that means he *has* to come to us for Christmas!"

My dad huffs. "That's getting a little ahead, isn't it?" he tells her. "Lochlan doesn't need that kind of pressure on him and neither does his young man."

'His young man.' That tickles me pink. Damn straight, he's mine. Or damn *not* straight, as Lili said.

"Besides," my dad continues. "I imagine he'll want to spend the holidays with his own family."

"It doesn't have to be Christmas Day itself," Mom says,

positively vibrating with excitement. "Anyway, he could be Jewish and not even celebrate Christmas?"

She looks at me, but I shake my head. "They're Catholic," I assure her, and my parents both look pleased. Not that it would matter either way to them, I'm sure. It just means that our families already have something in common, which is nice. "I'm sure he'd love to celebrate with us at some point over the holidays. But I'd like you guys to meet him before then."

"That would be wonderful," Mom says.

"Just so long as you invite me," Shelly adds threateningly. "I have to vet him."

I laugh and shake my head. "Yes, yes. Duly noted."

Rocky whines and tugs on his leash, which is our cue to start walking again. However, everyone is smiling, and it feels like the air is shimmering around me. The sun is beaming down, and the waves are crashing onto the shore. Gulls fly and squawk overhead, and I finish the last bite of my ice cream cone.

Life is good.

Out of nowhere, Shelly appears by my side with another wet wipe for my sticky fingers. She's given Orson to Greg, so that leaves her free to slip her arm through mine as we walk.

"I'm so happy for you, baby brother," she says genuinely. "I can't wait to meet him. I know you met at the puppy classes, but now it's a meet-cute story. So you need to tell me everything from the very beginning. No skipping any details! Tell me about the moment you first laid eyes on him."

My heart is so full. As I start describing that day in the park, I feel like the luckiest man alive.

Things can only get better from here, right?

CHAPTER 18

Dario

I feel like I've been walking around in a dream for days, and I don't seem to be waking up.

Good. After the nightmare I lived through, I think I'm owed some happy dreams.

Lochlan and I have met up a few times since things changed between us, and so far, the other shoe hasn't dropped. There's been no hint that he's feeling anything other than what he's told me. It's pretty scary to go against my gut instinct and trust him, but I have to try.

Because I'm so happy. I don't think I've ever been this happy in my whole life, actually. Ever since I left Shane, the best I've promised myself I could be was not *unhappy*. Floating around like I'm on cloud nine has come as quite a shock.

But a very welcome one.

My colleagues have probably noticed a change in me, especially the morning after Lochlan and I first hooked up when I brought in a massive box of donuts 'for no reason.' But nobody's called me out on anything yet. It's not really a 'water cooler moment' type of office where people stand around and gossip, though, luckily for me.

Still, I can't help but feel I'm walking on sunshine, like that eighties song. In fact, I have to catch myself sometimes to make sure I don't start skipping. After so many weeks of imagining what it might be like to kiss my new friend, then feeling ashamed for betraying his trust in that way, it's still incredibly hard to believe that this is reality. If I've somehow slipped into a parallel universe, I don't ever want to go back.

There's been so much kissing. And snuggling. And… naked snuggling. With orgasms.

Seeing as we jumped in with blow jobs right from the start, I'm totally okay that things haven't gone further than that. Because honestly, where we're at is still so new and exciting. It's thrilling, exploring each other's bodies and being so intimate.

Everything's different between us now, however, not just that we're having sex. Simply having dinner together or walking the dogs feels like it's got a completely different vibe to it. And I know we held hands before, but that was to practice being pretend boyfriends. When Lochlan has reached for me over the past several days, it's like there's electricity running between us.

I still can't believe he wants to be seen holding my hand in public, nor that he wants to do it all the freaking time. It takes my breath away.

Coming out was such a terrifyingly big deal to me, but he's so blasé, I'm almost envious of him. Except I'm not, because I want it to be that easy for him. For everyone, actually, but especially him. He's so damn pure. Why should realizing something new about his sexuality be frightening or cause him stress? He's right. Anyone who thinks being queer is a problem is the dumb one, not Lochlan.

But it's not just him coming out. It's him claiming *me.* Of being proud to be seen by strangers and people he might know with *me*. That's wild.

I'm still wrestling internally to feel worthy of that, but I'm forcing myself to relax and enjoy it whenever it happens. I want it so badly, and I'm slowly accepting that it's okay to get the things I want. That's allowed. In fact, it's wonderful.

"You heading out, Dario?" one of my colleagues asks as he passes by my cubicle. I blink and check the time on my screen. Wow, yeah. It's already five o'clock.

"Oh, sure," I say, frowning and wondering if I should finish what I'm doing or leave it until the morning. "Don't wait for me, though. I need to wrap this up."

He smiles and nods, wishing me a nice evening. Looking around, I can tell I'm the last one here, at least until the cleaning staff arrive. That's what happens when you lose yourself in daydreams, I suppose.

Except being with Lochlan *isn't* a daydream. It's as real as it gets, and I remind myself yet again that I deserve it.

Smiling to myself, I close the program I was working on. I go to shut down the whole machine, but then I notice I've got a personal email. Not many people or companies have my new address yet as I've been very careful when I use it and the things that I sign up for. So I'm apprehensive when I click on my inbox, but after a second I relax.

It's from Big Bark Bootcamp, specifically from our instructor, Zoe. The message isn't long and it's followed by a link.

Hi, Dario!

I couldn't find you on Instagram to tag you, but I thought you might like to see this. It's also been posted on our Facebook page, but you can't see that without an account, so if you don't have socials, I figured Insta would be best for you to see. Anyway, have a nice evening and see you on Saturday!

Zoe

I click on the blue link, which opens up to show me the most gorgeous photo of me, Lochlan, Rocky and Queenie from our last training class. Rocky is leaping in the air for a treat as the rest of us watch on, laughing. It strikes me that this is my first glimpse of seeing Lochlan and I from the outside. Even though we don't look like a couple, just seeing us side by side does something to me, bringing a lump to my throat.

We look so good together.

The caption is promoting our class's particular time slot, inviting people to sign up for the next course. But I'm simply captivated by staring at Lochlan and I for a good few minutes.

Until reality drags me from cloud nine, sending me crashing back down to earth.

This photo is on the *internet*. Zoe even said in her email that she sent me to Instagram not Facebook as I could see it here without the need for an account.

Anyone can see it.

Or search for it, if they have other photographs of me.

Nausea sweeps through me, and I push my wheely chair away from my desk, my hands flying over my mouth.

There was an extremely good reason why I deleted all of my social media accounts last year, and that reason hasn't gone away. Shane is just as tech savvy as I am. I have no doubt that he would have scoured the web for me when I left, trying to find out where I'd gone. He isn't allowed to show up at my parents' or tia's house without getting in trouble. My new place isn't part of the restraining order because he'd have to be informed of the address in order for him to be able to stay away from it. But I'd rather sacrifice that so-called protection to make sure he doesn't know the address.

In theory, there's no way he could know it.

But here's my face in this photo as clear as day, telling people which park we meet in every Saturday and at what time.

I think I'm going to be sick.

I run to the bathroom and steady myself over one of the sinks, taking long, deep breaths to try and calm myself. When I no longer think I might heave, I splash water on my face, then look at my reflection in the mirror.

Shane doesn't know who I am anymore. Actually, I don't think he ever knew the real me. Just the small, weak version of me that he carefully crafted by mentally beating me down into submission. I don't want to spend the rest of my life cowering from him.

But I do need to be sensible.

Drying my hands and face, I walk back to my cubicle, glad that the janitor hasn't arrived yet. I need some time to think. My knee-jerk reaction is to email Zoe back and ask her to remove the post. I don't have to explain why, I can just say 'for personal reasons.' She's lovely, I'm sure she'd understand.

On the other hand, I know that the damage has already been done. Nothing can ever truly be scrubbed from the internet once it's been put out there. More than that, though, I don't *want* the photo to be taken down. Yes, I need to stay safe. But I don't want to disappear from existence. That doesn't seem fair that Shane should get away with doing that to me.

And…this photo is just so beautiful. Even in my fear, I can't stop looking at it. This is proof that Lochlan and I exist as a couple. That we've occupied the same space and time. Will I look back and regret not preserving this moment?

Well, I can certainly ask Zoe for a copy of it for myself. As to whether I should ask her to take it down, it strikes me that's not a decision I have to make alone. In fact, I probably *shouldn't* make it alone.

I should talk to the other person in the picture. My partner. The person I'm seeing exclusively. My best friend.

My maybe-possibly-hopefully-not-fake boyfriend.

Realizing that I have someone I can rely on these days makes me feel slightly dizzy. I genuinely never thought I'd have something like this again. Or ever, I suppose. Shane might have been my boyfriend, but ultimately, he only controlled me. It wasn't a partnership. He didn't trust or respect me like Lochlan does.

Okay, so my mind is made up not to do anything until I talk with him. However, I do still think I should take action as soon as possible if I'm going to get it taken down to at least try and minimize its damage. The problem is, I know Lochlan is at work.

I also know that he's drilled into me many times that I should feel free to swing by whenever I want to. He's told me that family members and friends do it all the time. So long as they know that the alarm could sound at any moment and not to get in the way of that, it's fine.

I never thought I'd actually take him up on that offer, but as I stare at the photo a little longer, I know that I won't be able to get a moment's rest until I talk this through with him and get his opinion.

Making up my mind, I quickly log on to my camera app and check that Queenie is okay at home. I popped in to walk her at lunchtime, so she'll be fine for a few more hours. Not that this should take that long, I'm sure. But seeing her sound asleep in the living room calms my frayed nerves.

After that, I move quickly to shut everything down and get out of the office, not giving myself a chance to change my mind. Still, as I drive across town, my nerves grow and grow into something monstrous.

No matter how logical I try and keep my thoughts, by the time I park, I'm convinced that Lochlan is going to yell at me for bothering him. The only thing that gets me out of the car is the knowledge that I have to make a decision about the photo as soon as possible, and Lochlan is *in* that photo. He should get a say.

A small voice at the back of my head reminds me that I want his opinion and that I trust him. If he's going to be my maybe-possibly-hopefully-not-fake boyfriend, then I want to talk to him about important things. My therapist will definitely be proud I'm doing this.

I'm still a nervous wreck.

The firehouse is situated on a spacious street just off the highway intersection, which makes sense as it gives them easy access to the main road into town as well as the interstate. It's a large but quite unremarkable building, with sandy walls, terracotta tiles, and an American flag hanging from a pole out front. I see the truck, engine and ambulance all parked outside, so I'm guessing they're not out on a call.

My heart is thumping so fast and hard I'm worried it's going to explode out of my chest like a baby Xenomorph. But I force my feet to keep walking.

However, when a familiar barking reaches my ears, it's like all my fears melt away.

A gangly bundle of flailing Dalmatian limbs comes streaking around the corner of the big red engine. "Rocky, no!" a panicked voice I don't recognize calls after him.

"It's okay!" I yell back, crouching down to greet my other favorite four-legged friend. "I've got him. Hello, Rocky. Are you being a bad boy?"

Rocky throws himself on his back, demanding belly rubs from me as his tail whirls like helicopter blades. I laugh and oblige him, looking up as someone runs into view, presumably the guy who was worried about Lochlan's very naughty puppy racing into traffic. Not that there is any on this road right now, but I immediately appreciate his concern.

He looks younger than me, but some people have baby faces that follow them into their thirties, or so I've heard. He's an adorable blond either way, and he narrows his eyes at me as he rests his hands on his hips.

"Hi there?" he says, but clearly what he's asking is 'Who are you and why did this dog escape me to come find you?'

"Hi," I say, trying to swallow the nerves that are threatening to come back. "It's okay, I know him. I mean, I know Lochlan. Um, let's get out of the street, huh?"

As anxious as I am, I do want to get this excitable puppy away from the road, busy or not. So I stand and make eye contact with him like we've learned in class.

"Rocky, sit," I say firmly.

His focus is completely on me as he does as he's told, his tail only twitching a little as he waits for my next command. I reach into my record bag and slip my hand into the pocket where I keep Queenie's treats, grateful that I find them on my first try.

"Good boy," I tell Rocky, then point down by my feet. "Rocky, heel." He jumps to stand by me. "Good boy. Rocky, come." I don't look at the blond cutie. I just march away from the sidewalk and into the open front of the firehouse, stopping just over the threshold. When I think we're safe, I stop again. "Rocky, sit. Good boy!"

His butt barely touches the ground, but I'm already leaning down to give him his meaty treat, so I'll allow it. His tail goes bananas again and he swallows the morsel I give him with hardly a chew, barking once more in excitement.

"You must be Dario," the blond guy says, coming inside with us and folding his arms over his chest. He might be younger than me, but he's already more built than I imagine I could ever be. "Yo! Beast Man! Come here!" he bellows, before stepping closer to me and extending his hand. "I'm Teddy, nice to meet you."

"Yes, I'm Dario," I say faintly as we shake. "How did you…?"

"Beast won't shut up about you," a feminine voice says as an Asian woman comes into view. She's got high cheekbones that are accented more by how much she's grinning. Her ponytail swings as she dashes over to me. She might be average height and build, but she grabs my hand so hard I'm worried something might crack. "Holy shit, you're really here. And you're cute AF! No wonder he's gone gaga over you. I'm Lili, by the way. He might have mentioned me as the genius with the patience of a saint who made him realize he's a bisexual motherfucker."

I blink and try not to flinch as she releases my hand, but I do wriggle my fingers a little to encourage circulation again. "Lili, yes, I've heard a lot about you," I say.

"All amazing, no doubt," she says with a wink.

"Lochlan loves you," I tell her genuinely before if I can consider if that's something I should divulge. But it's true. He beams whenever he talks about his best friend, even if he's describing how she kicked his ass verbally or physically at something.

I'm about to wince at whether or not that was an over-share, when Lili squeaks and places her hand over her heart. "Holy fuck, you're adorable. No wonder he's obsessed."

"Who's obsessed with what?"

Two more guys round the corner of the engine, eyeing me curiously. They both look to be in their late twenties or early thirties and are ridiculously hot, just like everybody else I've seen from here so far. Is that some sort of require-ment for being a firefighter that I was unaware of?

The one who spoke has light brown skin and a mischievous sparkle in his eyes. His friend is white with soft auburn hair. The way the speaker nudges his elbow against the other guy, I suspect they're pretty good friends.

"Oh, hey! You're not Beast's new boyfriend, are you?" the mischievous one asks.

"B-Beast?" I stammer. I think that's what Lili said, too. But also…*boyfriend?* I try not to blush. We haven't agreed to that term yet.

I'm kind of hoping we'll get there. But I'm just so scared to commit to anyone again, even if he is as awesome as Lochlan. The idea of being tied down with someone…of being trapped…it's holding me back, even if it's completely illogical.

The auburn guy rolls his eyes. "Ignore Sawyer. He's a dick to everyone. Please don't take it personally."

"I wasn't being a dick!" Sawyer protests. "I was asking a question. *Nicely,* I might add."

"Guys, chill," Lili says firmly. Unsurprisingly, they listen to her. "This is Beast's friend, Dario. Dario, these assholes are Sawyer and Anton. Feel free to ignore them. We all do."

Teddy snorts, making Rocky bark and wag his tail.

"Hey," Anton says to Lili with a frown. "Not cool."

"I-it's okay," I assure him quickly. "I don't mind. It's nice to meet Lochlan's friends."

Urgh, I hope that's all right for me to say. Where *is* Lochlan? He might be mad that I'm saying stupid stuff in front of his colleagues. I'd be mortified if I embarrassed him in any way.

Speaking of which…

"Did someone say my name?"

My heart jumps in my chest as the man himself comes striding around the corner, grinning at his buddies. I have about half a second where my stomach drops in panic that I've made a terrible mistake.

Then Lochlan sees me, and I swear he melts like a human Popsicle.

"Dario," he says softly, as if there's no one else in the whole world watching us, let alone his colleagues in the firehouse. He drifts through the group, reaching his hands out to cradle either side of my face. "You're here! Why are you here? Is everything okay?"

I make a croaking noise, momentarily forgetting how to talk as I look into his beautiful green eyes. Around us there's a chorus of 'oohs' and 'ahhs,' but Lochlan ignores it, so I do, too.

"I…uh…"

Lochlan's expression falls. "What's wrong?" he asks more urgently.

"Nothing," I say, shaking my head within the gentle grip of his hands. "I mean…no, yeah, there is something I need to talk to you about. But—"

Of course that's the moment the alarm goes off. Every single one of them freezes and looks upwards as the voice comes over the intercom. "Station One-Thirteen. Search and rescue. Critter Canyon Park. Structure failure."

"The amusement park?" Sawyer says in confusion as they scatter like roaches.

"Less talking, more running!" a new voice bellows. As I scoop Rocky up and step back from all the people scrambling to get into their gear by the sides of the truck and the engine, a truly beautiful Black man strides into view. I'd guess he's in his forties or fifties, maybe, and it's clear from his body language that he's in charge. "Hello?" he says.

Oh…fuck. He's looking at me. "I-I'll get out of your way," I splutter immediately.

But Lochlan waves at the man and shakes his head. "Cap, that's Dario. He came to talk to me about something important. Can he ride along with us?"

I blink. That wasn't what I was expecting him to say. People do go with them on ride-a-longs, I guess. Lochlan's mentioned it before, but usually it's people's niblings on minor calls.

However, I can't help but latch onto the fact that Lochlan realized what I need to say is important and doesn't want to leave me hanging without hearing it. That touches my heart so deeply, a lump rises in my throat.

The captain pauses as he's about to mount the rig and narrows his eyes at me. "You wanna come along?"

My heart leaps. They would trust me like that? Lochlan wants me to come? I glance at him, and he nods furiously, grinning like this is the best day ever.

"Uh, yes, sir," I tell him. "I'd be honored."

The captain nods once, hauling himself inside the engine. "Shake a leg, then, son! You can bring the dog so long as he stays on his leash with you."

"T-thank you," I stammer.

Before I know it, Lochlan is helping bundle me and Rocky into the vehicle, wedging me between him and Lili with Rocky on my lap. The rig is already moving, but the driver—an older white gentleman I didn't spot earlier—catches my eye in the rearview mirror and winks at me.

"Welcome to the One-Thirteen!" he cries cheerfully as he flicks a switch and the sirens start wailing.

I look around. Everyone is grinning at me, but Lochlan doesn't seem to notice or care. He just slips his bulky arm around my back and hugs me to his side.

"Are you okay?" he asks sincerely.

For the first time since I saw that Instagram post, I finally relax and lean against his side. "I am now," I tell him truthfully.

The picture can wait. Right now, my man has claimed me in front of all of his friends—his work colleagues, no less. I feel like I'm walking on sunshine again.

Nothing bad can touch me right now.

CHAPTER 19
Lochlan

I'M STILL WORRIED WHY DARIO SHOWED UP AT THE HOUSE. Even though I told him a hundred times he'd be welcome whenever he felt like it—if we were out on a call, I know Nancy and Mrs. Bloom would take care of him—I thought it would be ages before he worked up the guts to actually do it.

So as much as I'm a little freaked out by what could have pushed him to come today, I'm also tickled pink that he made it at all. In fact, I'm damn proud of him. I know how his nerves like to get the better of him, so he must have been really brave to walk up to the station like that.

And Cap let him ride along! We do this every now and again, usually with someone's niece or nephew who's come for a visit. Gene is good at making sure they stay safe and out of our way, so I'm not worried about having Dario here. Actually, it's kind of thrilling to share my world with him.

I want to share everything with him.

"So what was it you needed to talk about?" I ask, shouting over all the noise as we race toward the call. Dario glances around at Lili, Tommy, and Lieutenant Rico. Cap and Gene are up front, but they can usually hear us talking. "Oh, unless it's private?" Damn it. I didn't think of that.

"Uh, sort of," Dario says. "It's fine, though. We can discuss it later. I just wanted your advice on something."

Well if that doesn't make me puff out like a peacock. Super smart Dario wants *my* advice? I'm not sure what I can offer that he doesn't already know, but you betcha bottom dollar I'll do everything I can to help him out with whatever's on his mind.

"Hopefully this call won't take long," I tell him, hoping he won't get anxious waiting around.

Dario shakes his head, though. "Whoever needs help is the priority. We can talk later. Honestly, it's nothing. I'm probably overreacting, and I just need you to tell me that."

He laughs nervously, so I squeeze him to my side. I don't want to agree that he's overreacting without knowing what's happened, but I still want to try and help. "It'll be okay," I promise him, willing that to be true. "I'm so happy you came to find me in any case." Now that *is* true.

For a second, we just look into each other's eyes, and it's like I can't even breathe. How is this amazing person *my* person?

Then Rocky jumps up and licks my face, breaking the spell. "Blurgh! Dude, not cool."

Lili and Tommy howl with laughter, while Rico shakes his head and reaches over to pat Rocky, calming him down and attempting to stop the pup from shoving his tongue into my mouth. Again.

I much prefer it when Dario does that.

"Look alive, people!" Captain Valentine calls from up front, catching our attention. "We're getting close."

I peer out of the window, seeing that we're speeding down the access road behind Critter Canyon. The sun is setting and it's going to be dark soon. Hopefully that won't jam us up too much.

This isn't the first job we've done at the park. In fact, Del and Yara get called out here quite a bit with people suffering from sunstroke, food poisoning, bee stings and other minor medical maladies. One time the Ferris wheel got stuck and we had to assist with the evacuation. But dispatch said something about structural damage, making me wonder what today is going to bring us.

A woman in a pantsuit is standing by the big chain-link doors that lead into the back of the park. She's holding a walkie-talkie and is waving us down. Cap lowers his window as we approach, but we all lean closer to listen as she calls out to us.

"Thank goodness you're here! Apparently, it's getting worse. Follow the security marshals, they'll direct you in the right direction."

"Thank you, ma'am," Cap tells her with a nod. "We'll do everything we can."

"Please hurry!"

I swallow then take a deep breath. Adrenaline is just skittering on the outskirts of my system, waiting to flood it. But not yet. I keep up my steady breathing, preparing myself for what's to come. Dario squeezes my thigh as Rocky watches me, subdued as he's no doubt picked up on the tension in the rig.

"You've got this," Dario says quietly, and my heart explodes like the Fourth of July. I know I do, but hearing him say it makes it ten times better.

We're coming to a stop, so I hastily bend down and kiss his cheek. "Thanks, baby," I say, not caring if my friends want to tease the shit out of me for being soft later. Let them. I know it'll only be because they're jealous of me and my gorgeous guy.

When the doors of the engine burst open, every other thought flies from my brain as I focus on the job in hand. "Stay here!" I bark at Dario and Rocky, even though I know Dario knows that. He still smiles warmly at me as I unwrap my arm from around his back.

"We will," he promises.

As my boots hit the ground, I immediately survey the area. There are already first aiders from Critter Canyon tending to people who look like they have minor injuries. From what, I'm not sure. But it looks like an evacuation of the park via the front entrance is already underway, judging from the fact that nobody else seems to be milling around.

Movement catches my eye, and I see a golf cart pulling up behind where the One-Thirteen has parked. The same lady with the walkie-talkie hops out and runs straight for us, which is impressive considering her three-inch pumps.

"Who's in charge?" she wastes no time in asking.

"I'm Captain Valentine. What seems to be the problem here, ma'am?"

"Cynthia Buchanan. I'm the operations manager here at the park." She shakes her head and looks disgusted. "I'm not entirely sure how it happened. But from what we can tell, a couple of youths were drunk off their asses and managed to somehow steal an ice cream truck, of all things, for a joyride."

"An ice cream truck?" Sawyer repeats incredulously.

Cap waves him off. "And that's what caused these injuries?" he says, indicating the people with cuts and bruises. One girl looks to have a broken arm, but if that's the worst of it, then I'd call that a win.

There's a special place in hell for drunk drivers, as far as I'm concerned.

"Yes, but that's not why you're here," Buchanan says, already marching off.

We're in a kinda intersection with popcorn stands and

toy stores around us. I notice that they've put the Christmas decorations up, creating a winter wonderland in SoCal. If it wasn't so deserted, the place would have a festive feel to it. The Ferris wheel is visible in the distance, as is the big runaway train coaster. But she doesn't take us toward either of those.

No, we're going in the direction of the Tunnel of Love.

"This thing is old, but I swear it's never failed a safety inspection," Buchanan is explaining as we hurry our way past the empty covered space where the park guests usually wait in line. The park's lights have come on as night has fallen, as it's open until late most days. I'm glad we aren't fighting against a power outage on top of whatever else is going on.

Aw, man. I remember coming here one time with my high school girlfriend. The ride is cheesy as hell, but it's actually a kinda cute place to bring a date to canoodle in the dark. The little boats that bob on the waterway only fit two people and look like flowers on lily pads. Inside, the tunnel has been updated with all sorts of crazy neon lights that make you feel like you're in some sort of psychedelic bayou with frogs and birds and dragonflies all coupling up around you.

Right now, the water is flowing into the tunnel's mouth, but I don't see any boats.

Buchanan is leading us around the fake mountain that the ride disappears into. "It was designed so gravity moves the boats along as much as anything," she's still explaining to us. "So you can see we're on a slope going downward right now. Honestly, I don't know how this could have happened. It's such a freak occurrence, but…well…look."

From memory, I think the 'river' twists and turns through the underground space until eventually coming out the other end where the guests disembark. Then some kind of crank guides the empty boats back to the start. As we approach the end of the tunnel, I'm starting to get a picture of what the problem could be.

"Holy shit," Lili mutters under her breath.

I'd almost forgotten about the ice cream truck that those stupid kids stole. But there it is now, smashed up and on its roof, sticking out of some shrubbery. That's not the issue, though.

All I can guess is that it mounted the curb then shot into the air and at such a freak trajectory that it hit one of the supporting beams on the giant Maiden Voyage swing-boat ride. You know, the kind that holds like thirty or forty people and rocks back and forth? With one of the four legs taken out, the entire thing has buckled at a strange angle. And the giant boat that's supposed to be attached at the top of that pyramid structure?

Yeah, that's made a bid for freedom, and it's currently lying twenty feet away, the exit of the Tunnel of Love crushed beneath it, water bubbling and leaking from whatever cracks in the rubble it can find.

"Jesus, Mary, and Joseph," I utter.

Staff from the park are helping people down from the boat swing. Extra flood lights are being set up around the area to help with the triage.

"Go," Cap says to Del and Yara, but they're already running.

"We're still assessing the damage," Buchanan says, her hand on her chest like that might slow her heart down. "By some miracle, we don't think anyone was struck on the ground when it got lose, or at least no one seems to have been seriously hurt. But there are a shit ton of concussions, cuts and bruises from the people on The Maiden Voyage when the truck hit the beam. Some people were thrown from the ride. I think they've all been transported already. I don't know their status." She shakes her head. "We're just not prepared for such a freak accident."

"That's why we're here," Cap assures her. "I assume more help is on the way, though?" He glances at Rico, who nods.

"At least three more stations are on the way, according to dispatch," he says before turning back to Buchanan. "What about the kids in the truck?"

"They were banged up pretty bad," Buchanan says grimly. "They're already en route to San Clemente General. The paramedics that fished them out didn't seem to think their injuries were life threatening."

I grunt, knowing I need to be professional right now. I'm glad the little shits should hopefully be all right. Honestly, though, I care way more about the dozens if not hundreds of other people they've endangered with their pathetic little stunt.

Buchanan isn't done, however.

"That thing smashed right into the exit of the tunnel," she explains, already hurrying us back the way we came. To her credit, Buchanan sets the pace, despite her impressive shoes. "I figured you'd need to see the extent of the damage before heading inside. But it apparently missed the flower boat coming out by a couple of feet and knocked it and its passengers clean out of the water. Then staff reported that several guests abandoned the ride and used the walkway to come back out the entrance, saying there had been some sort of cave-in up ahead. There could be one or two boats trapped under that, behind where The Maiden Voyage landed. But that's not the only issue."

"The water is still flowing," Cap comments with a frown. "Can't you turn it off?"

"We tried," Buchanan says. "But like I said, it was designed using gravity. The flow of the artificial river might have slowed, but I'm pretty sure it's still rising. If anyone's still in there…" She clenches her jaw. "I doubt the designers ever imagined anything like this could happen."

By the sirens wailing in the air, those are our reinforcements coming from the San Clemente fire departments. They'll be able to assist with the cleanup outside along with transporting injured guests back to the hospital.

It's our job to get to the people who are possibly trapped.

Possibly minutes away from drowning.

"Has the electricity been cut?" I ask as we approach the tunnel's entrance.

"The first thing we did," she assures me. "My security guys tried to go in once the guests started pouring out. But without the proper equipment—"

"No, you did the right thing," Cap assures her. "We don't need any more people in danger. Please keep the area clear and coordinate with the other units when they arrive. If the battalion chief shows up, he'll inform you of his presence and work with you. But we don't know how unstable it is in there and we need to ensure no one else accidentally stumbles into trouble."

"You got it, Captain," Buchanan says. "If you need anything at all, I'll be right here." She plants her feet and clicks on her walkie, firing off orders to her people to make sure we can do our jobs.

My heart is racing as we run as fast as we can in our bulky, heavy gear. If we're going to be going under water, it'll be better to ditch all the extras now so it won't weigh us down. But we still don't know exactly what we're facing.

Cap obviously thinks the same thing as he presses the button on our own radio. "Delacroix, Ortiz—what's your status? We might need you back up at the front."

"Reinforcements are starting to arrive here, Cap," Del says over the coms, his voice soothing even in a crisis. "We haven't loaded anyone into our rig yet, just triaging on site. Do you want us to head to your position?"

Valentine purses his lips. "No. You're most needed there for now. We'll let you know if the situation changes."

"Got it, Cap," Del says.

"Good luck," Yara adds.

Cap nods even though she can't see him. "You, too."

We turn on our headlamps as we plunge into the darkness. Without the colorful neon, this place might as well be as dark as a seaside cavern, especially as the sun has completely set now.

The fact that we're not dealing with the ocean is a relief. Tides can turn at a terrifying rate. But the steady stream of treated water flowing into this ride ain't no joke, either.

Like Buchanan told us, there are narrow black walkways either side of the rushing water we can use for access. Half of us take the left, the others are on the right. It's downright eerie without any lights on and the current feels so much more aggressive than usual as the water rushes by our feet.

"Fire department, call out!" Rico bellows, his voice echoing in the darkness. But it's not long before we start seeing the damage that's been caused by the rogue swing boat outside.

A bow of The Maiden Voyage has broken through the flimsy fake cave walls, tearing down all the insulation and plaster of Paris and whatever crap was back there. It's hard to tell from just the narrow illumination the flashlights are giving us, but it seems like several of the beams have caved in, creating a crisscross obstacle course.

Half a dozen empty boats have caused a jam up against the affected area, and they're slamming into each other as well as the unstable debris in an alarming way. The water has already risen above the walkway here, leaving us sloshing through it as we push forward.

"Fire department, call out!" Rico tries again from his position opposite me.

"Is anyone there?" Cap adds. He's leading the charge on my side, and when he gets to the first fallen beam, he leans carefully against it, shining his handheld flashlight as well as the one on his helmet to try and get a better look through the mess. "Call out! Anyone there!"

"Hello?" someone cries weakly from beyond the debris.

No matter how many years I've been on the job, my heart never fails to leap when we discover a victim is still alive in a disaster zone.

"Redwood Bay fire department!" Valentine yells back. "We're coming to get you! Can you tell me where you are?"

I hear a whimper that damn near breaks my heart. "I don't know," the voice says. It sounds feminine, young…and scared. "I'm here with my kid sister. The roof collapsed and rocked our boats so bad. We tried to climb out, but my sister slipped, and her foot is stuck. She can't even get it out of her sneaker. I think the water is getting higher. I tried looking around with my phone light, but there's crap everywhere!"

"It's okay. I'm Captain Valentine and I'm here with the One-Thirteen fire department," he says. "What's your name, sweetheart?"

"Carmen," the girl calls back.

"I'm Isabella," a younger sounding voice yells. "Please hurry. It's so cold."

"We're going to get to you as soon as we can," Cap promises. "Do you know if there's anyone else trapped in there with you?"

"No, it's just us, I'm sure," Carmen replies. "The other boat was so far ahead we barely saw them the whole ride. We could see the tunnel mouth when everything fell…" she trails off, unsure.

"We deal with what we know," Cap says determinedly to

us. "Our priority is the girls, but be on the lookout just in case there's anyone else."

"Yes, Captain," Rico says as the team gets to work.

Lili has already gotten the circular cutting saw out and Anton and Sawyer have the jaws to pry anything apart if necessary. Rico is working with Teddy to jam in the rescue air bags to make the area more secure, but they take time to inflate.

"We need to get in there," Cap mutters.

I'm already pulling off my coat and boats. "If we can't go through, I'll see if there's a way under."

Cap opens his mouth, no doubt to tell me it's too dangerous and to wait for the team to get more supports in place. But Carmen's shaky voice echoes through the tunnel again, barely audible over the rushing water.

"Mr. Valentine? Isabella's getting sleepy. She needs to stay awake, right?"

Cap's eyes widen. "Yes, girls. Stay with me. Why don't you tell me what you like to do for fun? Do you play sports or have a favorite band?" He looks at me and simply mouths 'go.' I don't need telling twice.

It's only when I hit the water and the current surges me toward the wall of piled up crap that I realize I have a new problem which never occurred to me until this moment.

Maybe the reason I always did this daredevil shit without a second thought was because I only ever had to worry about myself. Sure, I have my family, but I guess I never really considered how my parents or sister would feel if I never came home. No wonder my momma worries so much about me. I've been a real jackass.

But in this moment, I'm getting one hell of a wakeup call. If I die here today, who will take care of Rocky? What about all the things I never got to say to Dario? All the amazing things we never got to do together?

It's not like I've suddenly become a coward. It's more like a part of my brain has just this moment woken up and is screaming very loudly at me that this is a really dumb idea.

But then an actual scream pierces through the fog in my mind, focusing my attention once again.

"Something moved!" Carmen yells. "There's a metal beam pushing the boat down now!"

"Help!" Isabella screeches in panic. "The water's getting higher!"

"We're coming for you, sweetheart!" Anton yells back.

He must be thinking about his own little girl. She could be about Isabella's age. The idea of seeing her usually happy face pinched with fear wipes all other thoughts from my mind. I switch my handheld flashlight on, hoping it's as waterproof as it's supposed to be, take a deep breath, and go under.

It looks like a lot of the beams only fell as far as the walkways. But there are huge chunks of rubble littering the bottom of the artificial stream. It's difficult to tell how often I'll be able to come up for air. But I start by swimming under the first few girders to get me farther than the rest of my crew, then resurface as soon as I'm able. I breathe deeply and look around with my light. I still can't see the girls and there's so much junk in my way.

Between the noise of the rushing water and the power tools, it's hard to think straight. "Carmen?" I call out. "My name's Lochlan. I'm trying to get to you and Isabella through the water. Where are you?"

"We're here," she calls back weakly. It's hard to tell, but I think they're still several feet away. "Mr. Valentine said he was going to get more air bags."

That means they're not having much luck clearing a path. "Rico! You good?" I shout behind me.

"Still at it," he replies, which is code for 'It's not going great.' "How's it looking your end?"

"I'm going to keep moving forward," I inform him.

Despite my physical exertion, the water is still pretty cold against my skin. God knows how two young girls are faring when they're trapped and unable to move. Forget drowning. If I don't reach them soon, they could pass out from hypothermia.

Another deep breath, and I'm pushing my way through the underwater obstacle course. The current wants to push me forward faster, but I cling to what I can, making sure it doesn't force me somewhere I can't get back up again. It feels like it takes forever, but it's probably only a couple of minutes until my flashlight catches a glimpse of pink.

Leggings.

I shoot up, resurfacing with a gasp. Two girls scream. Their nerves must be frayed right now.

"It's okay, I'm here to help," I say quickly. "FOUND THEM!" I yell back at my team before smiling at the girls again. "I'm Lochlan. You must be Carmen and Isabella."

They nod, and I try not to look alarmed. I guess Carmen is taller anyway as she older. But Isabella's head is only a few inches above the surface and with the way the water's rushing through, the splashes around her face are already making it tough for her to breathe without inhaling droplets.

Before I start working on freeing the younger girl, I have to clear the scene. "Are you absolutely sure there wasn't another boat ahead of you guys?" I ask as I maneuver my way farther along the tunnel and shine my flashlight between the rubble.

"Really sure," Carmen says, and I believe her. The bow of the ship and the ride's exit are only about ten feet away from what I can tell. Thank fuck. That gives us one less headache, at least.

"Right, I think it's about time we got out of here, huh? Isabella, you're a little stuck, right?"

"My left foot," she sobs. "It hurts. I can't get it out."

"It's okay, it's okay," I say, holding onto one of the wedged beams to get closer. "I'm going to take a look now and we're going to have you free in no time. I want you to hold hands and focus on taking deep breaths in and out together. For five seconds each time. Isabella, if you feel anything, that will be me, okay? Try not to jerk or pull too much. We don't want to get in any more trouble that we're already in, all right?"

They nod. "Thank you, Mr. Lochlan," Isabella says with a trembling lip.

I squeeze her shoulder. "This is my job, sweetheart, and I'm really good at it. Can you both be brave for me a little longer?" They nod again. "Good job. Now, start taking those big breath in and out for me."

Wasting no more time, I inhale myself and use the beam to push myself under with my flashlight. It quickly becomes clear that it's this beam that has wedged a couple of chunks from the wall, trapping Isabella between them and the boat. I bet the poor thing has just been trying to tug herself free, but now I'm here, I think I can offer a different solution to get her out fast.

I come back up for air and wipe the water from my eyes. "Okay, team. I think what I need to do is push the boat *down*, then Isabella should be able to get her foot out. Carmen, is that pipe you're holding onto sturdy? Give it a good wiggle for me."

She does, frowning as she pulls hard on it, but it doesn't budge. I use that moment to also move into place, using the flashlight to help me find a good place to stand in my water-logged socks.

"Awesome," I tell Carmen. "Okay, wrap your arm around that pipe so it's tucked against your elbow. Yep, like that.

Now, can you both grab each other's wrists for me and hold as tight as you can? So tight it hurts, all right? As soon as I push the boat down with my feet, Carmen, you start pulling Isabella up. Isabella, it might hurt. Scream if you need to. But I'm going to get your foot free as quickly as I can, and Carmen needs to pull you up and stop you floating away or being pulled down by the chunks of wall. Do you guys understand everything I've just said?"

Isabella sobs and Carmen looks like she's going to puke, but they both grit their teeth and nod. The water is up to Isabella's chin. It's now or never.

"My heroes," I say with a grin, really meaning it. "Okay, here we go…one…two…three!"

I brace against the beam, praying to god it doesn't come down on our heads, and shove my feet down with as much force as I can. Poor Isabella lets out a bloodcurdling shriek, but within seconds she pops up out of the water like a Champagne cork.

"You did it!" Carmen yells, immediately wrapping her crying sister in her arms.

"ISABELLA IS FREE!" I holler back down the tunnel to my guys.

"NICE WORK, BELL," Rico yells back.

Isabella sniffs and takes a shaky breath. "Your name is Bella, too?" she asks me.

"Yeah, kinda," I say with a grin. "Guess that makes us twins, huh?"

I waggle my eyebrows at her and get a small laugh. Good. We're not out of the woods yet, and I need to keep their spirits up.

"Okay," I say, trying to sound like I'm in charge but also not to scare them with what's still to come. "All we have to do is get back past all the stuff that fell down, and my team are going to be waiting on the other side. Then we can get you medical attention and back to your parents. Were they here in the park with you?"

Carmen's lip trembles. "They went to get us all ice cream. I said this wasn't a scary ride and we were big enough to do it alone. I promised them I'd look after Issy. They're gonna be so mad."

She starts crying as well, but I shake my head and squeeze her shoulder again. "Oh, honey. That's exactly what you did! This was an accident, and you were a great big sister making sure you both got out okay. I promise they won't be mad. I think after all this, you both deserve all the ice cream you can eat. So let's go get it, huh?"

"Okay," they say in unison, still sniffling and shaking, but they haven't given up on me yet.

I detach the webbing from my belt and use it to wrap around our waists, creating a daisy chain. We have just enough slack between us that I'm satisfied we won't drag each other down as we weave our way through all the crap.

Now I just have to swim against the current and pull them both to safety.

No big deal.

"All I want you girls to do is swim, okay? Try not to touch anything as I don't know how stable it is. We'll have to go under the water a few times, so I'll need you to take big breaths, and I'll help tug you through, all right?"

"My foot hurts a lot," Isabella says shakily.

I'm not surprised. It's very likely broken. The cold water is probably stopping her from feeling it even more than she should.

"I know, Issy, but I need you to be tough. Who do you know that's tough?"

"Simone Biles?" Carmen suggests.

Isabella shakes her head, though. "Tough like Mom," she

says firmly. "Mom always says we can do whatever we set our minds to."

"And she's right," I say proudly. "Okay. Here we go!"

Fighting against the current soon has my muscles burning, and more than once the beam or chunk of wall I chose to try and haul us along shifts alarmingly on me. But inch by inch, we crawl our way back to where the flashlight beams of my crew are bobbing about.

"You're almost there!" Lili yells through the darkness over the rushing water. I realize she's also got in the water and is coming toward us. The guys must have cleared some of the way, making our escape easier. "Come on, girls. Come on!"

Once she clears the next major obstacle, the current sends her rushing toward us. But she kicks off something underneath her and ricochets to grab Carmen's hand as she's the one bringing up the rear.

With two of us now dragging the girls, we're able to move faster. Sawyer and Anton are reaching through the last web of crap, there to help all of us through with as little time under the water as possible.

And then it's over. Suddenly, multiple hands are reaching for the girls, heaving them out of the water. Someone's set up a floodlight to illuminate more of the tunnel, and the boats have been pulled back, tethered with ropes so they're no longer buffering against the fallen debris and making it less stable. My guys were actually able to clear quite a bit of it away and prop it up with the extra air bags Cap went to get. He's here now, pulling Lili from the water.

"No signs of any other guests," I tell him. "All clear."

"Good job, Bell," he says sincerely.

I give him a weak salute. "No problem, Cap."

The water has risen a couple of feet since I went after the girls. However, Sawyer and Anton have gotten them back onto the walkway where the paramedics are waiting on solid ground to wrap them in emergency blankets and get Isabella in particular off her injured foot. The medics aren't Del and Yara, but I wouldn't be surprised if there were multiple units here by now and our guys are busy helping someone else.

All that matters is that the sisters are on their way to the hospital now, soon to be reunited with their parents.

I cling to the edge of the walkway and catch my breath. After all my years on the job, I can safely say that I've never had a call like this before.

Turns out, it's not over yet.

The yap echoes through the tunnel, making me snap my head around. No…that couldn't have been…could it?

But then in the gloom, I see the whiteness bobbing in the water, making its way around the temporarily moored water lily boats.

It's Rocky, desperately swimming down the tunnel to get to me.

"What the hell!" I cry. I don't know where I get the sudden burst of energy, but I'm immediately powering upstream to get him. "Rocky, what are you doing here? Where's Dario?"

Ice shoots through my veins that has nothing to do with the frigid water. How can Rocky be here? I left him in the rig with Dario.

What's happened to Dario?

CHAPTER 20
Dario

"WE NEED AN EXTRA PAIR OF HANDS HERE!" SOMEONE YELLS from outside. There have been a lot of sirens around us, so I know more firefighters and paramedics have already arrived. I look up to see Gene glance back at me.

"You gonna be okay back there, kid?" he asks.

I nod before he's even finished asking. "Of course. We're fine."

Without another word, he nods back at me and slips out of the driver's seat of the engine into the night.

I take a deep breath, not sure why my heart is racing. It's not like I'm not responsible for anything, and the situation appears to be in hand from what I can tell. There's certainly a lot of activity going on closer to the accident site. However, there isn't that air of panic that I've felt before when I've driven past pile-ups on the freeway, for example. It might be naive of me, but I really hope that no one was seriously injured.

It's difficult to work out exactly what happened from where we're parked, and try as I might, my anxiety is getting the better of me. I'm worried about where Lochlan and his colleagues went, but I'm more worried about what they've found by now, or who. How he does this job is beyond me. I'd be crying all the time, I'm sure.

"Let's get a little air in here, huh?" I suggest to Rocky.

Without the ignition on, the A/C is off and it's getting a bit stuffy. I'm aware I promised not to venture from the engine, but I make sure to wrap the end of Rocky's leash an extra time around my fist and grip it a little tighter as I open the door ajar to allow some fresh air inside. And if I lean out and crane my neck to see what's happening down the street, that won't hurt anyone, right?

I haven't been here before, but it seems pretty obvious to me that there's a ride up ahead that's been damaged quite badly from the odd angle of the supporting beams. I bite my lip and squint, trying to see if I can fathom what's happened. Dusk has settled fast, but the park appears to have enough lighting for me to suspect it's usually open for business after dark. But it looks like some people are also setting up emergency flood lighting as well.

A wave of tiredness washes over me. Until that moment, I don't think I appreciated how the adrenaline from seeing the photo and worrying about Shane, then worrying about going to see Lochlan at the firehouse, *then* coming here with the sirens blaring was keeping me going. For a second, I consider closing the door again, huddling in the corner, and closing my eyes until someone comes back.

That's when Rocky tugs on his leash. Hard.

"Hey, no," I say firmly, waking up in an instant. "Rocky, sit. We have to stay here."

But the puppy has started going berserk, whimpering and thrashing around, trying to get down from the fire engine. I suddenly realize he might need to go potty, so I open the door fully and hop onto the ground, reaching so I can help him off the steps as well. But I'm not fast enough. He leaps onto the asphalt and starts straining against me.

"You can pee here," I try and convince him, but Lochlan has done a good job training him to go on the grass. I don't want to undo all that.

With a sigh, I look around. I don't think we'll get in anyone's way if we move to the nearby foliage. It's in the opposite direction of the accident site, after all, and I doubt Lochlan and the rest of the guys will be back any time soon.

"Okay, but we have to be quick," I warn Rocky, setting off the way he was trying to drag me.

With a yap, he starts running, his tail wagging so fast it becomes a blur. Thinking he's going to jump under the bushes and relieve himself, I give him enough slack to lead the way. But then he's pulling me down a side track, out of sight of the One-Thirteen's vehicles.

"Whoa, Rocky, stop!" I cry, but he just pulls even harder. I've never seen him like this before, so as nervous as I am to stray from where I was told to remain, I allow him to keep guiding me.

Something isn't right.

"What is it, boy?" I ask, aware he can't answer me. But he does bark again and scrabble to run even faster.

That's when I hear another bark.

When I first brought Queenie home, I did a pretty extensive search on where I was allowed to take her. So I know for a fact that dogs aren't allowed into Critter Canyon unless they've been snuck in on fire engines…or they're service dogs.

"Hello!" I yell as I start running faster, Rocky matching my pace easily. "Is anyone here?"

This side track obviously connects two busier parts of the park together and it does have a few street lights, but there are deeper pockets of darkness here, making me even more nervous. Either side is shrubbery with gorgeous flowers to make the walk pretty, but there are also three pioneer-style wagons ahead that are probably meant to add to the Old West aesthetic of the park.

Or there *were* three wagons. From what I can tell, the one farthest from us looks untouched, but the middle one has been shoved into the greenery at a wild angle, and the one nearest to us is a complete mess. It looks like most of the base has collapsed with only one of the massive wheels still attached, and the cream tarp has mostly detached, covering the broken bits of wood. I see tire marks on the ground and what could be part of a car bumper abandoned by the wreckage.

I still don't know what's gone on to cause so much destruction, but I have a feeling that whatever happened with the giant swing boat and this are possibly related.

"Hello?" I call out again, coming to a halt just before the carnage.

The tarp moves. A lump bobs around underneath. Rocky jerks on his leash, but I hold him back this time. If that's a frightened raccoon or something, it might lash out. But then I remember it was a bark that sent us running in this direction, so I hold my breath…

A golden Labrador puppy comes bounding out from underneath, all gangly legs and floppy ears. As they bark happily and charge over to us, I see that they're wearing a green vest. It reads 'guide dog in training.'

I gasp and run over to catch the little pup before they get too far. A quick glance at her collar tells me her name is Clover.

"Oh, good girl, Clover," I coo, taking a firm hold of her leash as well. "Was that you barking? Did you get lost? Are you—?"

A groan comes from under the tarp.

My heart threatens to stop, but before adrenaline can paralyze me, I lurch forward and yank back the heavy material. For a second, my brain can't process what it's seeing. It's not just that someone is pinned down under one of the detached wagon wheels. It's that I *know* that person.

"*Zoe?*" I splutter in disbelief.

A part of my frazzled mind remembers our teacher mentioning several times that as well as training puppies with us, she also works with guide dogs in training and often takes them to busy places to socialize them. But explaining why she's here isn't really as important in that moment as getting her free.

"Zoe! It's Dario. Hold still, let me try and lift this off you."

She groans again and twitches, but I don't think she's conscious. There's a nasty gash on her temple and blood everywhere. I'm sure I read somewhere that head wounds do gush a lot, but that doesn't stop me from panicking. She needs medical assistance, *now.*

"*HELP!*" I bellow at the top on my lungs as I reposition myself. "*CAN ANYONE HEAR ME?*"

I crouch down with the leash handles looped around my wrist, leaving my hands free to wrap around the wheel's rim. Gritting my teeth, I try and lift it up with everything I have, but it barely moves at all. I'm afraid of dropping it on her and causing more damage, so I carefully put it back down again, hoping I haven't worsened her injuries.

Despite my heart pounding like thunder, I strain my ears and try and hear if anyone heard me yelling. I doubt it.

"Okay, okay," I say to myself with two puppies anxiously sniffing at Zoe. I know she just moved and made some noise, but I still reach out and thrust two of my fingers against the pulse point in her neck. When I feel it fluttering, it reassures me a bit. However, it's clear she's in trouble and needs professional help as soon as possible. "Okay. I'm going to get help, Zoe. I'll be right ba—"

Her hand shoots out and grabs my wrist, her eyes flying open as she gasps for air. "Don't leave me," she croaks, tears escaping down her face. "Please, I…oh…"

Her eyelids flutter shut again, leaving me feeling alone again as I tremble from head to toe. "I won't," I promise her, even as I look around frantically.

I'm so scared it's difficult not to cry myself. I try my best to hold it together, though. Zoe is depending on me. I'm just not sure what's the best thing to do. Run for help or stay by her side like she begged me to?

Oh! How could I be so stupid? I have my phone on me! I can call 9-1-1 and tell them I'm at the park with a bunch of first responders and get the operator to send someone to us!

Feeling giddy with relief, I shift around and try to get my phone out of my pocket. But that's the hand with the dog leashes looped around my wrist. In trying to reach my phone, Rocky's one slips free…

Without warning, he explodes with a burst of energy, ripping his leash completely from my grasp and running back toward the fire engines.

"ROCKY, NO!" I scream in panic, watching in horror as he races into the darkness. But Zoe is still clinging to my hand even if her eyes are closed, and Clover is whimpering between us both.

I don't know what to do. *I don't know what to do!* The dispatch operator might be able to send us help, but Rocky is getting lost right this moment and anyway, finding a puppy isn't going to be a priority when people's lives are on the line.

It's a priority to me, though. It'll be a priority to Lochlan. I can't believe how badly I've let him down.

"HELP!" I scream as loud as I can again as I scrabble for my phone. *"SOMEBODY, PLEASE!"* Zoe lets out a sob and

screws up her face. She must be in so much pain. "It's okay, I'm here," I tell her, squeezing her hand tighter.

My hand is shaking so badly, I'm amazed I'm able to unlock my phone and type in 9-1-1 at all. But I'm soon connected to a human being who swiftly takes my details and assures me that someone will be with me as soon as they can. However, she warns me that everyone is pretty busy already so she can't guarantee when help will come.

"Just…please, hurry," I beg her.

She stays on the line with me, asking questions about Zoe and reassuring me that I'm doing a good job and help is on the way. But there's only so much she can do from the call center.

I don't know how much time is passing. I feel like I'm having an out of body experience, watching on helplessly as Zoe slips away from me. As Rocky runs off to who knows where. This park is enormous and so chaotic with all the emergency services trying to help all those people from the accident. I know he's microchipped, but if he gets lost…if he gets hurt…I could never look Lochlan in the eye again. He trusted me and I've let him down. I—

Zoe cries and tries to squirm under the giant wheel.

"Try not to move," I tell her urgently. "I know it hurts, but we don't know if you have a spinal injury. The dispatcher said I shouldn't let you move. Hold on for me, Zoe. Just… hold on." I hold the phone away from my mouth and scream again, hoping it might get someone here faster. *"HELP!"*

I'm ashamed as a sob escapes my own chest. I've never been so scared in my whole life, not even when Shane lashed out and hit me. I had no idea in that moment if he'd stop or if he'd keep going until he hospitalized me. If he'd do it again before I could escape and knock me down permanently.

Sure, I was terrified. But I was only trying to save myself then. Right now, it's like I have not one but two lives in my hands. I can't leave Zoe alone but something terrible could happen to Rocky because I wasn't holding his leash tight enough at just the wrong moment.

Is staying here the right thing to do? I know Zoe doesn't want me to abandon her, but what if nobody can get here in time despite the operator's help? Maybe I could find a paramedic. Should I have run after Rocky? What if—?

"Dario!"

My head whips around so fast I'm surprised I don't crack my neck. But as soon as I see Lochlan and Rocky running toward me at full pelt, another sob escapes and tears run down my face.

"It's Zoe!" I scream back at him, still not quite believing that he isn't a desperate figment of my imagination.

Did Rocky really go and get him for me?

I can puzzle over that later. Right now, all that matters is that I'm not alone.

The person I wanted to see most in the entire world just materialized in front of my eyes.

"Someone's here," I tell the operator. "I'm okay now. Thank you so much."

I don't know if I'm supposed to stay on the line or not, but I hang up anyway. Lochlan's here. Everything is going to be all right.

"Zoe?" Lochlan repeats as he and Rocky stumble to a halt in front of us. He's not wearing his coat or helmet anymore and he's absolutely drenched. I have no idea what could have happened, but I can find out later, no doubt.

I nod and look back down at Zoe as she takes shallow breaths, showing us that she's still alive. "She trains guide dog puppies, remember? Clover led Rocky here." I gulp. "Then I think he went and got you to help her, too. Oh, Rocky, you scared me. I'm so glad you're not lost."

"He's a good boy," Lochlan says to me with conviction,

but it's clear that all his attention is now on Zoe, as it needs to be. His eyes dart over her trapped body. "Were you on with dispatch?" he asks me.

"Yes," I tell him. "She said people were on their way. But everything's so crazy, she didn't know how long it might take."

He wastes no time in reaching for the radio on his shoulder. "Cap, it's Bell. I need medical assistance in the walkway opposite our rigs and another pair of hands if you can spare them."

"We're on it," a voice replies within seconds.

More help is coming. Rocky's okay. Hopefully, Zoe's going to be okay. I'm not on my own anymore.

I think the relief of Lochlan coming to the rescue has made me lose it. I watch on numbly as he moves to support her neck with his hands. It takes me several moments to realize that he's calling my name. I blink and look up at his worried face.

"Are *you* all right?" he asks.

I don't understand. Of course I'm all right. I look back down at Zoe. "We need to get the wheel off her," I say, like someone else is speaking through my mouth.

He shakes his head. "Not without a neck brace. Help is on the way. You did everything right, Dario. I'm so proud of you."

Those last words cut through my brain fog. I look into his green eyes, feeling the connection between us so fiercely it's like it's a physical thing.

In that moment, I know I love him. *Real* love, not the poisonous thing I was tricked into believing before. Like my soul didn't even know what it was searching for until he walked into my life.

Before I can wrap my head around it all, a pair of paramedics with a gurney and another firefighter rush onto the scene. I think I recognize the firefighter from the ride in the engine, meaning he's also from the One-Thirteen. Lochlan quickly confirms my speculation.

"Rico!" he yells as they approach. "Man, am I glad to see you guys. Did you clear the tunnel okay?"

"Yep, all good," he replies. "Definitely no one else in there. The rest of the team is assisting with the main triage site now. So, what have we got here? I'm guessing this is the path the ice cream truck took before hitting the swing boat."

Ice cream truck? What the hell?

"She's pinned, Lieutenant," Lochlan explains, even though that seems pretty obvious to me. But I guess his superior needs every scrap of information available. "Her name's Zoe Sharpe. She's our teacher at the puppy training class."

"We need to get a neck brace on her and assess her vitals," one of the paramedics says. He has a beautifully mellow voice that immediately helps calm my nerves. Lochlan carefully removes his hands so the medic can secure the brace. "How long has she been down for?"

He looks at Lochlan but Lochlan is looking at me. The female paramedic gently unclasps my hand from Zoe's. I don't want to let her go, but I guess I need to give them space to treat her. I realize they're expecting me to answer.

"I don't know how long she's been like this," I say as I unlock my phone and check my call log. "But I was on with dispatch for…just under seven minutes, and I found her a few minutes before that, and Lochlan was with me for a few minutes after I hung up."

"Was she conscious?" the male paramedic asks. His name tag reads 'Delacroix,' and I think I remember him sticking up for Lochlan back at the firehouse.

"Uh, not really," I tell him. "But she woke up at one point and grabbed my wrist, asking me not to leave her. She seemed to pass out again after that, but I kept an eye on her, she never stopped breathing."

"Good," Delacroix says warmly. "Thank you for taking care of her until we could get her."

"Is she going to be okay?" I ask.

"We need to get this wheel off her now she's been stabilized," the other paramedic—Ortiz—says. She looks up into my eyes and nods. "We're going to do everything we can for her, I promise."

"Thank you," I whisper. I'm trembling, so I hug myself in an attempt to get it to stop. "I tried to move the wheel, but I thought I'd do more harm than good, so I stopped."

"You did the right thing, Dario," Rico says. Hearing him use my name like that is so strange. But Lochlan beams at me, apparently unsurprised. It feels like that because these guys know Lochlan, they already know me. Accept me.

I'm honored.

"All right," Rico continues speaking to me. "Can I ask you to move safely out of the way and keep those pups with you?"

"Yes, sir," I tell him.

My grip on the two leashes is so tight, my knuckles are turning white. But there's no way I'm losing either of them again. Both dogs are whimpering and pawing at the ground, clearly picking up on our stress. But they stay with me, and the three of us watch the others get to work.

Rico and Lochlan position themselves on either side of the wagon wheel, crouching down with straight backs and gripping the edge like I did. Except they're both almost twice my size, so they're able to heave the thing off Zoe in one go, putting it to the side as Delacroix and Ortiz swoop in to roll Zoe onto a back board. She groans again, but to me that just proves she's still hanging in there.

"We'll get her transferred immediately to San Clemente," Delacroix explains as Rico helps him and Ortiz lift Zoe onto the gurney. "She's lucky you found her, Dario. We didn't have any other reports from this area."

"Yeah, you did good," Ortiz agrees with a wink.

I'm in such a state of shock, I just nod back. "Come on," Lochlan urges me, and we follow them back up the path along with Rico.

Zoe isn't out of the woods yet. At least she's in good hands now, so I can allow myself a chance to breathe and even hope for the best. Everything could absolutely turn out okay, and for that, I'm incredibly grateful.

I keep a hold of Clover as we hurry up the path, but Lochlan happily takes Rocky, telling him what a good boy he is and promising him steak for dinner. That makes me laugh weakly as we emerge from the side track, rejoining the main area of the rescue operation.

I think I'm finally coming down from the intense adrenaline rush of everything, and I feel a little dizzy. But before I can even consider getting unsteady on my feet, Lochlan is there to support me, wrapping me in his arms.

"Sorry I left the rig," I say, slurring a little with how incredibly tired I suddenly am. "But Rocky heard Clover. He's a real hero."

"You have nothing to be sorry for," Lochlan promises me, kissing the top of my head. "In fact, you were fucking incredible. Come on. Let's go join the others and tell them all about what a badass you are."

Chuckling weakly, I let him steer me and the dogs in the direction he wants to go. I look on in awe at the rest of the One-Thirteen who have formed a line and are helping people safely dismount from the wreckage of what used to be the swing boat.

Lochlan sags against me. "Holy fuck," he says weakly. "What a call. I need to get back out there."

He doesn't move, though.

I understand that he needs to go and do his job. But part of *my* job now is to take care of him. If he needs a minute to catch his breath to make sure he's safe to work again, I'll give that to him.

"Are you okay?" I ask him.

He looks down at me, such warmth and affection in his eyes it takes my breath away.

"I am now," he tells me, echoing my words from the journey here.

"Me, too," I promise him, leaning up to kiss him on the mouth. He doesn't even hesitate to reciprocate.

This evening might have started out with a shock, and being in the middle of a disaster zone is no joke. But in this moment, I feel like I'm exactly where I'm supposed to be in the world, with exactly the right person.

I was a fool to think everything we have could be threatened by something so silly as one photo on the internet.

Right?

CHAPTER 21
Lochlan

MY HEART IS POUNDING, AND MY BLOOD IS RACING. NOT unusual for a high adrenaline call, but I'm fully aware this has been like no other job I've ever done for one simple reason.

Dario was here with me. And my god, he was brave as all hell.

I knew that already. But seeing him jump into the fray like that was incredible. That asshole ex of his tried to break him down and make him feel worthless. It was all for nothing, though. Dario had the guts to break free of his control and start a new life. And today I saw that he has it in him to help rescue other people as well. Not everyone has that kind of strength.

Once it's clear that everyone has safely been removed from The Maiden Voyage, the One-Thirteen takes a breath before we start work helping clear the enormous amount of debris. That's when I suggest to Dario that he call a taxi and head home, as it's obvious we're going to be here a long ass time, possibly all night until the end of our shift at eight tomorrow morning. Dario says he'll take care of Clover for now, but he can drop Rocky back at my place on his way home. We have a spare of each other's keys for exactly this kind of dog-sitting emergency.

I know Rocky will probably be fine, especially as I've got the same kind of camera system set up at home as at the station and at Dario's place, so I can check in on him whenever. But before I can stop myself, I blurt out that Dario should pick up Queenie and come stay at my place. After everything we've been through, I want to keep him close, even if I have to work and can't keep him in my arms.

The thought of him chilling on my sofa, drinking my beer, eating my leftover lasagna and sleeping in my bed with both our dogs brings me a sense of calm that I know will mean I can do my damn job for the next several hours.

When he agrees with a shy but eager smile, I feel like my heart might actually burst in my chest with happiness.

The rest of my shift flies by after that. A crane has already been scheduled to come in the morning to deal with the wayward swing boat, but there's plenty our crews can do in the meantime to kickstart the cleanup. As with any business after a disaster, we're aware that Critter Canyon will want to reopen as soon as it's safe. The more we can power through after the initial aftermath, the better.

I'm grateful for the kinda mindless manual labor because it means my thoughts can mostly keep swimming around my favorite subject. But not just the general awesomeness of Dario this time. I can't get over how amazing he was going with Rocky to try and help Zoe. How he stayed with her while he called 9-1-1. That might not seem remarkable to some folks because that's what you're supposed to do in a crisis. But after years on the job, I can assure you that so many people get overwhelmed with adrenaline and freeze up.

My man might have just saved our teacher's life.

If I was on a high before when he came to the firehouse

and met my other family, that's nothing to how I'm feeling right now.

We have to tap out and bring the rigs back to the station so we can get them ready to hand over to the second watch when they clock in. I'm bone tired as I force myself into the shower then change back into my civies. However, when I check my phone before heading to my truck, there's a message from Dario saying that he was able to speak to a nurse at San Clemente General and find out that Zoe is going to be just fine. I sag in relief as I read that she's got a couple of broken ribs, a concussion, and a shit ton of bruising, but she's expected to make a full recovery.

Then there's a second message. Actually, it's mostly just a photo of Dario snuggled up in my bed with the three dogs on top of the duvet pressed against his belly and legs. He says that he's working from home today, so he'll be at *my* home whenever I get there.

I fucking run to my truck after seeing that, barely pausing to yell goodbye over my shoulder at whoever's still at the station.

The thing about adrenaline is that it can cause all kinds of reactions in your body afterward that you might not expect. Sometimes, it can make you sleepy, or starving, or cranky (probably because you need to sleep or eat). After one particularly nasty pile-up on the interstate, I rearranged my whole damn kitchen and somehow that made me feel less sad.

As I head home, I definitely make plans involving foot-high stakes of pancakes covered in maple syrup and sleeping for twelve hours.

But another side effect of getting your juices flowing is that they can *keep* flowing…down south…if you catch my drift. I'm glad everyone else on the team was just as tired as I was and didn't stop to talk to me for long as I was on the way out, because the truth is, I've been half hard since I got into the damn shower.

Now I'm so horny, I'm slightly worried if I'm okay to drive.

Thankfully, I make it back home without incident or even running any stop lights. I do have to go back and double check I locked my car, which I hadn't, but then I'm running up to my apartment as eager as a kid at Christmas.

I need Dario, now. More than ever before.

The dogs rush to greet me as soon as I open the door. "Hello, hello," I say as I fuss them. The blissful scent of freshly brewed coffee hits me, making me sigh contentedly. That's nothing, however, to the way my stomach swoops when Dario steps into the landing, holding a mug and wearing nothing but pajama pants. He said he was going to grab overnight supplies when he picked up Queenie yesterday evening, but in that moment, I decide I'm going to insist on him leaving some stuff like that here.

Seeing him so at home in my place does all kinds of funny things to my insides.

"Hey," he says softly, still looking a little sleep rumpled as he pads over to me with the coffee. "I wasn't sure what time you'd be back, but I put a pot on as soon as I woke up, and I saw there's bacon and stuff in the fridge if you want breakfast."

I pluck the coffee from his fingers and place it on the sideboard without even taking a sip. I can reheat it or pour a fresh cup later. Dario's thoughtfulness has sent me over the edge.

"I want *you*," I growl, slipping my hands under his ass and picking him up. His little squeak of surprise is adorable, but he soon gets with the program, wrapping his legs around my waist and his arms around my neck as his lips crash against mine. "You were so fucking amazing last night," I mumble as I start shuffling us toward the bedroom.

"I didn't do anything," he says with a laugh between kisses. "You're the hero here. I was so proud watching you work."

I growl again, somehow managing to get us over the threshold and shut my bedroom door with the dogs on the other side. Rocky and Clover might protest for a bit, but Queenie will soon calm them down.

She probably knows the human beings need some privacy right about now.

"I would like to implement a new rule," I say as I deposit Dario onto my mattress. He bounces and grins up at me.

"Yeah?"

"Yeah," I tell him as I crawl up his body, making him shuffle back and lie against the pillows. The bedding is still all over the place from where he slept here last night, and I realize it smells like both of us now.

I always want it to smell like that.

"New rule: no one is allowed to put my boyfriend down like that, not even him."

He blinks and suddenly looks more serious. "Boyfriend?"

My heart is pounding again. I cup my hand against his face and caress his cheek with my thumb. "I know we said we'd take it slow. But I think that's because you were worried I'd change my mind and realize I'm not into dudes after all. But that's not going to happen, Dario. I'm crazy about you, and I'd really, really like to tell the whole world that we're together. So long as that's what you want."

Tears pool in his eyes as he reaches up and mirrors me, pressing his palm to the side of my jaw. "I want to be your boyfriend more than anything. So long as you promise to be patient with me. I'm still scared, Lochlan. Still broken. I don't want to let you down, but I might not be able to help it."

I scoff and arch an eyebrow at him. "You're not broken. You're a survivor. No, you're like one of those fancy vases that they put back together with gold so it's even more beautiful than it was before."

Dario laughs, twin tears escaping down his temples into the pillow behind his head. But he's smiling up at me, so I know he gets what I'm trying to say. "Kintsugi. That's what the art form is called. It represents resilience."

"Well, there you go," I say smugly, pleased as punch that I remembered a smart thing even though I didn't know the word for it. "That's what you are. And Rocky and Queenie. Fighters, all of you."

Dario takes a shuddering breath and presses his lips together before speaking softly. "I'm not sure if I believe in fate or destiny or whatever. But I can't help but feel like the universe brought us all together for a reason, and for that, I'll never stop being grateful. I...I'd be honored to be your boyfriend, Lochlan. For real this time."

I lean back on my heels and punch the air. "WOOHOO!"

He laughs at my dumb ass, but then I drop down and start kissing him again until neither of us are laughing. We're moaning and panting and writhing.

I break away to yank my T-shirt off. "On the theme of not wanting to go too fast but possibly doing it anyway," I say as I reach for my nightstand. "I don't want to do anything you're not comfortable with. Getting naked with you is my new absolute favorite thing. But..."

When I pull out the brand-new box of condoms and bottle of lube, I watch him closely for his reaction. His eyebrows shoot up and he looks to understand what I'm suggesting. "You'd want that?" he asks quietly.

"Baby, I'm desperate for it," I tell him with a rueful chuckle. "I've been jerking myself raw to all kinds of porn. It hits different when you know what you're watching could become reality. My only question is if you're ready? No, wait, I have two questions. The second is what are you into? Whatever you like the most is the thing I want to do. Or *things*. There can be a wish list."

I waggle my eyebrows at him and am relieved when he laughs, even if he is still looking a little shellshocked. "I don't want to go in too hard too fast, though."

"We're way beyond hard, sweetheart," I say, shaking my head and rolling our thickened cocks together through our pants. He groans and closes his eyes. I use the opportunity to lean down and trace wet kisses along his throat. "Tell me your desires," I murmur against his skin. "You're safe with me, Dario. I want to make you lose your mind with pleasure."

He trembles underneath me in the most delicious way. "I…oh…um…well…you can always say no."

"I can," I assure him. "But I doubt I will. I think you like being in charge, don't you, baby? I love that. Boss me around. I'm a dirty boy, remember? Tie me up. Spank my ass. Whatever you like, and I'll tell you you're perfect and good and all mine."

He clings to my shoulders and buries his face against my neck. "Holy shit, Lochlan."

"You like the sound of that, huh?"

He nods then leans back enough to look into my eyes. "Where did you come from?" he asks in wonder.

"Homegrown in Redwood Bay, sweetheart," I tell him with a wink. "Been waiting here just for you. Tell me what you want, Dario, and I'll do it. I'll do anything for you."

For a moment, he simply slides his hand around the back of my head, drawing me close to kiss my lips softly and with reverence. "I want to do everything with you," he says, his voice cracking a little as his eyes search mine. "But right now…how would you feel about me topping?"

I'm relieved I did at least some basic research so I know

he means that he wants to be the one who fucks me. Lust flares through me at just the thought of it. "I've never done that with anyone before," I say, beaming down at him. "So it'll be extra special for us."

Again, he seems to search my face to see if I'm being honest. "A lot of gay men freak out at the idea of bottoming, especially if the other guy is, um, smaller. Less masculine. Until very recently, you thought you were straight. Are you absolutely sure?"

"People are dumb," I say, genuinely baffled. "Because I'm buff I'm not supposed to want something like that? Pshh. It's a good thing that I'm not gay or straight, but instead a mighty bisexual who wants his hot boyfriend to hurry up and fuck him in the ass already."

I tickle his sides and we're both laughing, but then he pushes me so I roll onto my back. I gulp as lust pulses through me. Both our chests are rising and falling as we breathe heavily, pupils blown with desire.

"Anything you want," I promise him again, making sure he's really listening. "Show me how you like it, gorgeous."

For a moment, he just breathes as his gaze trails seductively over my body. I watch as he slowly gets off me. His hands are shaking, but he doesn't hesitate as he begins untying my laces, easing my boots and socks off. When he unzips my jeans, I lift my hips to help him slide them down along with my briefs.

The fact that my cock bounces around like a goddamned wacky inflatable tube man, flicking pre-cum over my stomach, just makes me grin proudly. I need Dario to see how much I want him to be the one in charge here.

I want him to feel free.

We've been naked together several times now, but something feels different as I watch him slide his pajama pants off. It was obvious from the obscene tenting going on that he was already hard as well. However, the way he keeps his eyes locked with mine as he strokes his length hungrily is entirely new.

"*Christ*," I choke out. "You look so hot, baby. Is that all for me? Are you going to give it to me?"

"If you're good, dirty boy," he says as if he can't believe his own daring.

Good? I'll be fucking outstanding for him. Gold stars and everything.

"How do you want me?" I rasp. There are so many positions we can try. I've read that on all fours is often the easiest, but I want to face him. I want to kiss him. So I grab my heels and lift them as high as I can. "Like this?"

I don't know if I've ever felt this exposed in my entire life, but it doesn't make me vulnerable. I'm excited to share this with Dario. It's like I'm a wild animal, ruffling my feathers and showing my ass to my potential mate, hoping to be claimed.

Dario's jaw has dropped. "That's the hottest thing I've seen in my whole life," he says in a strangled voice before crawling back onto the bed and touching my thighs. "For now, can you hug your knees to your chest for me?"

"Like this?" I ask as I change position.

His expression is so sweet and soft. "Perfect, baby." My breath hitches and my heart floods with affection at hearing him call me that for the first time.

I want to be his baby just as much as he's already mine.

"Remember," he says seriously as he trails kisses down my inner thigh. "If you don't like anything, tell me stop. Even if you're not sure and need a second to think."

"I swear," I say, knowing he has to trust that I'm being honest with him if he's going to enjoy this. I'm pretty sure I'm going to love it all, though.

He hums and keeps mouthing his way down my body. I'm

slightly surprised when he skirts around my straining cock, but I don't get long to think about it. When his tongue swipes across my hole, I yelp, jerk, and blink rapidly, all at the same time.

"Whoa."

"Okay?" he asks.

I blink some more, very glad I had a thorough shower before I left work. "Uh…yeah. I think so. I really think so. Do it again?"

He chuckles, but within seconds he's back between my cheeks, giving my hole little licks like a kitten lapping up milk from a saucer.

I manage to keep ahold of my knees, but they fall further to my sides as I try and push my ass toward his mouth. He surprises me with a slap to the top of my leg, just where it meets my butt. I gasp and he grins. "Naughty."

His confidence is like a shot of the good stuff going straight to my head. I feel dizzy and tingly all over as I watch him dip back down and really go to town on the most intimate part of my body. I moan and wail and gnash my teeth as he kisses and sucks and licks, driving me wild. When his tongue starts pushing inside my tight ring of muscle, I'm sure I shake the whole building with my bellow.

"Yes, baby, *yes!*" I scream, gripping my knees so hard for him I'm sure I'm going to leave bruises.

I hope I do.

"Need you," I grunt. "Dario, please. Need you to fuck me now. Need to come."

"Shh, it's okay," he says as he comes up for air. "Not just yet, but soon. Hold on a bit longer for me."

"I will, I will," I babble.

He quickly squirts some lube onto his fingers, pushing two in where his tongue left off. Then he wraps the other hand around the base of my shaft and starts sucking the top. Not enough to make me come, but enough to make me wild.

Unable to hold them up any longer, my legs flop down, but he doesn't need me to spread so much like this. Instead, I thread my fingers through his hair as he bobs up and down, and grip the bed covers to try and keep myself anchored. I don't want to blow my load too soon and ruin this incredible moment.

I can't promise I'll be able to hold off for much longer, though.

"Dario, baby, please, for the love of god," I cry as he works a third finger inside me. It's a strange sensation, and I wonder if I should have played around with a dildo to be better practiced for him. But I think I prefer that this is all brand new for us to share together.

Especially when he starts to stroke my channel, and holy *shit* it's like he's found my on switch.

"Fuck, fuck, *fuck!*" I scream. That makes him laugh and pop off my cock with a filthy slurping sound.

"You like that, dirty boy, huh?"

I nod frantically as I squirm.

Without him working my dick, I'm less likely to come. However, I'm still frantically panting and writhing as he rubs my magic lamp.

"Would you really let me tie you up?" he murmurs, and I nod some more. "I could torture you like this for hours."

There's nothing restraining me right now, but I do nothing to free myself from my current torment, either. I'm in some kind of hellish heaven. The idea of trusting Dario like that—of being at his mercy—it makes something unfurl deep within me.

"Fuck me, please," I beg him. "I want to feel your cock in me, baby. I want your cum."

He leans up and kisses my mouth brutally. Then suddenly

his lips and fingers are gone, leaving me panting and trembling at the emptiness. But when my gaze focuses, I see him slicking up his cock with a fuck ton of lube, then he drizzles even more down my fluttering crack.

"Heels up," he says, and they fly back into my hands. I watch desperately as he positions himself between them, lining up his cock, then…

"Oh, oh," I whimper at the intrusion. It's strange but fucking awesome as he pushes farther inside me, claiming me, dominating me. He lets go of his length and places both his hands on my chest, digging his fingers into my flesh.

"Fuck," he gasps. "You feel so good, Lochlan. Oh my god. Is it okay?"

"It's incredible," I tell him truthfully, letting the sensation consume me. "You're incredible. You look so fucking beautiful right now."

He really does. His taut body is glistening with sweat and his dark hair is falling into his eyes as he looms over me. His lips are swollen, and his pretty eyes are wild with pleasure. He gnashes his teeth and seems to get as far as he can go inside me, and we both take a second to gasp for air.

That's not enough for me, though. I lean up, asking for his kiss. He gives it willingly.

With my legs held up to the ceiling in a restraint of my own making, he feels like he's so far up me he's going to puncture my stomach. But then he starts rocking his hips, and what little sense I still had goes flying out of the window.

All that's left is Dario as he thrusts against my prostate, lighting me up like Vegas at Christmas. I don't even know what I'm saying other than, "Yes! Please! More!" He's in no better state, so I hope he doesn't mind that I've turned into a blathering fool.

"Lochlan," he cries, stealing more kisses from me as we slam our bodies together. "I'm gonna come. I can't—"

"Come, baby, please," I urge him.

Within seconds, his back arches back and his mouth opens in a silent scream. I can feel his dick throbbing inside me, and even with the condom catching his load, it still feels so good.

I quiver as I watch him gasp for air and come down from his high. But before he's even started to soften, he's pumping more lube into his hand and jerking me off furiously.

"Come for me, baby. I want to see."

I screw my eyes shut and let go, fireworks exploding in the darkness as the most powerful orgasm of my life rips through me. I don't think I've ever come that much, not even when I was a horny teenager. It goes on and on until my hands drop my feet and my limbs come crashing down on the mattress. My body feels like it weighs a ton, but I'm so bathed in euphoria, I'll happily stay here forever.

At some point, Dario slips out of me, and we lay in the crumpled sheets, covered in sweat and cum. I hug him tightly to me, absently kissing his forehead when I have a burst of energy.

"I think I like boyfriend sex the best," I say eventually.

He laughs weakly. "Me, too,"

"I vote we have a lot more of it."

"Me, too," he agrees.

We stay in that moment that feels so perfect nothing could ever touch it.

That doesn't mean something isn't going to try, though.

CHAPTER 22
Dario

I HAVE A BOYFRIEND.

I thought I had a boyfriend before, but that wasn't real. Isn't it ironic that the guy I thought I was in love with turned out to be a fraud all along, and the man I began fake dating ended up being the real deal?

Life's funny like that sometimes, I guess.

There have been several times during the past week where I've found myself lost in thought, marveling at how infinitesimally small the chances of Lochlan and I meeting really were. Now I can't imagine my life without him.

It's probably all the daydreaming that caused me to leave my flash drive at home. Plus the fact that I'm spending so much time at Lochlan's now. I might have the bigger house, but he has more furniture, so it's kind of up for debate who has the better place.

Anywhere he's at is where I want to be, so I don't really care.

But I do care about my damn flash drive. My colleagues poke fun at me for not trusting the cloud to save important stuff, but clouds can be hacked. I like to ensure anything of real importance is only on a removable device with a physical firewall. Usually, I am extremely obsessive about where the drive is at all times.

Well, to be fair, I know exactly where it is. I left it in the USB port of my home computer after I took some work home with me to make up getting...*ahem*...distracted by Lochlan over the past week. I've never had better sex in my whole life, so I can't be too mad at myself.

Especially when I can easily nip home in my lunch break and have the added bonus of taking Queenie out for a quick walk. My manager doesn't need to review the project I've been pouring my time into until tomorrow, after all.

"Hey, girl!" I call out as I step inside the house. "It's just Daddy. Have you been a good doggy?"

I hear a scrabbling of paws on tiles before I see Queenie come bulldozing toward me, her wonky tooth poking out from under her lip as usual and drool flying everywhere. I laugh and crouch down to greet her as she snorts and slobbers all over my hands in excitement. I told her I'd be back tonight rather than at lunch, and I genuinely think she understands the difference.

After washing my hands, I head to my spare room and, sure enough, there's the drive exactly where I left it last night. Still, I'm flooded with relief as I rush to pull it out and put its cap back on so I can slip it in my pocket. Perhaps I should at least ensure *some* version of important work is saved elsewhere. I could probably protect it on my work desktop reasonably well even if I'm not using the cloud. I wouldn't mean to, but what if this drive dropped out of my pocket or got smashed? I wouldn't just be losing a lot of my hard work. I'd be putting the company at risk and letting my colleagues down.

Still, it's so hard for me to let go of all my old very valid fears of allowing myself to be vulnerable online. I remember what my therapist says, though, and try to be kind to myself in this moment. Right now, I have the drive and nothing regrettable has happened. I can think about alternative storage strategies another time.

A nice walk will clear my head. We'll only have about half an hour before I need to head back into work, but both Queenie and I will enjoy some fresh air in the park. I'll bring one of her frisbees to make sure she gets extra milage in as well.

I'm just going to grab her leash from the wall in the entrance hall when my doorbell rings. As we're heading out that way anyhow, I don't really think about who it could be. Lochlan is off today, but he knows I'm in the office as we spoke about it last night. Chances are it's another online delivery, so I just open the door.

Shane is standing on the other side.

I'm so shocked that I simply freeze, my brain grinding to a halt. I grip the door handle so tightly, it might be the only thing that's keeping me standing. My ears feel like they're full of drones, and my heart is beating so hard I think it might actually explode like the Death Star.

"Baby," Shane utters with an emotional sigh. "I've missed you so much."

Before I can register what's happening, he steps over the threshold and wraps his arms around me. I can't seem to move, like I'm frozen in carbonite. But he hums as he presses our temples together and inhales deeply.

"You smell different."

I smell different because I have Lochlan, Queenie and Rocky in my personal space all the time now. I smell different because I have a new home where I feel safe…or at least I did until about ten seconds ago. I smell different because I no longer wear aftershave I hate, but have to put on because he bought it for me, and if I don't spritz on enough to make myself feel sick, that means I don't love him.

Like he ever loved me.

That anger unlocks my tongue at least.

"Y-you shouldn't be here," I manage to stammer.

It seems like he ignores me as he lets me go and looks around my home, no doubt already judging it for not being to his taste. Also, the slightly tacky Christmas decorations I picked up from the store to celebrate my first independent Christmas. I have no doubt that even though I left him, he's going to berate me for not still decorating in a style he'd approve of, whatever time of the year.

However, that's the moment Queenie comes trotting out from the kitchen, no doubt wondering why we still haven't left for our walk. She stops dead in her tracks when she sees Shane, a low growl emanating from her throat before she lets out a couple of loud *'WOOFS.'*

"What the fuck?" Shane cries, jerking away from her with a look of revulsion on his face. Then he laughs and shakes himself like it never happened. "That's the ugliest dog I've ever seen."

My anger from before triples, spurring my feet to finally come back to life and do something. Even though I'm shaking from head to toe, I unglue myself from the entrance hall, leaving the door open as I march to plant myself between my precious baby and the insidious man who has forced his way into my lovely new home.

He won't be staying long.

"You shouldn't be here, Shane," I say more forcefully. "I have a restraining order against you. Get out." He doesn't need to know that the order doesn't technically cover this house.

"Yeah, that your mommy organized for you," he says in disgust. "Hon, I can't believe you let them twist you up like this. That you let them break us up! I've missed you so much. You broke my heart sneaking out like that. After all the time we spent together, how could you betray me like that? I've been losing my mind not knowing if you were even alive or dead."

Old, familiar guilt swirls in my chest. Queenie is still barking her head off, making it hard to think. I'm also worried about her bolting out of the front if she spies a bird in the bath. I don't want to close the door because I need Shane to understand that he's not welcome and needs to get the hell out right now. But I have to protect my girl first.

I huff and loop my fingers around her collar, walking her out back so she can wait in the garden. When I close the door and turn around, Shane has followed me into the kitchen. I know it's irrational, but I suddenly feel trapped. He's coming farther into the house rather than leaving.

"Aren't you going to apologize?" he asks.

Despite my fear, a laugh bursts out of me. "Apologize for escaping from you?"

His face drops and he looks so unbelievably hurt I almost doubt myself. It's interesting to see him now, like I'm looking at him through completely new eyes. I always thought he was so handsome, but there's a sharpness to his features that's clear to me now. A narrowness of his eyes and a meanness to his mouth.

He's the ugly one. Not Queenie.

"Escape? Miguel, how can you be so cruel?"

I wince at hearing my old name. I might have had it my whole life before I left him, but that person doesn't exist anymore.

He set that sweet boy's life on fire and almost burned him to the ground.

Dario is who rose from the ashes, stronger than ever before.

I don't feel strong, though, as Shane sinks into one of my new thrift store dining chairs. He shakes his head, resting his elbows on the matching table, and covers his mouth with one of his hands. Logically, I know it's all an act. But there's another part of my mind that reminds me he probably believes his own bullshit. He'll have himself convinced that I really am the one who hurt and betrayed him. That *he's* the victim here.

I swallow and try to hold onto my conviction. "You need to leave," I say again, but my voice shakes a little in spite of my best efforts. "We're not together anymore, Shane."

"And who's fault is THAT?" Shane explodes, rocketing to his feet and sending the chair flying backward onto the floor with a clatter.

There's the real Shane. It took no time at all for him to emerge, did it?

I flinch away from him, the urge to throw up washing through me for a moment before it passes. Queenie is barking nonstop outside, and my heart pangs for her distress. I made a promise to her that this home would be her sanctuary. That she'd never have to be afraid again.

Shane can't be allowed to ruin that. Not for her. And not for me.

But he's not done shouting.

"I did everything for you, Miguel, but it was never enough! I took care of you, provided for you, managed everything so you wouldn't have to worry. I *loved* you. I still do! But your poisonous family somehow managed to convince you that me being a good boyfriend was controlling. That I was *dangerous*." He scoffs, like nothing could be further from the truth.

All he does is remind me of just how dangerous he could be.

"You *hit* me," I snarl, my fists clenching.

He looks horrified. "I made a mistake—one *little* mistake —and you still can't bring yourself to forgive me? After everything we've been through?"

It's my turn to be horrified, but I'm certain my emotions are a thousand times more valid than his scripted performance.

"You think backhanding me was a *little mistake?* I could have had you charged with assault. Instead, I left. Why can't you accept that?"

He laughs hollowly. "I knew you'd be like this. In case you've forgotten, I would never have gotten that angry if you hadn't pushed me like you *always* do. Like you're doing right now! You push and *push* and then you wonder why I snapped."

"Then why are you even here if I'm so awful?" I yell at him.

His face softens. "Because you need me, Miguel. We were so good together. No one will ever love you like I do. I never stopped looking for you. Don't you want to know how I found you?"

I sneer, bile rising in my throat. I swallow it down, determined not to fall apart in front of him. "You found the photo I stupidly didn't get taken down from Instagram."

I curse myself. After all our excitement, I never even brought it up with Lochlan in the end. Things seemed so perfect. I didn't want to invite my past back in to hurt us any further.

Looks like it hunted me down anyway.

"I'm sure you researched the dog class," I continue, "then came sniffing around Redwood Bay until you could follow me home."

"You make it sound evil," Shane says with a wince. "I never stopped searching for you, Miguel. Hoping one day I could get you back in my arms again."

He bends down to pick up the chair, like he never came into my home like a bull in a china shop. But then he stands up and steps toward me, and something snaps.

"Stay back!" I bark loud enough to rival Queenie. Thankfully, Shane does pause. "You are in violation of your restraining order. You can't be within a hundred feet of me."

"Miguel, that's ridiculous—"

"*Stop saying my name!*" I scream, feeling like I'm about to blow. "You don't own me! I'm not yours! You are breaking the law, and you need to get out before I call 9-1-1."

"You invited me in!" Shane splutters.

"I absolutely did not," I counter.

A dark smirk tugs at his mouth. There he is again. The real Shane.

"What cop is going to believe you over me?" he asks.

For a second, my heart sinks. Time and space away from him has given me a new perspective of just how skilled a manipulator he is. What if officers come and he convinces them that we're simply having a disagreement, and I've become irrational and hysterical *as usual?*

But then it's like a lightbulb goes off in my head. The police will believe me over him, because I have *proof.*

As I was going to be at work all day, I switched the security system on before I left this morning. It's still on. The cameras are motion activated. I can go into the app and turn them on whenever I want, provided that the system is running. But otherwise, they won't record unless Queenie moves into view and sets them off.

Or I do.

They'll be recording right now.

A kind of calmness washes through me, and I take a nice deep breath as I fold my arms across my chest. "It's over, Shane. Don't come back here again. Don't try and contact me. We weren't good together, we were toxic.

Take my advice and find yourself a good therapist. Someone who will help you love yourself more, so you don't feel the need to bully someone else into loving you."

He looks aghast, and this time I don't think it's an act. "You've been blabbing to a fucking *shrink* about me? What have you told them?"

I sigh, feeling a tiny bit sorry for this messed-up man, but not anywhere close enough to forgive him. Of course he'd be more worried what some stranger he's never met thinks about him than acknowledging his ex-boyfriend is telling him to his face that he was abusive.

The fact is, though, that Shane might not be able to help his screwed-up ways. But that doesn't negate the fact that he traumatized me and physically assaulted me.

"My therapy sessions are about *me*, Shane," I tell him firmly. "No one else. They're about my life and how I want to live it."

"You always were selfish," he says scornfully. "Everything always *was* about you."

I almost ask, which is it? Does he want me to be talking about him in my session or not?

Then I realize that I wholeheartedly do not care.

"You need to leave now, or I really am going to call the cops," I say tiredly.

He moves so fast, I don't have time to react. In only a couple of strides, he's on me, seizing my elbow and giving me a shake. *"You* don't get to threaten *me!"* he snarls. Queenie is fully howling outside now. I can't help but whimper, terror racing through me.

Is he going to hit me again? Worse?

If I scream, will anyone hear me?

I've never felt so alone and afraid in my entire life.

Except in that moment, another sound joins the

cacophony. Amid the howling, whimpering and heavy breathing, I heard a tiny…yet determined…growl.

Shane and I both jerk our heads to look down at the same time to see Rocky with his teeth sunk into the bottom of Shane's jeans. I don't have time to process how this can be happening before Shane viciously tries to kick the Dalmatian puppy away.

"DON'T YOU HURT HIM!" I roar, twisting out of his grip and shoving him with everything I have. He staggers back in shock as Rocky lets go and hops away. He's not cowering, so I don't think he got hit. But he certainly starts howling, joining in with Queenie's song outside.

I scoop him into my arms, quieting him as he starts to lick my face. My frantic mind wonders if Queenie was loud enough to summon him all the way from Lochlan's house. But that's ridiculous.

Except that's the moment when Lochlan comes running into the kitchen, out of breath, and I wonder if Queenie's voice maybe *is* that powerful.

My heart erupts with relief. "Lochlan?" I cry. I hug Rocky tighter and realize that Queenie has stopped making a racket outside. Does she know that her other daddy is here now?

"Dario, are you all right?" Lochlan asks, stepping closer to me.

"Who the fuck is Dario?" Shane snaps, apparently recovered enough from mine and Rocky's counterattack against him. "Who the fuck are *you?*"

Lochlan folds his muscular arms, his T-shirt clinging to him like a second skin and leaving nothing to the imagination. Shane might be bigger than me, but that's not hard. Lochlan, however, *towers* over him.

"No need to ask who you are, asshole," Lochlan says with an arched eyebrow. "You're the douchebag who could only make himself feel like a man by wailing on his boyfriend. You need to get the fuck out of my town now, and don't let the door hit your ass on the way out." He tilts his head. "Or maybe do. I don't care."

Shane's expression has turned furious, and I'm ashamed that I can't stop myself from shrinking away just a little. "Oh," Shane says, wagging his finger like he's just about to get one over on Lochlan. "You're the guy from the photo! You and the mangy mutts." He looks between me and Lochlan, his eyes widening. "Who the hell do you think you are, homewrecker?"

"I told you, Shane, it's over!" I yell, feeling my backbone strengthen the longer Lochlan stands in front of me. "This is my home and the only one wrecking it is you!"

Shane sobs, and even my heartstrings twitch. *It's all an act,* I remind myself.

He's on a roll, though. "I've been worrying myself sick over where you are and if you were okay, Miguel. Only to find out that you've been *cheating* on me?"

Instinctively, I glance at Lochlan, immediately worried that he's going to believe Shane over me. But of course Lochlan's too smart for that. He just laughs and comes to wrap his arm around me as Rocky squirms in my arms, trying to lick both of us at the same time.

"Your lies won't work here, buddy," Lochlan says calmly. I press myself to his side, feeling as tall as the redwoods in this town. "You're not fooling anyone. You're just embarrassing yourself. Why don't you head on out now, while you still have some dignity?"

A muscle twitches in Shane's jaw, but he blinks and suddenly his eyes are wet, and his shoulders slumped in defeat. "Oh, Miguel. You've been brainwashed by this...*oaf.* I'll come back when you're alone so we can talk sensibly. Perhaps *I* should call the police and report a kidnapping."

"I'd like to see you try!" I cry, but Lochlan squeezes my shoulder and shakes his head.

"Let him go, baby. This pathetic little man isn't worth one more minute of your time. Trust me, he is never, *ever* coming back here again."

"Is that so?" Shane demands, spinning around and storming off to the front of the house. I break away from Lochlan and follow, wanting to make sure he really does finally leave my home. "Miguel is with me," Shane continues to rant, "and I will visit him anytime I fucking well please. Who's going to stop me? You?" He scoffs. "And what army?"

"You're right," Lochlan says calmly as I hurry after Shane to the door. "I don't have an army."

Shane steps outside and stops so suddenly that I practically run into him.

"I have a family," Lochlan says from behind us.

My jaw drops.

Out on the street, the entire One-Thirteen is parked right on my doorstep. The engine, the truck, and the ambulance, all just sitting there with their lights flashing blue and red all over my front yard.

Lochlan isn't on shift, so neither are the guys I know. Yet there they all are, leaning on the rigs or hanging off them in their civies. Other uniformed firefighters are mingled in the vehicles, and I assume that's the watch working right now. But then Sawyer sticks his head out of the engine's window with a shit-eating grin bright enough to power a warp core.

The horn blares so loudly, Rocky jumps out of my arms and goes running back to Lochlan.

"TOOT TOOT, MOTHERFUCKER!" Sawyer yells, giving me a wink.

My eyes sweep over the scene as Shane just gapes and Lochlan comes to rest his hand on my shoulder, Rocky sitting at our feet.

Sawyer's best friend, Anton, has a little girl on his shoulders who waves enthusiastically at us with a Barbie doll in her hand. Anton is glaring at Sawyer, presumably for dropping an F-bomb in front of his eight-year-old. But then he looks our way and salutes Lochlan and me.

Teddy is filming everything.

Del is standing close enough that I one hundred percent know that he's poised to leap into action should Lochlan need his help.

His paramedic partner, Yara, is walking around offering everyone cupcakes from a big Tupperware box that have got to be homemade.

Gene is holding hands with a woman who offers me the biggest, warmest smile as she cradles their baby on her hip and their other four kids brandish plastic light sabers at Shane.

Lieutenant Rico is watching the entire situation like a hawk.

Lili cracks her knuckles so loudly I can hear it from over here.

There's even a very fabulous-looking elderly lady who, despite the fact that it's the middle of a Tuesday afternoon, is dressed in a long, mauve cocktail gown and is dripping in diamonds. She holds a leash attached to an immaculately groomed shih tzu who's sitting at her feet, wagging their tail happily.

"Oh, what fun!" she announces to no one in particular.

A car door slams, yanking my attention to a white brunette woman striding away from a gleaming BMW toward my house. Captain Julian Valentine falls perfectly into step beside her. She looks to be in her early forties, sporting a nicely cut black suit and heeled boots that I automatically know she's not wearing because some man told her to, but because she enjoys men thinking she could step on their necks at any moment with them.

"Can anyone tell me what in the name of our lord and savior Ms. Chappell Roan is happening here?" she calls out, her voice not overly loud but clear as a bell.

"I-I have no fucking clue!" Shane calls back, indignation radiating from his vibrating body. "I came to visit my beloved boyfriend after a painful, enforced period of separation. Then this barbarian comes thundering into the house, chasing me outside, where I found all these delinquents. Who the hell are *you?*"

The brunette smiles, like a kindergarten teacher might indulge a toddler having a tantrum. She casually swipes the corner of her blazer aside, revealing a police badge that glimmers in the bright California sunshine.

"Captain Lucy Padilla," she says cheerfully as she walks up my garden path. "My new bestie Julian here told me there were reports of a domestic abuser breaking into this residence and terrorizing his former boyfriend. Would that be you, sir?"

Shane splutters like a pot about to boil over. "That's insane!"

"Actually," Lochlan pipes up. I glance over and see his huge grin. "There are doggy cams all over the house that have been recording the whole thing." He looks down at me and softens. "When the motion cameras activated, I checked in thinking I'd just see Queenie getting some lunch. When I saw some strange asshole making you upset, I knew exactly who it had to be. I promise, I wasn't snooping on you."

My heart melts all the way down to my toes. "I know you wouldn't. Thank you. My hero."

Shane is still fuming and spitting feathers. "You can't film me without my permission!"

"You did barge into my house and refuse to leave," I point out.

"Okay, mister," Captain Padilla says, a hint of amusement in her words as she reaches out to place her hand on Shane's back. "How about we discuss this further down at the station?"

"Are you arresting me?" he demands, jerking away from her touch.

She blinks once, her smile not faltering. "No. I'm asking you to come chat with me. If you don't want to do that, though, *then* I can arrest you."

Casually, she pulls her cuffs out of her back pocket. It's subtle, but I can feel Rico and Del edge just a fraction closer to us.

And then Shane snaps his head down to look at his foot.

Probably because Rocky has chosen that moment to cock his leg and pee all over Shane's shoe.

"Oh my fucking *god!*" he shrieks, jumping away like he's been scolded.

Lochlan drops his head back and laughs. "*Good* boy, Rocky," is all he says to his dog when he looks back down. But then he directs his attention back at Shane. "There goes that dignity, huh?"

Shane looks like his brain is giving him the '404 file not found' screen. As if he's sleepwalking, Captain Padilla starts steering him away from my house toward her car.

"That's what you get for messing with the One-Thirteen!" Lili crows as Shane walks past. Then suddenly all of the team are shouting and clapping and jeering.

"You come for one of us, you come for us ALL!" Sawyer yells, blasting the engine horn again.

"You belong in jail!" Yara shrieks before rushing over and insisting Padilla take a couple of cupcakes.

Anton's daughter waves from atop his shoulders. "Bye bye, grumpy man! Choose kindness next time!"

I don't even know when I start crying. I just know that at some point between all the applause and Shane being driven off in Padilla's car, I start sobbing against Lochlan's chest, not sure when I'm going to be able to stop.

"Oh, baby!" Lochlan cries in alarm, hugging me tightly. "It's okay. He's gone now."

"I know it's okay," I manage to tell him back between sniffles.

I don't care one bit about Shane. He really is gone, and I know in my bones that he's never coming back.

I'm crying because this morning I woke up with the knowledge that I now have a boyfriend.

What I didn't fully realize is said boyfriend comes with a whole found family ready to go into battle for *his* boyfriend, who they barely even know. But as I look around at them through tear drenched lashes, I know that they mean it, and I love them for it.

I love Lochlan even more.

Now I just need to work up the guts to tell him that.

CHAPTER 23

Lochlan

Watching Dario cry like this is the worst feeling ever. Worse than standing on one of Orson's Legos.

Thank god I checked the security camera app.

I like to keep half an eye on Queenie when Dario's in the office to put his mind at ease. He does the same when I leave Rocky at the station when we go on a call. But I know both of us are aware of respecting each other's privacy, so I never linger for too long. Nine times out of ten, I just find myself watching Queenie plodding over to her water bowl and back.

But not today.

When I first got a notification, I just assumed Dario had changed his mind and come home to walk Queenie after all and would be turning the cameras off momentarily. Perhaps his day had turned out to be less busy than he'd thought? But the second time I looked, I knew something was really wrong.

The other guy wasn't armed or anything, so I didn't think Dario was being robbed. But his body language was totally off, and within moments, it was crystal clear what was going on.

I still don't know how, but Shane found Dario.

There was no way in hell I was going to let him face that alone.

I never even meant to invite anyone else along to the 'Fuck Off Back To Where You Came From' party. I just dropped a message in our group chat saying that it looked like Dario's violent ex was in his house and, unless anyone was gonna stop me, I was off to do something about it.

It turns out nobody was interested in stopping me. They all dropped whatever they were doing and were across town in minutes. Captain Valentine didn't just call the new police captain. He also contacted the current One-Thirteen watch to see if they wanted to lend a hand if they weren't on a call.

He might come across as all mature and boss-like. But that petty bitch loves some good dramatics as much as the rest of us, if not more.

I was almost the first to arrive on the scene. Rico just beat me to it. So while Rocky ran inside to defend his other daddy, my lieutenant held me up for a few seconds, warning me to be careful and suggesting we wait for the police. We didn't know if Shane was still concealing a weapon, after all.

But wild hogs couldn't have kept me from running to my boyfriend's side, and I got in there as soon as I convinced Rico that I wouldn't do anything dumb. We both knew the chances of my actually keeping that promise were low. However, he probably sensed that unless he was going to physically restrain me, I wasn't gonna wait outside a second longer.

My natural instinct is probably always gonna be to protect the people I love, especially Dario. Not because he can't take care of himself, but because he has the biggest, most precious piece of my heart.

However, as soon as I stumbled into that kitchen, I could tell that Dario was holding his own. I hadn't been able to watch the feed as much as I would have liked when I was driving, so I wasn't sure what state I'd find them in.

I was terrified I might not find them there at all.

I never push Dario to talk about his time with Shane any more than he feels able to. But it's clear to me that if he hadn't escaped when he did, Shane would have done everything in his power to lock him away so he could live forever under his thumb. I don't think it was unreasonable to panic that Shane would be capable of kidnapping.

Hearing him accuse me of the very same thing made my blood boil. I understood why Dario got upset over that. But I knew that when Shane tried to walk out that door, he was going to be met by some of my best friends who were going to be just as unhappy to see him as me.

I didn't expect the whole damn squadron and then the cavalry to boot.

Neither did Dario, I'm sure. I hold him tightly as he clings to me, sobbing against my chest. He was so brave and strong, facing down his abuser when he thought he was all alone. But I don't blame him for letting it all out now.

"It's okay, baby," I murmur and kiss his hair. "I've got you." After a few more minutes, he starts to calm.

The One-Thirteen on duty obviously get a real call and has to hightail it, but not before they turf Sawyer out of the rig despite his requests to pull the horn again.

This is why he's not allowed to ride up front. Ever.

But with the men and women in uniform gone and Shane in custody on his way to the station, the atmosphere on the sidewalk becomes more relaxed. Some of Dario's neighbors have come out and are asking what happened. Luckily, I can tell that Rico and Del are answering their questions diplomatically to respect Dario's privacy as much as we can after such a public scene.

Dario takes a deep breath, wipes his face, and I pull a

tissue from my pocket to blow his nose. I always have stuff on me like that now because of Rocky. My sister taught me the value of good 'Mary Poppins' pockets after she had Orson.

Thinking of Rocky reminds me of our other loyal pup. "Where's Queenie?" I ask once Dario seems a little more composed.

"I put her out back so she'd be safe," he says. "I was worried Shane might try and kick her." His face crumples again. "He tried to kick Rocky. Lochlan, I'm so sorry—"

"Hey, hey, Rocky's fine," I assure him, pulling him back into a hug before he can spiral again. "I'll double check him later, but he's right here, wagging his tail."

"He bit Shane's jeans," Dario mumbles into my T-shirt.

I give a good belly laugh. "That's my boy," I say fondly.

Captain Valentine is approaching, and we share a nod as he reaches us. "Hey, Cap," I say so Dario knows we're not by ourselves anymore.

Indeed, he peeks his head up and sniffs. "Captain Valentine," he says in awe. "Thank you so much. You don't know what it meant to walk out here and realize you'd all come to help. I wish you didn't have to, but—"

"Ahh, we're all family here, son," Cap says, shaking his head. "Helping each other is what we do. Give it a couple of weeks, I'm sure someone will turn around and ask for a hand moving a couch."

"I'm not sure about that," Dario says with a cute little frown. "But if anyone needs their antivirus software updated, give me a shout."

Cap laughs and I hug Dario even closer to me.

"Our new police captain has asked you to come down to the station and give a statement, if that's all right?" Cap raises his eyebrows at Dario, who looks at me.

"Can Lochlan come with us?"

Cap grins. "Of course. I might have to draw the line at Rocky, though."

"He can stay here with Queenie," I suggest. "Shall we go rescue her from the yard and lock up?"

Dario nods. "I'll need to tell work where I am," he says glumly. "I hope I'm not in trouble."

Captain narrows his eyes. "If there's any trouble, you tell them to come talk to me."

As it turns out, Dario's manager is rightly horrified when he explains he's had a home invasion. I don't blame Dario for skipping over the part where it was his psycho ex who broke in. Knowing Dario, he won't want his colleagues to walk around on eggshells for him or treat him with kiddie gloves.

Luckily, his manager recognizes that going to the police is more important than getting back to the office. He promises to push some important meeting back, and tells Dario he can work from home the rest of the week.

While he's on the phone, I let Queenie inside. She'd been sitting at the back door whimpering, clearly keen to come in and check that Dario was okay. I'd heard her howling when I first gotten out of my truck, but she quietened down once I got inside and added my voice to the altercation. I guess she knows that I will never, ever let anything bad happen to her daddy.

As Dario closes the call, he stills for a second, looking at the phone in his hands. "So I guess you heard that my name's really Miguel."

That isn't what I'd been expecting him to say. "Oh, I knew that after I met your family," I said lightly. "A few of them had too many margaritas to keep it straight. But I figured you wanted to be called whatever you like most. Do you want to go back to Miguel if Shane's no longer a threat?"

He scoffs. "Unless he gets some serious help, he'll probably always be a threat to someone, sadly. I don't know if he'll get charged with anything but…I think you guys might have scared the crap out of him enough that he won't come back and bother me."

I step closer and wrap my arms around him, loving how he melts into my embrace. "That was the intention," I admit. "I wanted to show him that you don't just have one family looking after you now. You have three."

"Three?" he yelps, looking up at me in confusion. But it's obvious to me.

"Well, yeah. You already have your awesome family, and now you've got both of mine, too." I wink at him. "My mom and sister might disown me if I don't bring you over to meet them soon."

He swallows and searches my face for a moment. "This feels like a dream."

I lean down to kiss him. "If it's a dream, then I never want to wake up, baby. Now, come on. The sooner we go give your statement, the sooner we can get you back home and crash."

He nods and lets me lead him out of the house again, securing the dogs behind the door as we go. "We'll be back soon!" Dario calls through the wood to them.

I can see Gene and his horde have left, which is understandable. I can barely manage with one dog, yet he and his wife have five small human beings to contend with. But it looks like everyone else has stayed, and they all turn to look at us as we walk down the path, heading for my truck. No way I'm letting Dario drive right now. He needs to rest.

"Are you all right?" Del asks as we approach.

"That asshole got what was coming to him," Lili adds with savage satisfaction.

Rico nods. "He had no idea who he came to mess with. If you ever hear a peep from him again, you know we've got your back."

Dario looks around them all with wide, glassy eyes. "I don't know how to thank you all. You don't even know me."

"Psh," Yara says, skipping over to him. "Sure we do. You're Beast's boyfriend. Here, take a couple of these. You need the sugar."

"Why *do* they call you that?" Dario asks as he helps himself to two of Yara's chocolate and banana frosted cupcakes, handing me one.

"What, Beast?" I ask and he nods. "Because my name Bell with an 'e' on the end means 'beautiful' in French, so it's like the fairytale, Beauty and the Beast." I feel super proud to know a smart thing like that, even when Lili launches herself against my side and gives me a noogie.

"Plus, it would be ridiculous to call this big, dumb lug a pretty name like 'Bell,' huh?"

Dario turns to look at me with such a soft expression. "I think he's the smartest person I've ever met."

I know he doesn't really mean that. But hearing him say it still makes me all fuzzy inside anyway. I tune out as Lili, Teddy and Sawyer continue to rip on me. I don't mind it. "Bye, guys!" I call out, letting them know that they can keep joking among themselves if they like. All that matters to me now is how Dario's hand slips against mine, and we walk the rest of the way down the sidewalk to my truck.

Waiting beside it and looking like the Queen of England is Mrs. Bloom with Miss Margot Fonteyn. "So here's the young man you've been hiding away from me?" she says instead of something normal like 'hello.' I roll my eyes, but I'm still smiling.

"Dario, this is the One-Thirteen's neighbor, Mrs. Bloom and her dog, Margot. Mrs. Bloom, I'd like to introduce you to Dario Garcia-Perez—my boyfriend."

Maybe she was trying to pretend like she was annoyed with me, but she can't stop the big smile that breaks free as she eagerly waves Dario over to her for a hug. "Sylvia, please. Aren't you handsome? No wonder that horrid young man was trying to get you back. But I daresay you've gotten yourself a considerable upgrade with Mr. Bell, here."

I try not to blush. "Aww, thanks, Mrs. B."

She shoos me off, but she's still smiling. "Mr. Garcia-Perez, I insist that you come join me and Margot Fonteyn for dinner sometime next week. Perhaps when this one is off fetching cats out of trees? We can have a good old gossip."

Dario looks a bit taken aback, but he still beams. "I'd love that. Thank you, Mrs. Bloom."

"Sylvia," she corrects.

He lets out a little chuckle. "Sylvia," he agrees.

Eventually, we make it into my truck, and I start driving us to the police station. I keep my music low so it's not too quiet, but I also don't bug Dario with silly chit-chat, either. I'm guessing he might need some time to just sit with his thoughts.

It's not a long drive. Nowhere in this town really is. But a minute or so before we reach our destination, he speaks.

"Dario." I glance over at him and he nods. "Miguel isn't who I am anymore. I want to be Dario."

I thread our hands together. "You already are Dario," I assure him. "My boyfriend, the badass."

He laughs, but I mean it.

He's the bravest man I've ever met, and I'm proud to call him mine.

CHAPTER 24

Dario

THERE'S A FAT AND CHEERFUL LITTLE SANTA SITTING ON THE front desk when we arrive, holding a sign that reads 'Welcome to the North Pole!'. The sergeant greets us warmly and informs the captain over the phone that we've arrived.

Padilla meets us only a couple of minutes later. "Thank you so much for coming in, Dario," she says warmly as she shakes my hand. "Am I okay to call you Dario?"

I glance knowingly at Lochlan, who gives me an encouraging grin.

"That would be perfect, thank you."

She nods and turns to Lochlan. "And this is…?"

"Lochlan Bell," he says quickly, also accepting her hand. "Dario's boyfriend."

The shock of hearing him say that is starting to fade, but I wonder if there will ever come a time where it feels totally natural to me that such a gorgeous, kind, amazing man is proud to stand up and tell whoever will listen that he's my boyfriend. That I'm his.

Possibly not, but hopefully that means I'll never take how wonderful that fact is for granted.

They finish their shake, and Padilla beckons for us to follow her. "So, you're pretty new in town as well, huh?" she asks me as we head into a room with a table that could technically fit eight people around it, judging by the chairs. But it doesn't feel huge with just the three of us claiming one end. Lochlan and I sit, but she gestures to the coffee pot. "Can I get you something?"

"Yes, please," Lochlan says emphatically, but I shake my head.

"Um, have you got any herbal tea or anything? If not, water's just fine." I feel like I need something to calm my nerves right now, not wake them up.

"We have plenty of tea," she assures me, then sets about pouring two coffees and makes something fruity for me.

Lochlan squeezes my thigh and leans closer to whisper in my ear. "Look at you, asking for what you need. I'm so proud of you, baby."

I'm sure I blush, but I don't say anything back, afraid I might start crying if I do. Lochlan knows I'm listening to him, though.

"Thank you," I tell Padilla as she hands us our drinks. "And yes, to answer your earlier question, I've only been in Redwood Bay about three months."

"Three weeks," she says, jabbing her thumb toward her chest. "I was in a little place just outside of Seattle before this. But my folks are here, and they aren't getting any younger, and I just needed some damn sunshine, you know? When a promotion opportunity popped up for me, it seemed like fate. How about you?"

I know she's trying to get the measure of me. I don't blame her. Shane knows how to spin some wild lies. So I'm happy to chat for a while if it means the captain feels she can trust me.

"Uh, similar. It was the first job I got offered close to my family, so I went for it. I had to get out of Arizona."

"Ah," Padilla says knowingly. She clicks a pen and flips to a fresh page in her notebook. "And away from the charming gentleman who forced his way into your home today, I'm assuming? Why don't we start from the beginning. Tell me everything you can."

So that's exactly what I do. It's painful, and I'm afraid that every word I say could be the thing that makes her snap and accuse me of lying about who's the real victim between me and Shane. But Lochlan never lets go of my hand, giving me strength. Even when I tell parts of my story that make me cringe at how stupid and weak I was with Shane. In fact, he actually leans in and kisses my cheek just when I think I'm too ashamed to go on.

So I do go on. I describe how the last straw was Shane hitting me, how my amazing family didn't judge me, they just worked out the best plan to get me out of there. Then my name change, the restraining order, and finally moving here.

"I think that's all I need for now," Padilla assures me. "We'll be in touch with the Arizona PD to corroborate their involvement and get copies of their files. We'll need the footage from your home security system as well."

"Of course," I say as we all rise to our feet. I feel like my legs are made of Jell-O and that I could sleep for a week. But I know I just need to hold on a little longer, then I can go home.

With Lochlan.

"Do you think you have enough evidence to convict him?" he asks Padilla.

"I'm afraid I can never give guarantees," she says diplomatically as she begins escorting us toward the front of the precinct. "But I think the video footage combined with the witness reports are a solid starting point. Don't worry, Dario.

I'm going to have my ADA throw the whole book at him. Epilogue and all."

I smile tentatively, scared to get my hopes up. But I do know one thing for sure, and that's the last time I escaped Shane I felt so alone.

Now I have more families than I know what to do with.

"Thank you for coming in," Padilla says as we reach the front desk.

I shake my head. "Thank you for listening to me. For making me feel heard."

Her expression is sympathetic. "No matter what anyone might have told you in the past, you're important. I personally have your back now, kiddo. You have my number, call me anytime." She narrows her eyes. "Unless the Seahawks are playing. Then I might have to send you to voicemail." We all laugh lightly as she bats my arm with my own case file. "Seriously, take care. And try and stay out of trouble."

"I'll make sure of that, ma'am," Lochlan says earnestly. "Although, I'm not sure how much trouble there's going to be in Redwood Bay."

She scoffs and shakes her head. "That's what I thought about Pine Cove. I swear, sometimes small towns are crazier than big cities."

With a parting wink, she heads back into the belly of the precinct.

Lochlan and I both sigh at the same time, then chuckle weakly at each other. "Let's get you back to the rebel base," he says.

"Best plan I've heard all day, Commander," I tell him.

———

"Tell me what you need."

I blink and look at Lochlan. We're standing in my

entrance hall. The dogs are sitting at our feet, but they're just gently wagging their tails. I think they can both sense that I'm operating on low power mode, trying to conserve all the energy I can. I'm not sure I really remember the drive back from the police station.

"Uhh," I say as I look around what I can see of my house from here. I'm not sure what sparks the memory, but I suddenly slip my hand into my back pocket, sagging in relief when my fingers wrap around the flash drive. It would be a terrible sort of irony if I lost it after that talk I had with myself earlier about not losing it. "I should probably put this somewhere very safe."

"In your office?" Lochlan asks.

I nod, and he gently steers me there where I slot it back into the USB port. It'll be safe there with the door closed, especially with so many miniature intergalactic crews watching over it.

Lochlan then leads me back down into the kitchen where he opens the fridge. "Ah, perfect." He pulls out one of the protein shakes I have in case of emergencies where I'm in the zone and don't want to pause work to make a proper meal. It's a banana one as well, my favorite. I thank my past self for his forethought.

"What about you?" I murmur as he cracks the lid and presses it into my hand.

"I had a big lunch, I'm fine," he says.

I'm worried he's not being honest because he doesn't want to take the focus off me right now, and almost start to feel guilty. But then I remember that he's a grown adult and I trust him to look after himself. If he says he's okay for now, I believe him.

After I gulp down as much of the drink as I can stomach, Lochlan puts the lid back on, then brings it with us into my bedroom, placing it on my nightstand. The dogs haven't even followed us, so he has no objections when he closes the door. Wordlessly, he then crosses the room to me again where he begins gently taking my clothes off until I'm just in my briefs. He strips back the covers and guides me to lie down before tucking me in.

"Do you want company or to be alone?"

"Company," I reply immediately. "But…thank you for asking. That's so thoughtful of you."

"Of course, baby," he says, quickly stripping down to his underwear as well. "I'm here to give you whatever you need right now."

As he also climbs under the duvet, I roll to greet him, and we slide naturally into each other's arms. "You," I whimper, my emotions bubbling to the surface once more. "I just need you, Lochlan."

His kisses feel like heavenly clouds as his lips gently meet mine over and over again. He threads his fingers through my hair, humming happily. My chest aches with how much he means to me. How he probably doesn't even know how his actions today have gone such a long way to restoring my faith in humanity. It's almost as if I can feel the tough scars around my heart softening and fading.

All because of one man and the community he's a part of.

If I lose him because I was too scared to take a leap of faith, I'll regret it for the rest of my life.

Drawing back, I gaze into his eyes. He brushes my hair from my forehead and smiles sweetly. "What, baby?"

It's on the tip of my tongue to chicken out at the last second, but I must be brave.

"I love you," I say in a rush, hoping I haven't ruined everything. He was the one determined to speed things up. Yet there's always a chance…

Except of course there isn't. His face splits into a beaming grin and his eyes sparkle. "Oh, hell yeah! I think I fell in love with you the moment we met, you know? I just didn't realize it for ages. You've been my favorite person since that day in the park where my terrible son jumped all over you and I thought you were going to hate me."

"I could never hate you," I say, horrified by the idea. But he just laughs.

"I feel the same." He caresses the side of my face with such a feather-light touch, it sends shivers throughout my body. "I love you so much, Dario. Thank you for trusting me with your heart."

We begin kissing again, slowly at first, luxuriating in just being close with one another. But the heat starts creeping in, like a fire growing in my belly, and before long I'm moaning into his mouth.

"Need you," I mumble against his lips, scrabbling with the waistband of his briefs.

"Shh," he soothes me, rolling us so I'm on my back and he's hovering over me. "Is this okay? I want to take care of you."

This position used to make me feel trapped and worthless. But not with Lochlan. He knows that topping is how I feel good. But being under him right now just makes me feel cherished.

I nod, and he kisses my mouth some more. However, soon he's breaking off and reaching into my nightstand.

"Wait," I say, touching his arm as he withdraws the condoms and lube. "I…if you wanted…my test results are all negative."

It seems to take him a second to process what I'm saying, but then he beams at me. "You wanna go bareback?"

"We'll still need lube," I say quickly. "But…yeah, if you know your status and that's something you'd want?"

He drops the condom box back in the drawer as he leans down to kiss me hard. "I definitely want to feel everything with you, gorgeous. And we have regular health checks at work. I'm ready for lift-off."

I giggle at his silly sci-fi reference in the middle of a safe-sex talk, but also I think some of my relief is finally leaking out.

"Your departure is approved, pilot," I murmur before kissing him again.

I lay like a pillow princess as Lochlan gets our underwear off, then he straddles me for more kisses as he lubes up his fingers and starts stretching out his hole. I would have been fine just to frot after the day I've had. But if he wants to put the effort in to fuck, that feels pretty damn romantic to me in this moment.

He doesn't spend too much time on prep. It's not necessary as we've been at it a lot this past week and I'm not huge anyway. But I think right now we're both too desperate to be close more than anything else. Extra lube does most of the heavy lifting as he spears himself on my hard dick and starts lowering his way down.

"I love watching you," I whisper, running my hands over his damp chest as he sinks deeper. "I love seeing what I do to you."

He kisses my lips and grins. "I love putting on a show for you, baby. You feel so perfect. You know just how to treat me right."

It's simple praise, but his adoring words seep through my bones like syrup. "Tell me I'm good," I utter, tears leaking from my closed eyes.

"Dario, my baby," Lochlan says with a happy sigh. "You are the most perfect boyfriend in the whole wide world. I can't believe I'm lucky enough to call you mine. You're so good for me. So good *to* me. Everything about you is wonderful, but I know there's still so much cool stuff to discover. Thank you for being mine, sweetheart. Look at me?"

I take a breath and peel my eyes open. He smiles down at me, and I realize he's bottomed out already.

"I love you," he says earnestly, his gaze feeling like it's reaching into my soul. He rolls his hips and we both moan and gasp. "I love you, Dario. I love you so much."

"I love you, Lochlan," I tell him, a sob catching in my chest. "I love you, baby."

There isn't much talking after that. Lochlan does pretty much all the work as he cradles me and rams himself again and again on my cock. Neither of us last long, but I think he knows without me saying anything that this time I don't want to tease or draw anything out. I want to spill my seed inside him and mark him as mine.

He looks so stunning as he rocks on top of me and thrusts his huge dick through his closed fist. When he shoots all over me, I come inside him within seconds, feeling like my soul flies from my body.

I'm not sure how long we lie in a heap, panting and trembling together. When he eases himself off me, I moan, but don't have the energy to even lift a pinky let alone go after him. He returns soon enough, however, and I guess he might have cleaned himself up in the bathroom. He's got a warm washcloth that he runs over my junk and my chest so I'm not sticky. Then he dries me with a couple of tissues before fetching the protein shake I'd forgotten all about.

"Can you drink a little more for me?" he asks kindly.

When I nod, he helps me to sit up a bit and even helps me keep the bottle steady as I gulp a few mouthfuls down. After I've had enough, he puts it back on the nightstand, then cuddles up behind me as the big spoon, the duvet just heavy enough over us to feel comforting instead of suffocating.

It's like we're in a nest or a womb, so safe from the outside world as we regain our strength to rise from the ashes once again. Just before I slip into the warm darkness of sleep, I entwine our fingers and press our hands to my chest.

"My love," I murmur.

"My everything," he whispers as he nuzzles my neck.

I used to think that love was a weapon used only to control and tear down and punish.

I never knew it could be freedom itself. That it could lift you as high as the tallest redwood trees into the blue skies beyond.

Now I know what love truly is, I'm never going to let it go.

Epilogue

Seven Months Later
Lochlan

I didn't realize that Dario's back yard—sorry, *our* back yard—could fit so many people. I thought some of them would at least hang out in the kitchen, but apparently, they all need to be near the barbecue.

To be fair, the food is so amazing, I can't blame them. Dario and I have provided the usual burgers and sausages as well as a bunch of salads, but he also marinaded a metric ton of chicken in some kind of spicy orange juice and tomato sauce that is going down like a storm. Lili is also fighting him for space on the grill with her Korean barbecue ribs. I've already eaten myself silly and I still want more of everything.

But that's what holidays like the Fourth of July are all about, right? Good food and good people. What more could you want?

Well, the cold beer in my hand is also appreciated, as is the punch bowl of Tia Gaby's margarita that she's had to top up twice now. Lucky that most people don't live far away, but I can already tell that Uber is going to be getting a lot of business from this house tonight.

Our house.

Maybe I moved in a little fast, but fuck it. Dario and I were spending all our time together anyway. It didn't make sense for me to keep paying rent on my apartment when his place was three times the size. Or for Dario to buy more furniture when I had what he needed. Not to mention the yard we're standing in that Rocky loves.

He was getting too big to stay cooped up in my old digs as well. He was such a cute puppy, but I kinda forgot how huge adult Dalmatians are.

Right now, he and Queenie are happily trotting around, scamming as many people as possible for tidbits of food, or just plain stealing leftovers off unattended plates. It's pointless to try and stop them. We can balance it out by not giving them their regular dinner tonight and then hoping they don't decide to throw up on our bed.

I've come to realize that's what happiness is. Messy. Nothing is ever perfect, but when a guy like me is blessed with so much love in every corner of his life, that feels as close to perfection as possible in my book.

Following Rocky and Queenie around is Clover, who failed to become a guide dog when she refused to leave Zoe's side during her recovery. Looking at our former teacher now as she flirts with Yara, you'd never know that Zoe almost didn't make it out from under that rogue wagon wheel. But she's back to a hundred percent now, and Dario and I have actually become good friends with her.

My sister is sitting in one of the chairs, holding my brand-new sleeping niece and showing her off to anyone who's interested, which is most everybody. She's obviously tired as all hell, but Greg is running around tending to her every need, and I think she's enjoying that big time.

Orson is running around with Anton's girl, Rebecca, while Anton and Sawyer challenge a couple of Dario's tios at Uno. Tia Gaby is animatedly talking surfing with Rico. Mrs. Bloom is enchanting several of Dario's second cousins as Margot performs pretty tricks for them. Teddy is in charge of the playlist, but Cap keeps winding him up by sneaking over to the laptop and switching in Jimi Hendrix songs.

My favorite sight, though, is my mom and Dario's mom huddling in the corner with margaritas that never seem to run out, gossiping like schoolgirls.

This is what life is about. It doesn't matter what's in my bank account. I feel like the richest man alive.

I'm also celebrating something other than the national holiday. Well, technically *we're* celebrating. But I have a feeling Dario doesn't realize that.

Grinning to myself, I weave my way through the throng toward the barbecue, loving the way Dario's face lights up when he sees me. Even after all this time, it's like he still can't believe I'm with him.

When any idiot can see I'm the one who hit the jackpot here.

"Hey," I say warmly to both my boyfriend and my best friend. "Can I borrow Dario for a minute?"

Lili salutes me with her beer bottle. "I'll make sure nothing explodes."

"It's mostly all done now anyway," Dario says a little breathlessly as he wipes his hands on a dishcloth. "Do you think everyone's having a good time?"

I scoff. "They're having a *blast*. Don't worry, baby. Come on. I've got something to show you."

He frowns but follows me back into the coolness of the house and up to our bedroom where we can have a little peace and quiet. "Lochlan," Dario says firmly. "We are not having sex while everyone we've ever met is downstairs."

I burst out laughing. "Okay, well, that's definitely *not* everyone we've ever met. We can save that for our wedding day, yeah?"

Dario stills and I curse myself for putting my foot in my mouth. Even after everything, I know Dario still needs to take things a little slow. I wouldn't propose to him.

Yet.

Instead, I quickly fish out the picture frame I wrapped earlier and hid in my sock drawer. "I got you a little something."

He seems relieved it's not a ring box, which I'm glad about. Even if I have to wait twenty years, I know I'm going to marry this amazing man. But only when he's ready. When he finally stops waiting for the other shoe to drop and for me to realize I'm made some kind of terrible mistake.

That's never going to happen. So in the meantime, I will do all I can to convince him that I love him with everything I have.

"What's this?" he asks.

I laugh, but not unkindly. "That's kinda the point of wrapping it. So you can find out what's inside after opening it."

He rolls his eyes and snorts. "I meant why have you got me a present, dumbass?"

I huff and cross my arms. "How about you open it and stop ruining all my fun, loser?"

It's funny how a little banter does him good. When we first met, he wouldn't have found that funny. But we both know now with our whole chests that I'm not dumb in the ways it counts the most, and he's the coolest person I know.

He blushes and starts sliding his finger under the tape holding the paper together. The pattern has little green men and flying saucers on it, and I know he's enjoying that as he carefully reveals my gift.

"Oh," he says softly.

It's the picture Zoe put on Instagram of us. I know it caused a lot of trouble at the time, but ultimately, it was for the best. It flushed Shane out into the open and that asshole is currently doing two years for assault and stalking. I doubt he'll serve all of it. I might not have known him long at all, but it was enough to tell what a master manipulator he is. All I care about, though, is I think he got the message that if he ever comes back to Redwood Bay, he's going to be met by a world of hurt.

Dario didn't even tell me about the photo for ages. Eventually, he confessed that he felt like he brought Shane's return on himself by not asking Zoe to take it down straight away. Me pointing out that Zoe couldn't have done that anyway, as she was too busy trying not to die, knocked some sense into him extremely quickly.

I know that he's been working really hard with his therapist to stop blaming himself for the hell Shane put him through. But when he said he didn't ask Zoe to remove the photo because he loved it so much and wanted to talk to me about it first, I knew it was a big deal.

"Today is our eight-month anniversary," I tell him.

He frowns. "Of when we got together? You should have said something! I would have got you a gift, too!"

I shake my head and place my hands over his, cradling the photo frame between us. "You're my gift every day, baby. But no, not when we got together. It's the anniversary of the moment I saw you in that park. It's the anniversary of when the rest of my life began. I love this picture as much as you do. I don't want you to see guilt or failure when you look at it because none of what happened was your fault. I want you to remember your joy as well as mine. I want to hang it up and look at it every day. Because life isn't perfect. We're going to make mistakes and have to deal with bullshit that's not either of our fault. But we'll be okay because we'll face all that together."

"With Queenie and Rocky, too," he says with a sniffle. His eyes are wet as he looks at me, but also brimming with the love I know he feels for me.

"Of course," I tell him as I pull him into a hug. "Our little family of four. I'd fly to the moon and back for you guys. I'd travel across space and time just to keep you in my arms."

"Nerd," he says, making us both laugh because it's true. "I'd defy the Empire for you."

"That's because you're the bravest man I've ever met," I tell him softly.

We stay like that until we have to go back downstairs and host again. But as much as I treasure our time alone, I know we'll have plenty of that in the weeks, months, and years to come. This is the first time all of our favorite people have come together in one place, and although I'm sure it won't be the last, I want to appreciate it today while it lasts.

Family isn't just who you share blood with. Sometimes, those people are no family at all. Sometimes, family is a stranger you happen to meet in a park one day. Sometimes, it's a four-legged friend you've rescued and promised to take care of for the rest of their lives.

No, family isn't just blood. It's who you let into your heart. The people ready and waiting to swoop in and save the day just when you need them the most.

They're the real heroes. And my boyfriend and I are blessed to have the best of the best by our side.

Now and forever.

———

Thank you so much for reading Dario and Lochlan's story! Next up in **Redwood Bay Fire**, we have Zahir 'Del'

Delacroix, our charming paramedic, and the man who broke his heart right out of high school, Colton Ross. If you don't want to miss out on their second chance romance, pre-order **From the Ashes** today!

Turn the page to discover box sets of more heartwarming small town and found family series from HJ Welch, and contemporary fairy tale adaptations from Helen Juliet.

Thank you to my team!

Cover Designer: Jacqueline Sweet

Editor: Meg Cooper

Love, Support & Inspiration: Ed, AK, Rena, Charlie, Sarah, Hubby & our kitty cats

boyfriend Dair when he gets home from work. Hold on to your horses, Marine!

———

Troubled Waters

Bodyguard Scout Duffy doesn't know what's worse: the fact that his scorching one-night-stand, Emery Klein, is his bratty new client, or the fact that he doesn't even remember Scout. But Emery's life is in danger thanks to his out and proud charity work, and once he finally recognizes Scout, their chemistry in undeniable.

———

Homeward Bound

Swift Coal just found out he's a father, and his daughter (and her cranky cat) are coming to stay. His best friend's younger brother, Micha Perkins, has nowhere to go and a wrongfully tattered reputation. He's relieved when Swift asks him to be a live-in babysitter. He just has to hide his lifelong crush. Easy, because Swift is straight—right?

———

Bright Horizon

With sixteen years between them, baker Ben Turner and lawyer Elias Solomon have no idea their crush is mutual. But when Ben inherits his long-lost family's estate and becomes an overnight millionaire, Elias swears to protect the innocent younger man from the vultures circling him. To unravel the mystery of the inheritance, they must go to England to confront Ben's estranged relatives…and their feelings for each other.

———

Crossed Paths

Raj Bhat is done living in the shadows. It's time for him to take charge of his own destiny and tell the man he's fallen for how he really feels.

———

Midnight Sky

It's the night before New Year's Eve. Taylan Demir is all alone, and he's just lost his dog. Except when his handsome customer, Hudson Perkins, comes to his rescue, Taylan doesn't just get his dog back. He's suddenly got a hot date, and maybe someone to kiss when the clock strikes midnight.

———

Memory Lane

Angel Shields saved Jay Coal's life in high school, and Jay has secretly loved his straight best friend ever since. Now Angel's back in town with amnesia after a suspicious work accident and it's Jay's turn to rescue him. He pretends to be Angel's fiancé to see him in the hospital, but with his scrambled-up memory, Angel's not sure it's fictional after all. He just knows he loves Jay more than ever.

———

Thin Ice

Kamran's ex broke his heart, tricked him into aiding a bank robbery, and now he wants him to do one last job. There's only one way to say no: seek the protective custody of the biggest, grumpiest FBI agent ever, Lee Marshall. And pretend to be his boyfriend for a week-long family reunion in their giant mansion. Wait, what?

———

Calm Shores

Gorgeous, sophisticated Dante walks into Oliver's bar and orders…a boyfriend?! Dante needs a man to keep his mother from setting him back up with his awful, cheating ex, and Oliver is up for the challenge.

———

Fresh Snow

Emery Klein is throwing the best Christmas party ever, but his fiancé, Scout Duffy, and all their friends have something more exciting in mind.

———

Each Pine Cove book can be read as a stand alone and has its own happy ever after. But if you read the whole series, you'll see a lot of familiar faces!

Click here to get the Pine Cove eBook bundle

Click here to get the Pine Cove audio bundle

Spark

The last thing Joey Sullivan wants is to go back to his homophobic family, but he's penniless and has no choice. Recently single and heartbroken Gabe Robinson loves the town Joey hates. As a librarian and voluntary firefighter, he's used to helping people. When Joey gets a lucky break out of state, Gabe doesn't hesitate to take him on a road trip. The sparks that fly between them have to be just temporary, though. Joey can't wait to leave town and his family are eager to kick him out the door. Can Gabe's love save him from ending up on the streets? *Contains bonus epilogue.*

Burn

Songwriter Raiden Jones never thought he'd need a bodyguard. But when a malicious hacker starts destroying his career and threatening his life, he finds himself desperately in need of protection. That means ex-Marine Levi Patterson is stuck on tour with the bratty Raiden, their friction quickly turning sexual. Bisexual Levi is firmly in the closet and Raiden's never thought of being with a man before, but the chemistry is too fierce to ignore. Will the hacker ruin everything before they can work through their differences? *Contains bonus epilogue.*

Steam

Bad boy movie star Trent Charles is in need of an image makeover. Ashby Wilcott wants some peace and quiet after his ex-boyfriend cheated on him. They both find themselves in a remote ski resort, but Ashby refuses to fall for hot-as-hell Trent. Good thing Trent is straight, because Ashby is done with trouble makers. Except when Trent rescues Ashby from a sleaze, they find themselves pretending to be boyfriends for a wedding weekend. Ashby awakes a longing in Trent he's never felt before, and Ashby realizes Trent has a heart of gold. But can this fling last longer than the melting snow when there's a creep determined to tear them apart?

Blaze

Reyse Hickson might be an international pop sensation, but he's also forced to remain in the closet thanks to his homophobic record label. When gorgeous Corey Sheppard saves Reyse from a mugging, Reyse can't resist falling into his bed, if only for one night. However, a family emergency calls Reyse home, and it seems like the perfect chance for him and Corey to steal some secret time together. But it can't last. Reyse's label would never allow it. Can Reyse and Corey walk away from the best thing that's ever happened to either of them? Or is this love worth going down in a blaze of glory? *Contains bonus epilogue.*

Each Homecoming Hearts book can be read as a stand alone and has its own happy ever after. But if you read the whole series, you'll see familiar faces returning, and enjoy the spectacular ending of Blaze even more!

Click here to get the Homecoming Hearts eBook bundle

door, will Joshua and Darius's blossoming love be strong enough to save each other?

———

A Right Royal Affair

Nobody knows that Prince James of the United Kingdom is bisexual, and as he's sixth in line to the throne, it needs to stay that way. But when he meets the cheeky, outrageously gay Essex boy, Theo Glass, everything could change. Against his better judgement, James asks Theo to help him put on a royal charity ball to remember. Can they resist their mutual attraction for a whole week alone in a picturesque castle, or will true love bloom?

———

Hair Out of Place

Raphael d'Oro is a secret prince who has spent his entire life exiled in a London penthouse. But now he's in a race against time to get back to his tiny European nation to claim the throne that's rightfully his and save his people. Good thing he has his insanely hot older bodyguard to take care of him. But Griff Thompson would never want someone as inexperienced as Raphie, would he? Even *if* they keep finding themselves in places with only one bed…

Click here for the Fairy Tale Collection eBook

Click here for the Fairy Tale Collection audio

About the Author

HJ Welch is an author of contemporary MM romance series, including the international bestselling Pine Cove series. She lives just outside of London with her husband and three balls of fluff that occasionally pretend to be cats. She began writing at an early age, later honing her craft online in the world of fanfiction on sites like Wattpad. Fifteen years and over half a million words later, she sought out original MM novels to read. By the end of 2016 she had written her first book of her own, and in 2017 she achieved her lifelong dream of becoming a full-time author. When she's not writing she's usually dancing, singing, filming music videos, taking long walks, working on jigsaw puzzles, drinking prosecco, or talking about Taylor Swift.

She also writes contemporary British MM fairy tale adaptations as Helen Juliet.

You can contact Helen via the following:
Newsletter: https://www.subscribepage.com/helenjuliet
Website – www.hjwelch.com
Facebook Group – Helen's Jewels
Instagram – @helenjwrites
BlueSky – @helenjuliet.bsky.social
Book Bub – @HJWelchAuthor
Facebook Page – @HJWelchAuthor